Applause for L.L. Raand's Mid

The Midnight H
RWA 2012 VCRW Laurel Wreath winner *Blood Hunt*
Night Hunt
The Lone Hunt

"Raand has built a complex world inhabited by werewolves, vampires, and other paranormal beings...Raand has given her readers a complex plot filled with wonderful characters as well as insight into the hierarchy of Sylvan's pack and vampire clans. There are many plot twists and turns, as well as erotic sex scenes in this riveting novel that keep the pages flying until its satisfying conclusion."—*Just About Write*

"Once again, I am amazed at the storytelling ability of L.L. Raand aka Radclyffe. In *Blood Hunt*, she mixes high levels of sheer eroticism that will leave you squirming in your seat with an impeccable multi-character storyline all streaming together to form one great read."
—*Queer Magazine Online*

"*The Midnight Hunt* has a gripping story to tell, and while there are also some truly erotic sex scenes, the story always takes precedence. This is a great read which is not easily put down nor easily forgotten."—*Just About Write*

"Are you sick of the same old hetero vampire / werewolf story plastered in every bookstore and at every movie theater? Well, I've got the cure to your werewolf fever. *The Midnight Hunt* is first in, what I hope is, a long-running series of fantasy erotica for L.L. Raand (aka Radclyffe)."—*Queer Magazine Online*

"Any reader familiar with Radclyffe's writing will recognize the author's style within *The Midnight Hunt*, yet at the same time it is most definitely a new direction. The author delivers an excellent story here, one that is engrossing from the very beginning. Raand has pieced together an intricate world, and provided just enough details for the reader to become enmeshed in the new world. The action moves quickly throughout the book and it's hard to put down."—*Three Dollar Bill Reviews*

Acclaim for Radclyffe's Fiction

In *Prescription for Love* "Radclyffe populates her small town with colorful characters, among the most memorable being Flann's little sister, Margie, and Abby's 15-year-old trans son, Blake…This romantic drama has plenty of heart and soul." —*Publishers Weekly*

2013 RWA/New England Bean Pot award winner for contemporary romance *Crossroads* "will draw the reader in and make her heart ache, willing the two main characters to find love and a life together. It's a story that lingers long after coming to 'the end.'"—*Lambda Literary*

In **2012 RWA/FTHRW Lories and RWA HODRW Aspen Gold award winner** *Firestorm* "Radclyffe brings another hot lesbian romance for her readers."—*The Lesbrary*

Foreword Review Book of the Year finalist and IPPY silver medalist *Trauma Alert* "is hard to put down and it will sizzle in the reader's hands. The characters are hot, the sex scenes explicit and explosive, and the book is moved along by an interesting plot with well drawn secondary characters. The real star of this show is the attraction between the two characters, both of whom resist and then fall head over heels." —*Lambda Literary Reviews*

Lambda Literary Award Finalist *Best Lesbian Romance 2010* features "stories [that] are diverse in tone, style, and subject, making for more variety than in many, similar anthologies…well written, each containing a satisfying, surprising twist. Best Lesbian Romance series editor Radclyffe has assembled a respectable crop of 17 authors for this year's offering."—*Curve Magazine*

By Radclyffe

Romances

Innocent Hearts

Promising Hearts

Love's Melody Lost

Love's Tender Warriors

Tomorrow's Promise

Love's Masquerade

shadowland

Passion's Bright Fury

Fated Love

Turn Back Time

When Dreams Tremble

The Lonely Hearts Club

Night Call

Secrets in the Stone

Desire by Starlight

Crossroads

Homestead

Against Doctor's Orders

Prescription for Love

Honor Series

Above All, Honor

Honor Bound

Love & Honor

Honor Guards

Honor Reclaimed

Honor Under Siege

Word of Honor

Code of Honor

Price of Honor

Justice Series

A Matter of Trust (prequel)

Shield of Justice

In Pursuit of Justice

Justice in the Shadows

Justice Served

Justice for All

The Provincetown Tales

Safe Harbor

Beyond the Breakwater

Distant Shores, Silent Thunder

Storms of Change

Winds of Fortune

Returning Tides

Sheltering Dunes

First Responders Novels

Trauma Alert

Firestorm

Oath of Honor

Taking Fire

Wild Shores

Short Fiction

Collected Stories by Radclyffe

Erotic Interludes: *Change Of Pace*

Radical Encounters

Edited by Radclyffe:

Best Lesbian Romance 2009–2014

Stacia Seaman and Radclyffe, eds.:

Erotic Interludes 2: *Stolen Moments*

Erotic Interludes 3: *Lessons in Love*

Erotic Interludes 4: *Extreme Passions*

Erotic Interludes 5: *Road Games*

Romantic Interludes 1: *Discovery*

Romantic Interludes 2: *Secrets*

Breathless: *Tales of Celebration*

Women of the Dark Streets

Amor and More: Love Everafter

Myth & Magic: Queer Fairy Tales

By L.L. Raand
Midnight Hunters

The Midnight Hunt

Blood Hunt

Night Hunt

The Lone Hunt

The Magic Hunt

Shadow Hunt

WILD SHORES

by

RADCLY*f*FE

2016

This Trade Paperback Original Is Published By
Bold Strokes Books, Inc.
P.O. Box 249
Valley Falls, NY 12185

First Edition: March 2016

Credits
Editors: Ruth Sternglantz and Stacia Seaman
Production Design: Stacia Seaman
Cover Design by Sheri (graphicartist2020@hotmail.com)

Acknowledgments

When I was small, I wanted to be a cowboy, or an astronaut, or a doctor on horseback. I wasn't drawn so much to adventure as I was to the idea of getting away to a place where life was what you made it—I never minded being alone, and a few good friends were enough for me when I needed company. I learned to love the "wilds" at an early age, camping every summer with my parents in the Adirondacks in an untamed stretch of mountains before the state park system discovered it. That meant no water except what came from one hand pump carried a bucket at a time down a dirt road, no showers, no toilets (flush or non), and no rules or regulations. The same ten families or so returned every summer to this uncivilized spot on the shores of a chain of lakes to spend a few weeks with nothing to do but fish, read, explore, and escape. This place was a sanctuary all on its own—for the people as well as the wildlife. As I wrote this book, I thought of Putts Pond and how little I appreciated the specialness of the experience at the time, and am ever grateful to my parents for their idea of the perfect vacation. So this one is for them.

Many thanks also go to: senior editor Sandy Lowe for keeping the show running while I write, editor Ruth Sternglantz for keeping an eye on the work as I go, editor Stacia Seaman for finding all the things I missed, Sheri Halal for a super cover, and my first readers Paula, Eva, and Connie for encouragement and inspiration.

And as always, thanks to Lee for every new adventure. *Amo te.*

Radclyffe, 2016

To Lee, for making life a surprise

CHAPTER ONE

Austin was right in the middle of scripting a fight scene between Charos, the demon overlord, and Ciri, the Guild Hunter, when her cell phone vibrated. Wincing, she pulled her attention from the storyboard to check the number, already calculating outcomes. Depending on an assortment of variables, a phone call from *Private Number* at three a.m. had the potential to shoot the rest of her night and probably the next day all to hell. *If* she was unlucky, and *if* she took the call.

Between the third and fourth rings, Austin mentally factored in the likelihood there was a family emergency—low probability, no one in her family blocked their personal numbers, and if her parents or brother were in trouble, one of the others would call—versus an automated or highly motivated human solicitor for lowered credit card rates or zero-interest car loans—a slightly higher possibility, safely ignored—against a callout from the company. While the last would not be unusual, seeing as how disasters invariably happened in the wee hours, she'd just gotten back in-country after handling a high-profile personal injury suit in Malaysia and hadn't even scheduled the after-action report meeting yet. She couldn't be that unlucky.

She let the call go to voice mail and inserted a text bubble next to Charos's sneering, horned head.

Today is the day you die, Guild Hunter.
I've heard that before.

She sketched Ciri's smirking face in profile, the sheathed sword with its magically bejeweled pommel extending from the leather scabbard between her shoulder blades, her signature braid flowing over her shoulder. Red eyes for Charos, along with thin black lips, a scale-covered snout-like face, and curved protruding canines completed the panel.

Her cell danced on the drafting table again and she caught it with her free hand before it toppled to the rough plank floor.

"Germaine," she said, carefully keeping her irritation from her tone as she penciled out the next sequence.

"I'm sorry to bother you, Doctor," Eloise's cultured tones announced.

"You know by now," Austin said for perhaps the hundredth time, "you can skip the honorific. A doctorate in engineering might make me capable of changing the oil in my car, if I really wanted to, but beyond that, my therapeutic skills are limited."

"I'm quite sure I've heard you referred to as a miracle worker." Eloise laughed, her melodic voice belying her analytical mind and death-defying efficiency. "I'm afraid we might have a situation that needs your very particular attention."

Of course she did. There'd be no other reason for the VP of Operations of the U.S. division of General Oil and Petroleum to be calling personally at *any* time of the day or night. Austin set her drafting pencil aside, pushed her wheeled stool back from the table, and pivoted away, staring across her cabin to the dark windows that looked out over the Hudson. "How much of an issue? I've only been back in the country a few days, and I was hoping to go off the grid for a bit."

She didn't add that she had a deadline in a few weeks for the first draft of the graphic novel she was adapting from a paranormal urban fantasy series. That part of her life was private and bore no relationship to what she did for GOP. Even her family didn't know about her secret career, not that they'd put much stock in it. They'd far rather see her embroiled in a big burn or a high-profile media extravaganza with the potential for fireworks—no matter how metaphorical. Drawing and texting comics was something for teenagers.

"Rig 86 has a breach," Eloise said coolly and without apology for derailing Austin's plans, giving no indication of precisely how serious the situation might be.

Serious was a given. The company had land and offshore drilling sites throughout the world, and breaches were not uncommon. Usually they were small, confined, and repaired before anyone outside the company was really aware of the potential problem. If they were calling Austin, the company was worried.

"How large?" she asked.

"At the moment, a flow rate of only a few thousand barrels a day."

Austin walked through the living room to her bedroom beyond, opened the closet door, and pulled out her go bag. "Chance for containment?"

"Uncertain at this time."

She transferred shirts, pants, socks, and underwear from the rough oak dresser against one wall into the bag. Her toiletries and work boots were already loaded. Anything else she needed, she'd buy wherever she was going. Her wallet was on the dresser and she slid it into her back pocket. "Escalation potential?"

"Moderate at this point."

"Where is it?"

"About fifty miles from the Maryland shore."

"Damn." Why didn't these spills happen in unpopulated areas far from TV cameras, fishing waters, and beaches?

"Your flight has been scheduled to leave Albany at six," Eloise went on as if they'd been discussing a board meeting. "You'll transfer to a regional plane at BWI that will take you to Rock Hill Island. The present point of operations is at the Hilton nearest there."

"Who's the incident commander?"

"Ray Tatum. He's aware you'll be arriving."

"How long do we have before we need to go public?"

"We'll make that assessment when you arrive."

"You have a marine meteorologist available?"

"We will have. She's flying in from Philadelphia at about the same time you are."

"All right. I'll be in touch."

"There is one other thing," Eloise said in the same cool, even tone.

Austin tensed. Eloise was about to drop the hammer. "What would that be?"

"There's a large wildlife refuge on Rock Hill Island and surrounds. It's a well-known stopover for migratory birds and this is apparently the beginning of their nesting season. The area is a popular tourist destination."

"Where is it relative to the rig?" Austin locked the cabin, tossed her bag in the back of the Jeep, and climbed in.

"The island is almost directly in line with our rig and presently represents the outermost point of contact should the spill progress toward land."

"In other words, a PR nightmare." And now she understood why she'd been called at such an early point. Eloise wouldn't say it, but the company was counting on her to keep a lid on news of the breach. What she needed to do was plug the leak in terms of publicity, and if this wildlife refuge became threatened, to minimize the bad press.

"I'm sure you'll handle it."

"What do we know about this place and the people?" It was probably too much to hope they'd find someone sympathetic—environmentalists generally were opposed to any kind of drilling and, once an accident occurred, took full advantage of the situation to lobby against the whole industry.

"I'm afraid not very much," Eloise said. "I have people working on that now, but you'll probably never need to interface with them."

Austin read between the lines. *Make sure the environmentalists don't get wind of the threat.*

"Right." Austin backed down the drive. "By the time I get there, the problem might already be solved."

"Precisely."

"Right." Austin disconnected and drove toward the river, a black ribbon under the moon, quiet and still and deadly. *Right.*

❖

"We'll be landing through a bit of a storm moving in from the south," the pilot announced. "Might be a bit bumpy for a few minutes, so I'll ask everyone to keep your seat belts on and close up your electronics at this time."

Gem flagged the page in the latest population report she'd received from the Carolina Coastal Observatory, closed her iPad, and slid it into her computer bag under the seat in front of her. She'd known the storm was coming and had caught the earliest flight out of Hartford she could before the anticipated fog rolling in with the front grounded planes along the East Coast. She'd been lucky to get one of the last coach seats still open. She didn't mind stormy weather—in fact, she often stood on the shore waiting for a front to roll in just to watch the beauty of the clouds roiling in the sky, dark blues and purples swirling and dancing, as if an invisible artist mixed the colors on a wild palette in a frenzy of creation. She loved the way the wind buffeted her hair and plastered her clothes to her body, the stinging bite of the first needle-sharp raindrops bringing every sense and cell to life. The sea felt it too—cresting and crashing as to the call of the wind. While she was often the only human on the beach, life around her pushed on as if in a race with the storm to lay claim to the shore. Terns and gulls scurried along the edge of the frothing waves, plucking up the sea creatures that struggled valiantly against the battering push and pull of the tides.

Even when the rain blew in solid sheets of icy water, she'd often stay, the scent of fresh pure air and the untamed sea filling her with wonder and peace. She loved those solitary moments when she knew in her bones her life was nothing but an inconsequential point in a vast continuum of time.

As much as she loved those moments of abandon, she detested flying in airplanes. The unnaturalness of it, being contained in a metal canister, breathing recycled air and other things she'd rather not consider, reminded her of how land bound she was and how different from the creatures she envied.

As the plane began to descend, she remembered the first time she'd told her mother she wanted to be a bird.

"Why is that?" her mother had asked patiently, never laughing at any of her wild fantasies.

"Because they can go anywhere they want, and they're never really alone, even when they're by themselves in the sky."

Her mother studied her and nodded gravely. "You know what we call that, honey?"

She'd shaken her head.

Her mother had patted her hair. "We call that freedom."

Freedom. Yes, but even the free flying creatures she loved were not really free, but bound by some innate instinct that directed their life cycle and bade them return to certain places every year, against all odds or adversity. They followed the call of some distant drummer, on a stage too ancient and too primal for her to ever understand. But she'd keep trying, and keep envying them.

The plane bumped down, bumped again, and the deceleration pulled her forward in the seat until the plane came to a halt. She glanced out the window, but it might as well have been midnight rather than just after seven a.m. Thick fog blanketed the runway. The lights from the terminal barely penetrated the murk. They were lucky they'd been able to land at all. She could have been diverted to Philadelphia or worse, where she'd end up spending days trying to get to the coast.

Still, her connection was undoubtedly going to be grounded.

As soon as the flight attendants opened the doors, she grabbed her computer bag and carry-on and trooped out, breaking away from the crowd as quickly as she could and heading for the rental car area. The lines snaked away from every counter, two and three people deep, as the departure board flashed *canceled* after nearly every flight.

She picked the shortest line and hoped for the best. She would have dearly loved a cup of coffee, but she wasn't giving up her spot for anything. She flicked through email while she waited, answered a few, and as she drew closer to the counter, began to hear snippets of conversation between stranded passengers and harried service representatives. The news wasn't encouraging.

A middle-aged man in a rumpled white shirt, business pants, and a monogrammed briefcase slung over one shoulder by a hand-tooled leather strap announced angrily, "Look, I've got to have a car. I have an important meeting in two hours and I'm going to have to reschedule that as it is."

"I'm really sorry, sir, but our only remaining vehicles are reserved, and we can't release them—"

"Have you looked outside? Those people with reservations aren't going to be arriving. I'm here now. I need to have a car."

"I'm very sorry, sir," the woman said again, her tone unbelievably calm considering the morning she must be having, "but we are not authorized to release any of the reserved—"

"I want to see a manager."

"I'm afraid he won't be in—"

"Never mind. I'm sure one of the other agencies can take care of me." He spun around, knocking into the woman behind him. She stumbled back and collided with Gem.

"Oh!" Gem's phone slipped from her hand and, off balance, she made a clumsy grab for it.

"Sorry," a dark-haired woman said in a husky, rich alto. Somehow, Gem's phone was miraculously scooped from the air by a long-fingered hand. "Got it."

Gem straightened and met bittersweet chocolate eyes shot through with gold. "Thanks."

"I think it was my fault you dropped it. Sorry about that."

"Not your fault. It's a bit of a mess, isn't it?"

The woman shrugged. "That's what we get for trying to outsmart Mother Nature."

Gem grinned. "But we'll keep trying."

"Undoubtedly."

The stranger was about Gem's age, dressed in khakis, a pale-blue cotton shirt, and casual boots, and carrying a worn leather satchel in one hand and an equally travel-weary computer bag slung over the other shoulder. Her collar-length, layered dark brown hair verged on black. The angular slant to her arching cheekbones, deep-set eyes, and bronze skin tones hinted at the Mediterranean somewhere in her ancestry. Her lips parted in a full, confident smile, and Gem felt herself blush. She was staring. She never did that.

"I think you're up." Gem nodded toward the counter. The woman looked over her shoulder and back at Gem as if reluctant to end the conversation. Gem was certain she was making that part up, but an unusual spark of interest shot through her nonetheless. "Good luck."

"Appreciate it." Austin didn't expect to have any better luck than the fellow who'd knocked into her. Dozens of other passengers milled about in the same fix and no one seemed to be getting any vehicles, but she'd waited this long and might as well try. She smiled at the petite redhead behind the counter. "Hi."

"Your name please?"

"I don't have a reservation." Austin paused. Her flight had been short, but Eloise had called hours ago. Given the time it had taken her to drive to the airport and catch her plane, maybe Eloise had used her crystal ball. "I don't think."

"I'm sorry?"

"Check under Germaine." She spelled it, glad she'd automatically lined up at the rental place the company always used.

"Oh. I have it." The redhead smiled for the first time in twenty minutes. "You're lucky. It came in right before the rush hit."

"Better lucky than good," Austin said.

The agent laughed again and raised a brow. "Sometimes it's nice to be both."

"You're right." Austin grinned. She enjoyed flirting with women. She enjoyed women, when she could. At the moment, she couldn't, so she signed the necessary papers and stepped aside to file them away in her briefcase. The blonde she'd bumped into stepped up to the counter.

"I'm afraid I don't have a reservation. And I suspect that's not a good thing."

The cute redhead sighed. "I'm so sorry. We simply don't have any other vehicles."

"Do you think I'd have any better luck elsewhere?"

The redhead looked down the counter at the long lines at every rental car agency. "Honestly, I don't think anyone without a reservation is going to get a car today. You'd be better off using your time trying to find a hotel room. There won't be many of those left either."

"Well, thanks anyways."

Austin collected her keys and caught up to the blonde as she wended her way through the mass of people milling about. She'd been stranded plenty of places in her travels around the world, and more than one stranger had helped her out with directions, impromptu rides, or in a few cases, even offered her a room when she would have been sleeping on a bench otherwise. Returning the favor only seemed right, and the fact that the blonde was beautiful had nothing to do with it.

"Excuse me," Austin said as she drew alongside the blonde. "I'm not sure we're going in the same direction, but if we are, I've got one of the last vehicles leaving today. Maybe I can give you a ride somewhere."

The blonde stopped and regarded her contemplatively.

Austin grinned. "I know you don't know me, but I've got references if you need them." She patted her briefcase. "ID provided on demand."

The blonde laughed and held out her hand. "I'm Gillian Martin. Most people call me Gem."

Austin took her hand. "Austin Germaine. Nice to meet you. Again."

"It is."

Gem's tone was thoughtful, and Austin somehow knew she meant it. An unfamiliar pleasure stirred in her chest. She traveled constantly, met new people the world over, but rarely connected with anyone. She had gotten used to being alone and was rarely aware of being lonely. But right at this moment, she realized she had been. "So, about a ride?"

She heard the hopeful note in her voice and didn't care. Her breath caught as she waited for the answer.

"I'd very much like a ride, but unfortunately, I doubt we're going in the same direction. I'm headed to a little place off the coast no one except avid birdwatchers tends to visit this time of year." She cocked her head, her gaze sweeping down Austin's body. "I don't suspect you're one of those."

"I'm afraid not." Austin never discussed her work for the company and had even less reason to talk about her other work. She often felt as if she led a secret life, and the person she was there, no one actually knew. "Where is this place?"

"It's called Rock Hill Island. It's—"

"About two hundred miles from here as the crow flies," Austin said, "or it would be, if not for the fog. Would you believe me if I said I was headed there myself?"

Gem laughed and shook her head. "As a matter of fact, no. Why ever for?"

Austin grinned and chose a half-truth. "A working vacation. I've got a deadline, and I like to get away where I can concentrate and be waited on at the same time."

"Well then, it appears it's fate. I'd love a ride."

"Perfect." Austin didn't believe in fate, but she did believe in luck, and at least for the moment, hers was looking up. That was likely to change when she reached Rock Hill Island and liaised with Ray Tatum, but until then, she'd enjoy a beautiful woman's company while wearing the secret skin that fit her best.

CHAPTER TWO

Gem kept pace with Austin's slightly longer stride as they searched for their vehicle among the rows of numbered rental cars. They finally found the late-model Nissan Pathfinder and stowed their gear in the rear. She climbed into the passenger seat as Austin slid behind the wheel, started the vehicle, and switched on the navcom.

Austin slid her phone out of her pants pocket, scrolled through with her thumb, and punched in an address on the console. "What do you know? The hotel address pops. Looks like we've got directions."

Gem scanned the readout alongside the route map. "Yes, and if we weren't driving through soup, we'd probably be there in the three-plus hours predicted. Obviously, the electronic gods haven't picked up the weather report yet."

"Double the time estimate, if we're lucky." Austin backed out of the space and joined the queue leaving the garage.

"Road trip." Gem sighed. She hadn't planned on a day in the car, but at least she wasn't sitting on a hard plastic seat in the airport or calling hotels looking for a room. "I used to love them when I was a kid. On occasion, I still do. But I'm really sorry you're going to have to drive through this."

"I'm used to it. I live in the Catskills, and fog is a way of life starting in October."

"I can spell you whenever you need. I'm a New Englander too. Although give me snow over fog any day."

"Agreed."

"I hate to even ask, but if we can find a place with coffee—"

"And breakfast," Austin added.

Gem groaned as her stomach grumbled. "Yes, please."

"Once we get off the interstate, we ought to run into some diners. That work for you?"

"Diners always work for me."

Austin smiled. "Perfect."

Gem liked the way Austin's quick grin softened the carved line of her jaw and caused a few crinkles to appear at the corner of her eye. Austin drove with an easy sense of confidence and casual focus, radiating the aura of a woman used to *doing* and being in charge of whatever the action was at the moment. She'd said she had a deadline—she must be some kind of writer. Funny, she looked more suited for a fishing boat somewhere, or riding a four-wheeler up some mountainside, than sitting behind a desk.

"If I didn't know you were a writer, I would've pegged you as an outdoors-woman," Gem said.

"You wouldn't be far off," Austin said carefully. Generally when it came to personal disclosures, she didn't have any problem blurring the edges of the truth with people she was likely never going to see again. Or even those she might. Confidentiality was built into her, professionally and personally, from an early age. Her father had been active-duty military when she was growing up, and some of his missions had been classified. He'd been closemouthed about what he did, even after he'd moved into more administrative sections. Her mother was a physician, and she didn't talk about her work very much either. Austin had learned not to probe or to share her own secrets.

When she went into consulting, confidentiality was a given, but working for GOP took that to new heights. She'd signed endless papers binding her to silence, at considerable legal and financial penalty should she break confidence, not that that was ever going to happen. Protecting the reputation of her client, any client, was a point of honor, and she'd learned that from her mother and father too.

Still, maintaining professional barriers bled over into her

personal life, where privacy exacted a price. Women found her secretive and aloof, and often translated that into unemotional and cold. She knew because she'd been told more than once by women on their way out of her life. Maybe they were right. No one had broken her heart when they'd left, and maybe that was because she wasn't the type to invest emotionally. She'd simply rationalized she hadn't wanted anything serious, but maybe she wasn't actually capable of it. Not that any of that mattered now. Friendship, at least, she ought to be able to manage without compromising principles or comfort. "I live year-round in a three-room log cabin in the mountains between New York City and Albany. It's rustic."

"Define rustic," Gem said, intrigued. She knew plenty of environmentalists who lived off the grid, but this woman didn't strike her as that either. She had a patina of sophistication about her, despite the plain khaki pants, unironed cotton shirt, and beat-up leather flight jacket. She could just as easily see her in a tuxedo cradling a champagne flute in her sure, strong hand as she could with her booted feet up on a rough pine railing.

"I heat the place with a wood-burning stove in the winter, so I spend a lot of time doing things like chopping wood, doing my own repairs, and chasing bears away from my recycler."

"Internet?"

"I'm not that far off-grid. Satellite, which does the job most days."

"What do you do when you're not working?"

"I ride a little bit when I have time." Even though there was hardly any time when she wasn't working, one way or the other.

"Horses, you mean?"

Austin nodded. "Motorcycles, ATVs too."

"Let me guess. Snowmobile?"

Austin grinned and turned off the main highway when the in-dash voice instructed her to detour around slow traffic ahead. "Guilty. You?"

"I live just outside Hartford and have an adjunct position at Yale. I ski, and I can always be persuaded to take a long weekend doing just about anything outdoors, any time of the year."

"What do you teach?"

"Virology."

"Are you a medical doctor?"

"No, PhD microbiologist. Well, that and an ornithologist."

Austin glanced at her, one eyebrow quirked. "Really? That's an interesting combination."

Gem smiled. "It sounds that way. I went after the birds first."

"What makes someone want to study birds?"

Gem hesitated over her standard answer, having learned most people didn't really understand a love of birds. Birds weren't like domestic pets or even farm animals—not cuddly, or people oriented, or hobby-farm material.

"Is that an insulting question?"

"No!" Gem blushed. "I always wanted to be a bird. This is as close as I could get."

Austin nodded as if she really understood. "They do seem to have a great life—except I always wonder if they know their existence is just one long struggle to survive. Not just birds—all creatures."

Gem detected a hint of pain that surprised her. "People too?"

"Maybe us most of all." Austin blew out a breath. Where the hell had all that come from. She had always been aware of her mortality. She'd learned that in a hospital bed before she could even put the pain and terror into words. But she'd gotten through all that, gotten over being the weak one in the family, the one who wasn't quite fit enough to fit in with her high-achieving, risk-taking family. "Sorry. I think this soup is getting to me." She glanced at Gem. "Tell me about the birds. What do you study?"

"I started out with population studies and migratory patterns, and that led me into the study of bird-borne disease."

"That's where the virology comes in, I take it."

"Yes. Now I consult with the U.S. Fish and Wildlife Service on all kinds of environmental crossovers involving birds."

"Really." Austin slowed as a string of taillights ahead of her blinked in the murky light. Warning bells rang. She'd had more than enough contact with Fish and Wildlife agents, since they were usually the first called in environmental contaminations. Like oil spills. "So research is your primary focus?"

"Yes and no. I'm more of a field agent than a bencher. Right now I'm involved in a national study group looking at the presence of avian flu in migratory birds. We think the recent outbreak among chickens in the Midwest was transmitted from a locus in migratory wild geese."

"And that's what you'll be doing on Rock Hill Island?"

"Mostly. It's the height of the migration season, and we're expecting a large number of species to make a stopover. We're banding and cataloging, charting flock size and flight paths, and—" She broke off, laughing. "And I can't imagine any of that is of interest to you at all."

"Actually," Austin said quietly, "I think it's very interesting. How extensive an area will the birds be occupying?"

"Probably twenty-five miles of shoreline, and inland of course. We have observation stations scattered throughout the refuge. I'll have one of those cabins."

"Sounds rustic," Austin said.

Gem laughed at the way the conversation had come full circle. "I'm going to let my inner geek show. It is pretty primitive, and it's wonderful. Not totally uncivilized, mind you—we have running water and I can get cell service most days—but there's no one around for miles. Waking in the morning to nothing but the sound of birds and the wind—and this time of year, rain a lot of the time—is my idea of heaven." She laughed again. "Out there, I swear sometimes I feel like I really will grow wings."

Austin glanced at her, not a hint of mockery on her face. "You want to, don't you?"

"More than anything," Gem said softly.

"Do you fly?"

"Only when forced."

Austin grinned, a damnably handsome grin, Gem noticed. That was odd for her too, noticing women she hardly knew in a physical way. But then the whole day was a little out of time—here she was, enclosed in a vehicle with a near stranger, muffled by a blanket of fog as if the rest of the world didn't even exist, headed along a road she could barely see. She had every reason to be uncomfortable, or at least as guarded when meeting new people as she usually was—no one would ever confuse her with an extrovert—but here she was, chattering away, and enjoying herself. For once, she'd just let things be and not try to analyze everything. What was it Kim always said—she felt with her head and not her heart? Today, she'd just shut off the little voice that cautioned her to be careful, not to give away too much, not to want too much, and just enjoy an interesting and attractive woman's company. "I always feel like I'm in a cage strapped in with rows and rows of strangers."

"How about small planes?"

"Not really fond of them."

"No, really small planes. Like a four-seater."

"No experience. You?"

"I have a license," Austin said. "I think it's a lot like being a bird when you're in a single-engine four-seater."

"I can sort of imagine that."

"We should go up sometime. You might like it."

Gem almost said yes and caught herself when her inner voice kicked in. Conversation was one thing—socializing was something else again. She didn't do socializing. She had her fieldwork, her research, and her professional relationships to more than fill her days. She had a nice uncomplicated friendship with Kim for the occasional dinner or a movie or even less occasional sex. Come to think of it, there hadn't really been any sex for quite some time. When had she stopped caring about that? But if she didn't miss it, it really couldn't be very important. Did she really want to complicate her life by spending time with someone new?

"Sorry," Austin said. "That probably seemed to come out of nowhere. It's just when you mentioned birds, I immediately thought of flying."

"You don't need to apologize."

Austin fell silent.

Ordinarily Gem preferred silence—she loved being alone with her thoughts or hearing nothing but nature's symphony. But she missed the earthy richness of Austin's voice instantly. Or maybe she missed the connection that had developed so effortlessly she hadn't had time to be wary. "Are you a good pilot?"

"My father flew fighter jets in the Middle East. He taught me." Austin glanced over, her eyes glinting in the reflected light from the dash like a hawk's eyes catching the slanting rays of the setting sun as it swooped down over a field to grasp its prey. "I'm a damn good pilot."

"Do you have your own plane?"

Austin hesitated, then nodded. "I do. A Cessna TTx."

"Uh-huh," Gem said blankly.

"Cruising speed two hundred and thirty-five knots, range twelve hundred nautical miles." Austin's tone was teasing.

"Should I confess I'm completely ignorant of all things mechanical?"

"It's the eagle of single-engine aircraft. Imagine the majestic wingspan, the speed in flight, the soaring power. Better?"

"Much." Warmth spread through Gem's chest. She pushed the pleasure aside. Austin was just one of those people who knew how to charm. It wasn't personal. "Why aren't you flying it today?"

"It's a working getaway and I'm planning to hole up, mostly. The plane would just be sitting on the tarmac the whole time." Another partial truth—the other part being she had no idea how long she'd be here or where she might have to go after this. She didn't want to leave her plane at the local airport if she ended up flying cross-country.

"So tell me about your work—you mentioned a deadline. Fiction?"

"Actually I script and illustrate graphic novel adaptations."

"Really? What kinds?"

"This one is a paranormal urban fantasy series."

Gem caught her breath. "That's so cool. Which one?"

Austin figured Gem was being polite—even her brother, who she'd thought would be interested, had written her work off as a weird hobby. Not high-profile enough, she guessed. Still, it was nice that Gem didn't immediately change the subject.

"The Guild Hunter Chronicles by—"

"Audrey St. James. I love Ciri!"

"You've read them?"

"Oh yes, and a lot of others too. Would I know your work?"

Austin laughed. "I doubt it. I think most of my readers are about fifteen and male."

"I bet you're wrong. Give me a hint. No, wait. Let me guess."

"Hold that thought." Austin narrowed her eyes at a flickering sign up ahead that appeared for a millisecond and just as quickly disappeared. "I think there's a diner coming up. I could really use some food and fuel."

"Me too. But I'm not letting you off the hook."

"You like uncovering things, don't you?" Austin eased toward the side of the road and pulled off into what felt like a bumpy gravel lot, although she couldn't really make out the surface as she angled into an open place in front of a long aluminum-sided building that looked like a giant bullet. Lights glowed in a row of windows. An honest-to-God diner. She could've wept.

"I've always loved secrets," Gem said, "as long as I was in on them."

Austin turned off the motor. Too bad her secrets were ones she couldn't share, especially not with a wildlife biologist whose number-one love was likely to be endangered by Austin's employer in a matter of days. But who knew? So far the day had gone better than she could have imagined, despite the lousy weather and the delay. It had been months since she had spent this much time alone with a woman when they weren't rushing to get to bed. The time with Gem had been more satisfying than most of those couplings. Maybe her luck would hold and the catastrophe would be contained by the time she arrived on Rock Hill Island.

CHAPTER THREE

W ow," Gem said as she pushed through the steamy revolving-glass doors and glanced the length of the diner. The counter was lined with mostly solitary men hunched over heaping plates of food and big ceramic mugs of coffee. The booths were filled with an assortment of people who looked as if they were desperate travelers like her and Austin, looking for some light, warmth, and food. A few families, scattered couples, and the occasional lone elderly individual, probably a local, filled the rest of the places. "This place is jammed. Where are all the cars?"

"I think they're out there, you just can't see them through the fog." Austin pointed to a waitress clearing the table in the only empty booth and put her hand on Gem's back. "Let's grab that one."

Gem tensed at the unexpected touch and headed down the aisle, imagining she could feel the heat of Austin's palm on her skin. Which of course, she couldn't possibly. All the same, when they reached the booth and Austin moved away, she missed the fleeting contact. She must have been imagining the proprietary nature of the gesture too. Dismissing the flight of fancy with a flicker of inward irritation, she pulled off her windbreaker and hung it on the curved iron hook attached to one of the wooden poles rising from the end of each bench. She slid onto the red vinyl seat, and Austin settled across from her. Austin had shed her jacket before she began driving and hadn't bothered to put it on when they stopped. The shoulders of her shirt were damp from mist that was quickly turning to rain. "Do you think we're going to be able to make it today?"

"I'm planning on it." Austin pulled out her phone. She wasn't just planning on it, she had to get to the coast and meet with Tatum. No matter what route she had to take. Well breaches were unpredictable. The whole scenario could change with every passing hour. The leak might already be contained, and she could turn around, once the weather cleared, and go home. That was the optimistic outlook. Or the breach could have widened and thousands of gallons of oil could be flooding the ocean right now. "If I can get a signal, I'll check the weather. Maybe we can skirt around the front."

Gem pulled out her own phone and started scrolling. "I don't see a wireless connection in the diner—no surprise there, since I'm not altogether sure we haven't wandered into Brigadoon—" Austin chuckled and the warm, deep peal touched off an unexpected thrill of pleasure Gem couldn't quite define. Whatever the source of the heat unfurling in her middle, it was nice. Kind of scary nice. "My cell signal is pretty iffy too. Like, there and gone again. Mostly gone."

"Same here," Austin said grimly. Being out of contact had gotten to be a way of life. Some of the places she traveled for GOP, especially in Southeast Asia, did not have sophisticated broadband networks or any kind of cellular coverage. She was used to making decisions based on the info she had at hand, with or without input from the home front. That's what they paid her for—to make decisions in the company's interest. Their contract was a matter of trust, and her reputation, pride, and self-respect rested upon her upholding her duty to the company. Right now she was in the dark, and in the wind, and not a damn thing she could do about it. She slid her phone away. "Nothing to do but keep with the plan until we get some more intel. Then we'll reassess."

Gem regarded her thoughtfully. "I'm on board with that."

A middle-aged brunette waitress appeared beside them in a tight black skirt, a low-cut silky white shirt that strained over full breasts, and a wraparound black nylon apron with deep pockets that held a pad, pens, a half dozen straws, and a handful of packets that were most likely sugar. "You two know what you're having or do you want menus?"

Gem said, "Coffee."

Her desperation must have showed because the waitress laughed, a deep earthy rumble that was unself-conscious and sexy all rolled into one. "Goes without saying." She quirked an eyebrow at Austin. "You too?"

"Absolutely. And scrambled eggs and toast."

"Got it. How about you, honey?" She directed her query to Gem, her eyes dancing and her generous mouth tilted into a teasing smile. "What have you got a hankering for?"

"Uh...blueberry pancakes and poached eggs. And coffee." Gem hoped she didn't sound like an infatuated teenager, which was how she felt. God, what was with her today—first an innocent, casual touch from Austin awakened her long-dormant libido, and now the waitress in a diner turned her into a gawking adolescent?

Still laughing, the waitress scrawled something on an old-fashioned order pad—no fancy computer terminals in sight—and headed toward the pass-through to the kitchen to hang their ticket on the line with half a dozen others.

Gem rubbed her eyes and muttered, "It must be the fog. It's done something to my mind."

"Oh, I don't know," Austin remarked drily. "She's pretty hot."

"Stop." Gem kept her eyes closed.

Now Austin laughed. "Your secret lust for sexy waitresses is safe with me."

"Diners," Gem said. "I love *diners*. Good plain food, lots of it, and fast service."

"And don't forget the waitresses," Austin added.

"I won't." Opening her eyes, Gem grinned. "Now stop trying to divert my attention. Back to the small matter of graphic novels. I don't recognize your name, so I'm guessing you use a pseudonym."

"Twenty questions, huh?" Austin liked Gem's persistence, and the spark in her eyes was captivating. She suspected whatever the object of Gem's focus, she'd be relentless in her pursuit. For a heartbeat, she let herself imagine what that would be like—to have all of Gem's contagious energy and intensity focused on her. As if she were all that mattered. That rarely happened to her—oh, she was used to being at the center of a woman's attention, at least for the few moments when they played the game of chase and catch, but then she was always the chaser. Never the caught. Never, she suspected, the truly wanted.

"I bet you're really good at what you do," Austin said.

Gem's brows rose. "I…I hope so. Why did you say that?"

"You don't give up—and you enjoy discovery. That drive to know, to understand, must be important for someone doing research."

"I can't imagine why else anyone would do it," Gem said. "Most of us spend years searching for an answer to a problem, and sometimes it never comes."

"But you don't quit."

"Not yet," Gem said lightly. "And you're diverting again."

"Like I said—you don't quit." Austin smiled ruefully. Considering what might be waiting for them on Rock Hill Island, Gem's quick, inquisitive nature might be problematic. Gem would be watching the same reports of maritime wind and ocean currents as Austin, only Gem would be tracking the approach of the migratory birds while she would be charting the potential direction of spread of an oil spill. They'd probably be in an unknowing race against time to see who discovered it first, unless the spill was so large by the time she arrived, the company would be forced to go public. If Tatum's first-response team could get containment lines in place and trap the oil or redirect it up the coast away from the sanctuary, she might have a chance to keep the whole thing under wraps. Then the world would never know—just another mechanical failure that happened and was handled all the time. And most importantly, Gem would never know she'd been lying to her almost since the start. Sins of omission, but sins all the same.

The storm was against her. Tatum and his crew were experts at containing spills, and Eloise was adept at managing the company's official PR statements, but Tatum was blunt and oftentimes belligerent if challenged by those he considered to be opponents. He couldn't be trusted to deal with the press on-site. If—more likely when—word got out, she needed to be on scene to defuse the situation. Otherwise they'd have environmentalists camping out onshore and a media storm the company paid her to prevent. She didn't like thinking about Gem as one of those environmentalists who might be crying for blood, and it hadn't happened yet. Right at that moment, there was nothing she could do to change what would happen. And she wanted to see the light in Gem's eyes turned on her just a little while longer. "In the comics world, like it or not, testosterone rules. An androgynous name works better on the cover, so I went with a pen name."

"Austin would probably fly in terms of being genderless," Gem said musingly, "but it's a little too sophisticated, and I see you as someone a little…hmm…flashier in your artist persona."

"Flashier, huh?" Austin cocked her head. "Not sexier?"

Gem ignored the trickle of electricity down her spine and pretended she didn't notice Austin flirting. But she noticed all right. Austin veered between serious and outrageously playful, and the constant back and forth was so unpredictable as to be enticing. Like intermittent reinforcement—and Lord, now she was analyzing her own behavioral responses as if she were a test subject. When had she forgotten how to simply enjoy herself? "So, are you mostly doing paranormal?"

"Pretty much any kind of sci-fi fantasy. I prefer action-adventure type stories. Easier to script. More exciting to draw."

"Well, I know you're not doing the *Y: The Last Man* series, which I love. I've seen Vaughan's picture and I know that's not you."

"You weren't kidding." Austin nodded appreciatively. "You do know your comics."

"I mostly read the graphic adaptations of authors I'm really fond of. I like to see the characters given form." She laughed. "The women always look different than I imagined—but we've come a long way from the Wonder Woman years, not that I don't still love those too."

"You mean with the big breasts and tiny waists? I dunno about that."

"Well, I'll give you the big breasts. But at least now the female heroes have muscles and are a lot more into physical confrontation. I love a woman with a sword."

Austin swallowed her coffee wrong and choked. "Really?"

Heat climbed into Gem's face. What was she doing? She hadn't been this open and unguarded since Christie, and that seemed like another lifetime. That *was* another lifetime ago. She'd sworn she'd keep a careful distance from people, and she hadn't suffered for it. Why she was suddenly dropping all her barriers with a near stranger, especially a somewhat mysterious, if terribly charming stranger, was inexplicable. "I was being literal."

Too bad. Austin almost spoke aloud but was glad she hadn't. Gem looked uncomfortable, and maybe she should take that as a warning herself. Gem wasn't the kind of woman she'd pick up for an hour or two in a hotel room on a long layover somewhere. She didn't do it all that often, but when the constant travel, unrelenting pressure of defusing one crisis after another, and the endless self-questioning got to be too much, her choice was to drink until she slept or have sex until she didn't think. When she'd found herself drinking a little too much four or five years before, she decided sex was a better antidote. She didn't turn to it frequently, but when she did, she enjoyed the game, took pleasure in the flirtation and the seduction and ultimately in the final, if fleeting connection. She'd already gone beyond the point of flirtation with Gem. She liked her. Anything beyond that would only be complicating what was likely to become a very difficult situation. "Literally, then…you might have seen the *Sisters of Revenge* series. It's about a cadre of—"

"Women warriors dedicated to protecting women on a planet where the captives of territorial wars are sold into slavery. I know that one. Did you—?"

"That would be mine."

"You're kidding. You're Ace Grand?" Gem rocked back in her seat and laughed aloud, her face transformed by pleasure. "That's amazing. You're awesome!"

Austin just stared, stunned by a whirlwind of sensation, dizzy as if she'd stepped into a rainbow of color and heat. She'd never met a woman capable of such spontaneous delight. A tightly coiled tendril of hope, long lost and deeply hidden, stretched tentatively toward Gem, testing the possibility of connection. Everything else—the job, the constant pressure to excel, to succeed, to be *better than*—disappeared. The unrelenting need to measure up and not be left behind faded.

How would she ever hold on to this feeling? What could she possibly do to make Gem look at her this way again? A tight ball of regret filled her chest. Before very long she'd likely destroy any chance she had of being the benefactor of Gem's favor. Knowing she would lose yet again, she determined to hold on to every glimmer of pleasure as long as she could. "That's me. But you don't have to call me Ace."

"Ace. Yep. It suits." Gem leaned forward, gripping the coffee cup the waitress had placed down a minute before. "I love your stuff. The characters are incredibly vivid, and the dialogue really jumps. The adaptation you did of Young's *Demon Darkness* series was fabulous. Really true to the novels, and the physical depiction of Andromira was…Sorry, I know I'm being a fangirl, but—well, I'm a fan."

"Hey," Austin said, trying not to preen, "don't apologize. I'm really glad you like comics. I don't meet many people I can actually have a conversation with who do."

"Do you do signings?"

"Not very often. My schedule is pretty jammed." Austin couldn't very well tell her that most of the time she had to squeeze her graphic work in between trips to one part of the world or another to neutralize a potential global disaster. "I don't get much exposure to the audience."

"There, you see? That's why you don't know there are lots of people like me who really enjoy comics."

"You're probably right. I'm very happy that you proved me wrong."

"Well, I doubt proving you wrong could become a habit." Gem smiled. "You strike me as being someone who knows what you're about."

"Thanks, I think." Austin saw no point in telling her she was wrong. That she'd never entirely been able to shake her childhood, when she'd known she'd failed to meet her parents' expectations, and she still carried the scars, not all of them physical, as reminders.

"So…" Gem paused as the waitress deposited their food, left a check, and hurried off. "Do I get a sneak preview of Ciri? I can't wait to see how you see her."

Austin grabbed the pen the waitress had left on the table by the check and folded over a corner of the paper placemat advertising local garages, contractors, and pet sitters. She quickly sketched Ciri holding her sword overhead with both hands, her long braid flying behind her, bolts of lightning shooting from the blade, and a banshee war cry enclosed in the balloon above her. She tore the paper in half and passed it to Gem. "There you go."

She held her breath while Gem turned it back and forth, as if she could see beneath the flat page to the rest of the action. When she glanced up at Austin, her eyes glowed. "If I show up at your hotel room and demand to see more, will you think I'm a crazy stalker?"

Austin forced a grin, knowing that wouldn't be the reason Gem hunted her down. "I think I'll probably be safe."

"Mmm." Gem folded the paper carefully and tucked it into her pocket. "I'll remind you you said that."

CHAPTER FOUR

A re you sure you don't want me to drive for a while?" Gem asked as she buckled into her seat and Austin got behind the wheel. She'd almost hated leaving the warm cocoon of the diner, where she'd felt a little removed from her ordinary life and a little bit out of control. She wasn't quite herself, and the unexpected freedom was exhilarating. Austin continued to fascinate, by turns charming and amusing and then, suddenly, quiet and reflective—as if she were struggling with some larger question and finding the answers elusive. Gem loved puzzles, although her interest didn't usually extend to people. She'd learned a painful lesson when it came to people—she was terrible at reading them and vowed never to be in a position where her flawed ability to discern another's true intentions would matter. If she didn't care, she couldn't be hurt. Austin had already made her forget her sacred promises—from the beginning, Austin had been a mystery Gem wanted to unwrap.

"I'm good for now. But thanks." Austin eased out onto the highway. Traffic was light, but the visibility was almost zero. The mist had turned to a steady, light rain and fog blanked the sky, making the day nearly as dark as night. They'd been on the road half the day and were still only a third of the way to their destination. "If we keep making the kind of time we have all day, I'll take you up on it."

"We could surrender," Gem said. "Pull into a Motel 6–type place and ride this out. The rain may not let up, but eventually the fog will lift. We'd probably end up arriving at about the same time, and the driving would be easier. Probably safer too."

"We might have to eventually." Austin didn't have any intention of quitting, but she couldn't really come up with a plausible reason why she needed to reach Rock Hill Island ASAP. "But the fog has to break eventually, and we might get lucky sooner rather than later. You okay with being cooped up in here awhile longer?"

"I'm fine. I've never minded coops." Gem smiled. "And the company is excellent."

"Yes, it is." Austin glanced over and smiled. "Is there someone you need to update on your situation?"

"Someone…oh, at the sanctuary, you mean?" Gem shook her head. "No, not really. Our study group is funded through a national program in association with the sanctuary's foundation. I'm actually in charge of the research program, and I planned to arrive a few days early. I wanted a little time alone just to enjoy the place before the work got started."

"To wake up to nothing but the sounds of the wind and birds," Austin murmured.

Gem flushed, glad Austin's attention was on the road. "My inner geek is showing, isn't it."

Austin looked her way and shook her head slightly. Her expression was solemn, unexpectedly serious. "Not at all."

"Well," Gem said, her throat unusually tight, "the other investigators have been here before. If anyone does show up before me, they'll settle in fine on their own. How about you?"

"Sorry?" Austin said.

"Is this a solitary vacation, or do you have friends in the area?"

"Oh." Austin preferred to say as little as possible about her plans—the less said, the less she had to embellish. And the less guilty she'd feel about not explaining her real purpose for the trip. "No. Just me."

"You are serious about holing up, then."

"Once I get into the drafting stages of a project," Austin said, happy to retreat to safer ground where she could answer without subterfuge, "I tend to hibernate until it's finished."

"How about I give you my number when we get there," Gem said, "and if you decide a change of scenery will improve your concentration, or you just need a break, you can call me. I'll show you around the sanctuary. It's quite beautiful this time of year."

"I...thanks."

"You're welcome," Gem said quietly, a little taken aback at her offer. She could tell herself she was just being friendly, just returning Austin's generosity in giving her a ride, and that would be true—partially. But it was more than that, if she really wanted to look at it. She liked Austin's company. She wanted to see her again, although that didn't seem likely given what Austin had just said. Reaching out to someone—someone who interested her in a personal way—just wasn't something she did. More often than not, she was the one gently saying no to proposals from women to get together. She wasn't unfriendly, and she enjoyed the company of women, but so very often, those invitations came with the unmistakable undercurrent of interest in something she had no interest in. She didn't want a date. Not that she wanted a date with Austin, and Austin hadn't given her any indication she was at all interested in anything like that.

She just enjoyed her company—her easy confidence, her gentle teasing, even her occasional silences that hinted at some hidden hurt. Those glimpses of internal struggle might intrigue her most of all. And if she was honest, she'd have to admit that she wanted to know those secrets. She didn't want to say good-bye at the end of the trip and never see her again.

That desire for more was astonishing and a warning she ought to heed. She had no time and no place in her life for anything remotely resembling a personal relationship. Oh, she had a relationship with Kim, but they'd been comfortably seeing each other for almost two years and neither one of them had taken it to a truly serious level. As far as she knew, Kim didn't see anyone else, and neither did she, but they'd never actually discussed being exclusive. She mentally examined the possibility that Kim might be seeing someone else, something she'd never given any thought to before, and didn't feel the slightest bit of jealousy or threat. She suspected Kim would feel the same about her. They were fond of each other, compatible in their interests, both socially and professionally. Sex had never been a huge part of their relationship and was less and less so as time passed. They were comfortable—or at least she was. Safe and comfortable and unengaged. She knew for certain that the most intimate times she'd spent with Kim never stirred the bone-deep excitement of sharing a simple meal with Austin. She'd never believed in the concept of chemistry, but being around Austin was changing her mind. Her skin literally tingled when Austin's mellow tones brushed over her. And that must spell danger. Retreat was surely the wisest course.

"I know you're busy," Gem said, "so, please, don't feel obligated—"

"It's not that. If I can escape," Austin said quietly, "I'd love a tour. But I can't make any promises."

"Fair enough," Gem said, surprised by the somberness in Austin's voice. She almost sounded as if she had no control over what was going to happen. Maybe that was just her way of describing being caught up in her work, something Gem definitely understood, but there was a level of regret in Austin's tone that tugged at her. Impulsively, she reached across the seat and squeezed Austin's forearm. "I mean it, no pressure. I understand about work, about getting lost in it. About needing to finish a project."

Without warning, Austin caught her hand and held it. Her fingers were as strong as Gem imagined, warm and smooth. Hers automatically threaded between Austin's, and the fit was perfect. Her breath caught in her throat. No, she'd never felt anything quite like this, not even before she'd put up the barriers to guard against getting too close.

"I don't feel pressured," Austin said. "Not the way you think. Not by you. It's…a little hard to explain."

"Then don't. Call if you can. I'd…" Gem grabbed a breath, took a chance. "I'd like that."

A muscle jumped along the edge of Austin's jaw, her profile in the reflected light of the dash going still and hard, as if flesh had been replaced by marble: cold and beautiful and untouchable. "So would I."

"Well then—all we really need to do is—"

A loud bang reverberated through the vehicle.

"Hold on!" Austin grabbed the wheel as the big vehicle swerved and skidded. "Damn it."

The SUV lurched onto the shoulder and Gem's seat belt tightened across her chest, pinning her against her seat. Her pulse jumped and she peered out the windows into the surrounding gloom, desperately trying to see. "What is it?"

"A flat, I think," Austin said through gritted teeth. "Something must have been in the road. I didn't see it." The vehicle bumped along the shoulder and finally came to a stop. "You okay?"

"Yes, fine." Gem released her seat belt and massaged her shoulder where the strap had bitten in. She bet she'd have a bruise.

Austin punched the hazard button and lights flashed on the dash. "I hope we've got tools."

Gem opened the large glove compartment and sorted through what was there. "Manual. Rental papers. No flashlight."

"There has to be a spare and a jack," Austin said. "I'll go take a look."

"I'll come with you."

"You might as well stay in here. There's no point both of us getting drenched."

"Visibility is terrible," Gem said. "I don't want you outside working without some way to warn other vehicles. At least I can use the light on my phone to signal that we're out there."

"Let me assess the damage first. Then we'll go from there."

"Promise you won't try to fix it by yourself."

Austin sighed. "Has anyone ever mentioned you tend to be pretty stubborn?"

Gem smiled. "That would not be a news flash. Now, promise?"

"Promise. Two minutes."

"I'm counting."

Austin slipped outside, leaving her alone in the silence with nothing but the metronomic flicker of the hazard lights and her own confounding thoughts. The fog sat against the windows, pressing in like a malevolent force. She shook away the foreboding. She'd never been afraid of the dark, never been afraid of the unknown. The only thing she truly feared was falling victim to her own desires, and being wrong again.

The rear hatch opened and when she looked back, a shadow moved in the gray mist. Austin. "All right?"

"Fine. Just be another minute."

After what seemed like fifteen minutes rather than one, Austin tapped on the side window and Gem powered it down. Rainwater blew in, dampening her hair and face. She pushed wet strands away from her face. "How is it?"

"It's flat all right. We've got a new spare and tools. We're well enough off the road that I think I can change it safely. It's gonna be messy and will probably take me some time. It's a mudslide on the shoulder."

"You think Triple A is out of the question?"

"On a day like this? They're going to be so busy dealing with fender benders and breakdowns, we could be sitting here for hours. It's just a flat. I've changed plenty."

"I can't say I'm an expert at it, but I take direction pretty well. I'll help."

Austin's hair was soaked, lying in thick, dark slashes across her forehead. Her shirt was plastered to her chest, clinging to muscles and the curve of her breasts. Water dripped from her chin and the angles of her jaw. She was gorgeous. Gem swallowed and steadied her voice. "It'll go faster with me helping."

"I'm already soaked. Really, there's no point in both of us—"

"I'm coming." Gem grasped the handle and pushed open the door an inch. "Let's get this done."

"You win." Austin stepped back and caught Gem around the waist as she jumped out. "Watch your step, okay? The shoulder slopes away right behind us and I can't tell how far down it goes."

The rain pelted Gem's face, an icy blast that startled her with its ferocity. The storm was coming in harder than she'd expected. She gripped Austin's waistband to steady herself. "I'm good now."

"Come on." Austin offered her hand and, for the second time in less than an hour, Gem took it. The action felt as natural as anything she'd ever done, and as rare. She couldn't remember the last time she had touched anyone with such a feeling of rightness.

Austin led her back along the side of the vehicle. She'd left the hatch up and directed Gem in front of it. "You can duck underneath if the rain gets too bad."

"Do you have a rain slicker?" Gem asked, zipping her windbreaker.

"In my bag, but I might as well save it at this point. I'm already drenched."

"You're going to freeze."

"Don't worry," Austin said. "I've been out for a lot longer than this in plenty of worse places."

Gem wanted to ask what she meant. But she had more important things to do. Like keep them from being hit while they were stopped. She pressed the light icon on her phone. "I only have a half charge."

"You should save it. I'll be okay."

"At least let me hand you tools."

"Only if you stay out of the road. I don't want some jackass to come plowing along and hit you."

Her concern, and her possessive tone, brought heat rushing to Gem's skin and kindled a slow burn in deeper places. She brushed the damp hair from Austin's cheek. Her face was hot, her eyes blazing. Gem had the insane urge to kiss her. She swallowed hard. "I'll be careful."

But she feared it was already too late for that.

CHAPTER FIVE

Austin wrenched off the last lug nut and held it out in Gem's direction. Water trailed down the middle of her back and pooled in the hollow of her spine. Her pants were sodden. Her shirt adhered to her skin like a cloying lover. She was a mess, but she'd gotten the damn thing off. "Here you go."

"Got it."

Gem's fingers slid over hers, hotter than they should be considering the freezing, driving rain. Maybe she was just imagining the rush of warmth traveling up her chilled extremity from the brief touch. Just like she'd imagined the heat in Gem's eyes, gleaming in the glow of the taillights a few minutes before. The memory of that heat was enough to cast out the cold as she knelt in the mud, cranking the jack under the big, heavy SUV. Thinking about Gem kept her mind off all kinds of things, things she probably *should* be spending a lot more time worrying about. Like what was happening out in the ocean on Rig 86, and whether the oil had sheened the ocean surface. If that happened, they'd have to contact the authorities and begin ocean- and shore-containment procedures. She kept expecting her phone to vibrate—Eloise chasing her down, wanting to know where the hell she was. Since she had no way of changing any of that right then, her guilt about wanting to think only of Gem eased a little. Who could blame her for wanting to quell her misery by daydreaming about a beautiful woman who was amazing in every way? Gem's enthusiasm, her joie de vivre, her humor, and those flashes of heat that came from nowhere and seemed to surprise her as much as Austin were the stuff dreams were made of.

Too bad not all of her secret pleasure was guilt free. She doubted Gem would look at her the way she did if she knew of her other job, even though it was legitimate and necessary. Yes, she was hired to avoid bad press for the company, but minimizing civilian panic and averting economic instability were essential too. Sure, she was paid to keep a lid on the bad press, but she was also paid to prevent rumor and escalations of doom that could literally destabilize the world. No one wanted stock markets plunging at word of offshore oil leaking and potentially costing billions of dollars when it might not come to pass. When and what news to release to the world wasn't her call alone, but her technical input was a big part of it, and she was the wall between the press and what was happening behind the scenes. Eloise and her bosses were too smart and too scrupulous to subvert the law, but within the bounds of the law, they protected the company. And why shouldn't they? Much of the world depended on the oil business too.

"Not that that would matter to Gem," Austin muttered as she yanked off the wheel and leaned it against the side of the SUV. She doubted Gem would have much sympathy for big corporations. Too many true disasters—pipeline ruptures, well failures, transport ship leaks—had caused countless wildlife deaths and contamination of waters and marshlands and beaches throughout the world to argue that the oil industry hadn't damaged the environment. She couldn't argue against those facts. They existed too. She'd known a lot of people like Gem, people devoted to the sanctity of the environment and its inhabitants, who'd made it their life's work to protect it. She respected the work they did and tried to walk the thin line between protecting her client's interests and preserving the integrity of nature. She believed her job was necessary, or she wouldn't do it. The fact that her parents appreciated the risk involved, and approved of her work, never mattered. Much.

She hoisted the muddy wheel and carted it to the back of the SUV. She set it down, leaned in, and pulled out the spare.

"Are you almost done?" Gem asked. "You've got to be miserable."

"Theoretically, this next part should be easy," Austin said grimly. She dumped the flat into the well in the rear of the SUV. "Let's hope so."

Gem gripped her arm. "You're sure I can't help you out some?"

"It's gotten a lot darker," Austin said. "I could use your light if you don't mind getting wet. I think you can still stay under cover of the hatch and keep mostly dry."

"I've been wet before," Gem said. "Wildlife biologist, remember? The birds don't care if it rains. I won't melt."

"Sorry. You're right. I mean, maybe not about the melting, but I get you're not a delicate flower."

Gem laughed. "Definitely not. More like a wildflower."

"Yeah, I can see that." Gem did look wild and beautiful, with damp blond curls framing her face and her blue eyes alight. Austin traced her finger along the angle of Gem's jaw where raindrops beaded in a delicate chain and slowly brushed them clear. Gem's eyes widened again, and that spark of heat flared. An answering fire surged in Austin's belly. Hell, what was she doing? She turned away and grabbed the spare. "Okay, you're up."

Gem followed Austin, switched on the light on her phone, and held it down in front of her. Austin knelt on the stony, muddy shoulder and wrestled the spare onto the wheel hub. If that was the easy part, she hated to think how hard getting it off had been. She hated thinking of Austin exposed to the wicked wind and driving rain for so long. She edged a little closer and tried to use her body to shield Austin from the downpour.

"Okay. Hand me the nut." Austin held out her hand. "Give them all to me—you don't need to be out here too."

"I'm good. Wildflower, remember?" Gem dropped the first nut into Austin's hand and pulled the hood of her windbreaker closer around her face. She was still reasonably dry, although her jeans were soaked from the thigh down, below the bottom of the jacket. Austin's clothes were so thoroughly soaked she might as well have been standing naked—and that was an image she didn't want to dwell on. Or actually, she kind of did—which was worse. Traffic had slowed to a trickle, most people probably having given up and pulled off to wait out the storm in roadside motels. The occasional vehicle, usually a pickup truck going too fast, shot by and sluiced water in their direction. Austin didn't even seem to notice the additional deluge, but Gem wanted to shout after the crazy drivers to smarten up. "I wish I had some way to keep you drier."

Austin looked up, blinking rain from her eyes. "I'm okay. Really. Almost done."

A minute or two later, Austin released the jack, pulled it out from under the vehicle, and rose. "Come on, let's get out of here."

Gem hunched under the raised hatch and kept her light on while Austin stored the tools back in the wheel well and closed up the back.

"You need dry clothes," Gem said.

"I'll have to change inside."

"Fine. Get what you need." When Austin hesitated, Gem said, "I won't look."

Austin grinned. "Damn."

Gem gave her a little shove on the shoulder. "Hurry up. Even your eyelashes are dripping."

Austin pulled her satchel closer, rummaged inside, and came out with a shirt and jeans. She bundled them up and thrust them under her arm. "Come on, I'll help you back inside."

Gem poked her lightly in the center of her chest. "I can make it. Go get in yourself."

"Stubborn," Austin muttered, but she closed the hatch and they both headed back to the front.

Gem shed her windbreaker before she climbed in and draped it over the back of her seat so it could drip onto the rear floor. Austin stood outside with her door open. "It'll be faster to take my clothes off out here, and I won't get the seat all wet."

"As long as you're quick." Gem swiveled in her seat and peered out the back. "There's no one coming right now. If someone does, you need to jump inside."

Austin laughed. "They probably won't even see me."

"Oh, they'll see you," Gem said. And so would she, because she planned on keeping an eye out behind them, and that meant she'd be looking past Austin toward the road. But it wasn't as if she was intentionally spying or anything. She just didn't want anyone seeing Austin naked except her. Her mind stumbled on that thought. Oh, for heaven's sake, she really did need to get a grip and get back to reality—any number of women had undoubtedly seen Austin naked and likely would again. And she wasn't going to be one of them. This road trip would end soon enough and she'd be her careful, rational self again. Just the way she liked it. The way she wanted it.

Austin stripped her shirt off over her head without even unbuttoning it, balled it up, and tossed it into the back of the SUV. Whatever she'd had on under it went along for the ride, and she was suddenly, gloriously naked from the waist up. Her teardrop-shaped breasts were neither large nor small, with small, tight nipples beaded in the chill. Damn near perfect—no, check that. Perfect. Her chest and shoulders were subtly muscled, and if she had a tan, it was an all-over one. Gem's stomach tightened.

Austin glanced in, grinned, and opened her jeans. When she hooked her hands in the waistband, Gem dragged her gaze away. Lord, she must seem like a voyeur. Maybe she was, a teeny bit, because watching Austin undress was definitely enjoyable. She wasn't cold any longer, that was for sure.

Austin swiveled onto the front seat and shoved down her jeans. Her boots went flying onto the floor on the driver's side. She was fast, but not so fast Gem couldn't see her muscular form emerge. She was lean and long, which was no surprise. Her skin blushed red from the reflected dash lights. Her torso was tapered, her hips narrow, and below...Gem carefully didn't look there. Within seconds it seemed, Austin pulled her jeans up her long legs, lifted her hips, and snugged her pants around her waist. When she raised her arms to tug on her shirt, Gem kept her eyes up, but she'd already seen the long, irregular scar that wrapped around Austin's torso just below her left breast. Slightly indented, darker than the surrounding skin, the scar was not deforming, but a symbol of something serious nonetheless.

Austin shoved her shirt into her pants and leaned down to pull on her boots. "Thanks for keeping lookout."

"No problem."

Austin adjusted her seat, glad to be warm and dry, and glad Gem seemed to have enjoyed watching her change. She wasn't usually self-conscious or really even aware of how other women perceived her body. She rarely gave it much thought. She kept in shape more because of the nature of her work than anything else, climbing around rigging, hustling from one place to another, and when at home, keeping up the property and stockpiling firewood for the winter. When she was with another woman, her focus was on them, and usually that's the way they liked it too. She wasn't above being pleasured, she enjoyed it, but those times her partners were less than reciprocating never really bothered her.

She wondered how Gem saw her and hoped she liked what she saw. That was unlike her, but none of this was really like her. The silence grew, and she thought she knew why. "I was born with a heart defect. That's what the scar's from."

"And the surgery fixed it," Gem said, her heart beating faster. Of course the problem was fixed, it had to be. Austin was in great shape, and…the idea of Austin being ill, being hurt, was frightening in a way she didn't want to think about.

"It took a couple of goes. The first time was just a few days after I was born, so they tell me. Then again when I was eleven," Austin said, her hands loosely clasping the wheel, "but, yeah, all's good."

"That must have been really hard." Gem's heart hurt imagining Austin's childhood being shadowed by such a serious illness.

Austin glanced over at her. "Long time ago."

Gem nodded, hearing the pain but recognizing Austin's attempt to make light of it. Still, the specter of a young Austin dealing with the fear and discomfort filled her with sympathetic sorrow. Wishing to chase away the shadows, or maybe ease her own sadness, she cupped Austin's jaw and brushed away a trickle of water trailing down her cheek with her thumb. Austin held so very, very still, Gem was reminded of a wild thing, caught and wary and waiting to be freed or destroyed. Freedom was so very often only a breath away from death. "I'm sorry."

"Thank you."

Austin leaned ever so lightly into her palm, or perhaps she imagined that too. If she did, she didn't care. She couldn't pull away. She drew Austin's face closer and kissed her, and when Austin didn't move back, she let her lips linger, feeling the coolness of the rain disappear from Austin's soft lips and heat surge against her mouth. She slid her fingers into Austin's hair, wrapped them around the back of her neck, and stroked her nape as she stroked her mouth. A soft groan escaped from deep in Austin's chest, and her lips parted in offering. Gem teased a little inside, tasting her, and traced the warm inner surface of her lower lip with the tip of her tongue.

Austin groaned again and gripped her shoulders, her hands hard and wonderfully demanding. Her tongue met Gem's, hot and firm, turning the kiss into something deeper, something hungrier. Gem gripped Austin's shirt, clinging to her. Her breasts tightened and her blood beat hard in the pit of her stomach. Her breath came faster, her head grew light. She wanted to climb into Austin's lap and press against her. She wanted to feel her everywhere. She tugged at Austin's shirt, found hot skin and hard muscles. She groaned.

Austin jerked back. "Gem. God. Traffic. This isn't safe."

"I know." Not safe for more reasons than Gem could count. She braced her palms against Austin's chest, holding herself away or she'd kiss her again. She gasped in a breath, another, until she felt like she could speak. "Traffic. Right. God, sorry."

"I hope not." Austin curved a hand behind Gem's head and yanked her close. She kissed her hard, hard enough for Gem to open her mouth and take her in again. God, she wanted to be naked, she wanted Austin's mouth and hands all over. She wanted in a way she hadn't wanted since before she knew better. She got a hand between them again, stroked the few inches of skin she'd bared on Austin's stomach. Needing to feel. Needing. Austin's hips lifted and Gem's vision blurred. "Okay, we need to stop."

Austin groaned. "I know. You feel so damn good."

"We can't stay here. And we can't…" Gem gestured to the front of the car and the wheel and the gearshift and the insanity of what they were doing. She laughed, her voice shaking. "And you know. We can't."

Austin slumped back, her hands on her thighs. "Yeah. I know. We can't." She glanced over, her face stark with hunger. "But I want to."

CHAPTER SIX

The silence stretched to fill the car, the air as thick as the swirling mist outside. Ordinarily Austin didn't mind silence. She enjoyed the quiet, letting it give her mind a place to empty and her body to relax. So much, maybe too much, of her life was spent on the move, but she didn't stop long enough to wonder if that was what she really wanted. She and Gem had shared long stretches of silences throughout the day, and even with the absence of words she'd been attuned to Gem's presence—her quiet breathing, the companionship and warmth reaching her as if Gem had extended a hand to touch her. This silence was different, a chasm of uncertainty filled with all they hadn't said. Her head pounded with her own voice and what she imagined Gem was thinking.

When in doubt, revert to talking about the weather.

"I think the fog's lifting," Austin said.

"We're on a roll, then. I'm catching a cell signal," Gem said, staring at her phone. She flicked through a few screens. "NOAA predicts a chain of fronts moving through over the next few days." She laughed a little mirthlessly. "I believe we're about to experience the calm before the next storm."

"I don't mind if it gives us a shot at getting to the coast." Grateful for any sign of normalcy, Austin leaned over and switched to an alternate route on the GPS. "What do you think? Shall we try to skirt around this and take the coast road south? If it doesn't work out, it could end up taking us longer."

"I don't mind taking a chance," Gem said quietly.

Trying to decipher some hidden meaning to that statement and deciding anything she guessed would be wishful thinking, Austin turned off onto a local road that would take them to the shore road on the ocean side of the peninsula. During the season the narrow two-lane was congested and traffic crawled for miles as the chain of tiny coastal towns strung along the shoreline filled with tourists, but in mid-September, they were preparing for the long off-season, when many of the local stores closed, the motels shuttered, and the year-round inhabitants scrambled to make a living or went on public assistance until the tourists returned in spring along with the birds.

Birds. Gem's passion.

"Tell me about the birds," Austin said.

"What about them?" Gem sounded slightly suspicious, as if she couldn't fathom why Austin would ask.

"Anything." *Anything just so I can hear your voice.* Austin glanced at her, wondering if her desperation showed in her eyes and not really caring. They had so little time. She just wanted them not to be strangers for a little while longer. "Why do they migrate in the first place?"

"We don't really know—we can only surmise from their behavior." Gem chuckled. "Like with so many things. Anyhow, something signals them to migrate. That cue isn't necessarily the same for every species—sometimes it's the shortening of the day, or the change in nighttime temperatures, or a reduction in their food supply. Certainly genetics plays a part. The exact combination of factors probably varies from species to species, but even first-time migrants know where to go when the time comes."

Despite wishing the damn birds were flying anywhere but right toward them, Austin was fascinated. By the phenomenon all on its own, and by Gem's enthusiasm most of all. "Do they always come back to the same places when they migrate?"

"Many do—especially the long-distance migrants that travel from Canada as far south as Central America. Some locations, like the area around Rock Hill Island, are what we call migrant traps. Popular stopovers for large numbers of birds." Gem smiled. "And of course, favorite spots for researchers, conservationists, and amateur birdwatchers."

"Migrant traps." Austin winced inside. Perfect. Not only did she have to worry about shore contamination, she had to deal with a threat to a pivotal location for people and wildlife.

"Mmm. That's part of the reason we study the flyways, so we can identify these areas of high species concentration and protect them. The island sanctuary is one of the stopping points along the Atlantic Flyway." Gem hesitated. She loved talking about birds, and she didn't mind skirting around the topic Austin obviously didn't want to discuss any more than she did. Like the elephant sitting in the backseat leaning over their shoulders. The kiss neither one of them wanted to acknowledge. She was grateful for the surcease. Maybe in a few more hours she'd be able to sort out her own feelings about it, but right now she was as surprised by the kiss as Austin probably was. Other than that first insane kiss with Christie ages ago, she'd never done anything so uncontrolled. And this time, she'd done it with a clear head, absolutely for herself and no one else. Unlike that first time, when she'd done it more out of desperation to save things with Paul than anything else. This time she'd kissed a woman first because she wanted to. She'd wanted to touch Austin, taste her, delve inside her. The question was why, and she hadn't an answer. "Do you really want to hear about all this?"

Austin nodded. "I do. So, this Atlantic Flyway—I'm assuming that's not a euphemism."

"Not at all. There are quite a number of flyways traversing North America, well-traveled migratory pathways with established stopovers for various species. It's made it easier for conservation groups to protect endangered species by identifying and preserving sanctuaries."

"Like Rock Hill Island."

"Yes—the Audubon Society has been the big mover and shaker there, but plenty of smaller groups and institutions do the same thing."

"I remember when I was a kid," Austin said, "watching the geese fly south in huge V-shaped formations. The sound was so amazing. I always felt a little sad—I don't know why." She shrugged. "Maybe I just wanted to be somewhere else too."

The melancholy in Austin's voice tugged at Gem's heart. "Where was that?"

"Vermont," Austin said. "My mother is a trauma surgeon at UVM."

"Is that where—" Gem trailed off.

"Where I had my surgeries? Yes."

"And now?" Gem didn't have the right to ask, but she couldn't help herself. She wanted—needed—to know in some deep primal place that Austin was safe.

"I'm good. Perfect health."

Austin grinned and looked more like the charming rake she'd appeared when teasing Gem in the diner about the buxom and seductive waitress. Had that only been half a day ago? Time seemed to have fractured into before and after *the kiss*, and the universe had taken on a whole different color. Despite the fog, the before-kiss time had been suffused with sunlight and blue skies, at least in Gem's imagination. The after-the-kiss was a deep purple morning sky on the edge of the sea as storm clouds rolled in. Reminding herself she loved both and never feared a gale, she went with her instincts. "It must have been really hard as a kid, though."

The silence surged back and Gem held her breath. Their truce was so fragile, like a fledgling first attempting to fly.

"I didn't have the stamina of other kids, so sports were out. In my family…that was tough."

"A competitive lot?"

Austin's laughter was sharp-edged and humorless. "About everything. My father was active Air Force and flew fighter jets in the Gulf. He met my mother there—she was Navy reserve and got called up as a medic. She got out between wars when my brother was born, but she never left the front lines. My brother's some kind of athletic savant—he never met a sport he didn't excel at. Got drafted to both a Major League Baseball team and the NFL. Played both for a while and finally settled on baseball. Plays for the Yankees."

"Richie Germaine is your brother?" Now that she thought about it, she could see the resemblance. Germaine was a star on and off the field—smart, handsome, and mega-talented. He also had a world-famous model for a wife, and they were frequently the subject of media attention.

"Yep, that's my big brother. I never could catch up in the physical arena—by the time I was finally done with the surgeries, it was too late for me and school sports." Austin grimaced. "Or much of anything else my family valued."

If they hadn't been in the car and weren't still mired in the after-kiss awkwardness, Gem would have hugged her. She could so easily see the child who, through no fault of her own, hadn't fit in a highly aggressive, competitive, physical family. Austin seemed to be the last person in need of protecting, but Gem ached with a well of protectiveness all the same. "Well, you've made up for it now. You're pretty damn famous yourself."

Austin laughed, and this time her obvious pleasure softened her features, making her seem younger and far less cynical. "Yeah, that's me—crowds follow me wherever I go."

"Told you," Gem said, inordinately happy just to have made her laugh. Maybe the after-kiss strangeness would fade away now too.

"So," Austin said, "enough about my uninteresting past. Tell me what kind of birds you're expecting, and when."

"I'm mostly interested in waterfowl—ducks, geese, swans, pelicans—especially since many of them overnight on pastures en route where they might come into contact with domestic fowl. And of course, all the shorebirds are key to follow. Many of them endangered." Gem stretched, beginning to feel the stiffness in her back and thighs from the long hours of inactivity. "The saltmarsh sparrow is a favorite of mine. And don't try to tell me you're dying to know more."

"Come on," Austin protested. "It's interesting. Do you band them or something?"

"Some, yes. We also document the flocks through satellite tracking, geographics, and sometimes with little tracking devices called geotrackers. And we ask birdwatchers to call a hotline if they sight a banded bird."

"I had no idea," Austin muttered, and she really should have. She'd dealt with environmental rescue teams more than she'd like, but she'd never talked to the biologists—usually just the incident commanders. She needed to get a lot closer to the ground to understand the personalities involved and what was at risk. "How long do they stay?"

She hoped the answer was not very long. If the spill was ongoing but slow, even if they couldn't contain it immediately, they might be able to set up enough blockades to stop or divert the movement of the surface contaminants to shore. Then if the birds were gone, the impact would be far less. Cleanup procedure would be a lot less complicated if they didn't have to deal with wildlife salvage.

"They don't all arrive at once, of course," Gem said. "We'll be seeing nesting flocks for the next few weeks."

"I see." Of course she couldn't catch a break. But then, maybe she would. Maybe Ray Tatum would give her good news. And she needed to contact him soon to get a sit rep. "We're still a good three hours from the island at the speed we're going. If the weather clears a little more, I'll be able to make better time, but I'm not counting on it."

"Whenever you're ready, I can eat," Gem said.

"Let me know when you've got some kind of signal again too. I need to make some calls."

"I'll keep checking." Gem remembered Austin had mentioned there was no one she was meeting, but she didn't pry. It was none of her business who Austin needed to call, a stark reminder she didn't really know anything about her. Or rather, what she *did* know were not the things one ordinarily learned on first meeting. Sure, she knew where Austin lived, more or less, and she knew what she did for a living, and she'd learned a couple of things about her family. But she didn't know her age, she didn't know her taste in music, or her favorite food, or her favorite color, or, God—if she had a girlfriend. Weren't those the things you were supposed to talk about when first getting to know someone? Obviously, she was failing at Relationship 101. But she did know some things about her—she knew she was confident, capable, a good listener, protective, a little possessive, secretive at times, and, beneath the strength, plagued by sadness. Austin was fascinating, alluring, and a fabulous kisser. And about that kiss…

"What happened back there," Gem said before she could second-guess herself, "was pretty unusual for me."

Austin cut her a look. "The tire changing or the kiss?"

Gem smiled fleetingly. "I've done both a few times before. Actually the kiss more than the tire thing, but I usually wait until, you know, we've had a date or three or so to jump. So to speak."

"We had breakfast at the diner. That's kind of the date."

"It was." At a loss, Gem searched for exactly what she wanted to say. She didn't want to apologize. She wasn't sorry. The kiss had been everything she hadn't realized she wanted—exquisitely sensual, passionate, a tangle of sensations that disengaged her mind and left her with nothing but feelings. Wonderful, wild feelings she wanted to recapture. Of course, she wasn't about to mention she wanted to do it again. That and more. She needed to examine those emotions a lot more carefully before she found herself in way too deep. The kiss was one thing. Sex with a near stranger was something else again.

"It was a hell of a kiss," Austin added. "Just saying."

Gem laughed, exhilaration coursing through her. The heaviness and uncertainty that had weighed on her evaporated. She felt as light as a bird must, drifting on an air current. "That's an understatement, Ace."

Austin caught her breath. *Ace.* No one called her that. She liked it. "You okay with it, then?"

"Mostly. You?"

"Sure, yeah." Austin slowed and pulled in to a small lot in front of a single-story building with a sign out front proclaiming *Erma's Family Diner*. She turned in the seat and faced Gem. "I mean, I'm not usually taken by surprise that way. I…I liked it a lot."

"So we'll just agree it was good, and we're okay."

Austin wished it was that easy. What she hadn't said, couldn't say, hung in the air like a thundercloud only she could see. She couldn't divert that storm, not yet, and she didn't want to tarnish the memory of the kiss, not when it was likely to be the only one she had. "Absolutely. We're great."

CHAPTER SEVEN

W e might catch a break after all," Austin said, looking out the window beside their table. Although the sky remained gray and heavily overcast, the rain had stopped while they'd looked at menus and ordered. Unlike the diner that morning, this restaurant was nearly empty at the height of the dinner hour. Although not large, the main dining room felt cavernous with only a few tables occupied, or perhaps it was the silence at their table creating the vast empty sensation in her chest. Austin resisted the urge to shake her shoulders to throw off the cloak of melancholy. The ominous weight wasn't going to be dismissed with a casual gesture. The easy connection between her and Gem had disappeared, and the tension taking its place twisted in her middle like a giant claw.

So much for talking away the unease between them. She'd said everything was okay between them. So had Gem. But the awkwardness intensified with each passing minute. Gem toyed with the stem of her wineglass, her expression pensive. Austin wished again she could read her mind. She wished a lot of things, and wishing for what she couldn't have was something she thought she'd given up a long time before. Apparently, she'd been wrong. She reached across the table and caught Gem's free hand. "Hey."

Gem looked up, her eyes widening. "Sorry? What?"

Just the sound of her voice eased the knot between Austin's shoulder blades. "Are you really okay?"

"Yes and no. Mostly uncertain." Gem smiled faintly. "Lousy company. I'm sorry."

"No need to be. Anything I can do?" Austin grimaced. She might be a little too late for that. "Or am I the problem?"

"I hate to say it's me and not you, but that's the truth." Running her thumb over the back of Austin's hand, Gem shook her head. "I'm just trying to figure myself out, and believe me, that's never been easy. When it really counts, I'm a mystery to myself. It's hell when you keep secrets from yourself."

Austin sat back, reluctantly releasing Gem's hand. She wanted to keep holding it, but she couldn't keep inviting that connection with all that went unsaid between them. All *she* hadn't said. "I'm sure there's a million things about you I don't know, but you don't seem secretive to me. In my experience, people with secrets to keep rarely talk about themselves—or when they do, they never say anything that matters."

Gem's brows rose. "What matters, do you think?"

"To you?" Austin smiled. "Your birds, your work, your love of solitude. You enjoy being alone, but you're easy to talk to. You like people but you don't need someone around twenty-four seven. You're independent and comfortable with your own company."

"Well, at least I've given a good first impression," Gem said lightly, but her expression remained contemplative. Her gaze was reflective, as if she was looking inward or somewhere far off into the distance.

Austin waited, her heart thumping, feeling like a fraud. She was the one keeping secrets, even though she'd been more open with Gem than anyone she could ever recall—at least once she'd learned not to expose her innermost thoughts to her family. Could Gem tell the disclosures were a little one-sided? They never seemed to have casual conversations. Every moment seemed so important. Maybe that was why she couldn't pull back, didn't want to let the silence—the distance—grow. Gem brought every fiber of her being to life. Could anyone blame her for not wanting to let that exhilaration fade away?

"The last few years," Gem said at last, "my main goal has been to keep my life on an even keel, to be happy with what I have—the friendships, personal and professional, and my work. I thought I'd achieved a pretty good balance, all things considered."

"And today changed all that?" Austin didn't want to hear Gem regretted the intimacies they'd shared, but she wanted to hear Gem's truth, whatever that might be.

"Well, some of it." Gem reached for her wineglass, took a long, slow swallow, and cradled the glass in both hands. "I would characterize myself as being slightly unbalanced today." She looked up, gave a rueful smile. "The kiss might have been a bit of a tilt."

Austin grinned, happy to see even a little of the worry ebb from Gem's eyes. "I have to admit I like you unbalanced."

"I'm glad to hear that, because I think it's all your fault."

"Mine?" Austin kept her tone light, but she watched Gem's face and read the seriousness there. She prepared herself, pretty sure she was guilty of whatever Gem was about to accuse her of. "What have I done?"

"Somehow you made me stop thinking about balance and... and comfort." Gem nodded as if in sudden understanding. "That's it, I think. I don't want to be comfortable around you." Her eyes brightened. "I want to be a little crazy. Which I guess I was."

Austin swallowed, urgency coiling in the pit of her stomach. "If it helps, you're not alone. You make me pretty crazy too."

"Is that a bad thing?" Gem asked, as much to herself as Austin.

"What do you think?" Austin sensed they were talking about the future as much as the past, and she had to let Gem decide if the kiss was something to risk repeating. She couldn't voice her own desires, not this time. Not with this woman.

"I wish I knew." Gem sighed. "I don't know what to make of it."

"Do you have to understand it?"

"I don't know. I think so. I'm usually careful, cautious. I don't leap before I look, hard and long. At least, that's who I've been for the last eight or nine years at least."

"And before that?"

A pained expression flickered across Gem's face. Her

eyes darkened again. "Before that I was young and naïve and impressionable. Some might say stupid."

"All of those things go along with being young, don't they?"

"Were you ever young and stupid?"

"Careless," Austin said immediately. "Reckless. Risk-taking. So, yeah, stupid fits."

"Have you ever done anything you knew in your heart wasn't what you wanted, but you did it anyway?"

"I don't know." Austin blew out a breath, looked inward. "I'm not sure I know what's in my heart." She searched Gem's face. "But I can't imagine you've done anything you can't forgive yourself for."

"Forgiveness is a panacea for some ills that shouldn't be masked." Gem's mouth set into a hard line. "I don't believe that forgive and forget is always the best course. Sometimes we have to remember so we don't repeat our mistakes."

A chill doused the fire kindling in Austin's belly. "What can't you forgive?"

Gem was quiet for so long Austin knew she'd overstepped.

"I'm sorry." Austin held up a hand. "That's really personal, and being locked up in a car with me for a day doesn't make us close enough for me to ask—"

"*I* kissed *you*, remember?"

"Oh yeah, I remember." The heat surged back, a hunger in Austin's depths that refused to be silenced. "I remember kissing you back too. And if it makes any difference, I've been thinking a lot about doing it again."

"So have I. So I think that gives you the right to ask. I don't have to answer, after all."

"You're right, you don't. Your secrets are yours."

"I was married," Gem said abruptly.

"You must have been young." Austin wasn't as surprised to learn that Gem had been married as she was to learn she wasn't any longer. She couldn't imagine anyone letting Gem go.

"Nineteen. He was my high school boyfriend—more than that really. Our families were close. We'd known each other all our lives.

He was my best friend growing up, and it just always seemed a given that's what we would do."

"Sometimes when we're young we don't question what we want or why we think we want things," Austin said. "And it sounds like the two of you had something."

"I loved him," Gem said musingly. "A certain kind of love, at least, and I wanted that to be enough. Even when there were times I thought maybe it wasn't."

When Gem hesitated, Austin retrieved the wine bottle and poured another inch into Gem's glass, giving her a chance to decide to keep talking or not.

"Thanks." Gem picked up her glass. "We'd been married about three years, I guess, when I couldn't keep pretending everything was all right. I was applying to graduate school and Paul to law school. Of course we were trying to find a way to stay in the same location if possible."

"That's a lot of pressure on any relationship."

"That's what I thought too, when things started feeling…off. We weren't communicating, and the sex…well, the sex—" Gem shrugged. "Let's say it went from not great to not much at all. At first I minded, because I missed the connection, but not enough to push the issue."

"You didn't have any experience with women?"

Gem sighed. "I didn't have any experience with anyone except Paul. For a long time I thought it was me, not doing something right or not reading the signals correctly—but he kept saying everything was fine—and finally I stopped asking."

"Until…" Austin said gently.

"Right. Until he suggested we needed to explore the boundaries of our relationship. That it would be good for us, individually and as a couple."

Austin gritted her teeth. If she had Gem, she'd never want anyone else to touch her. She forcibly relaxed and kept her voice level. "He wanted to open up the relationship?"

"Yes. Or rather, sort of," Gem said bitterly. "He had someone specific in mind. Someone we both knew. One of my best friends, as a matter of fact."

"That couldn't have been easy."

"No, it was surprisingly easy. Christie, that was...is...her name, had always thought Paul was terrific. The perfect guy, she used to say. She was always looking for someone just like Paul."

"Did you have feelings for her, besides friendship?"

Gem drained her wineglass and, when Austin reached for the bottle, covered the top with her hand. She couldn't quite believe she was admitting all of this. She'd never even told Kim the whole story, and God, they were involved. But Kim had never asked, and she'd never been shaken out of her comfort zone enough to want to revisit any of it. Austin shook her up, all right. One simple kiss had her reeling, more than three years of dating Kim had ever done. "No, I'm good. Really. I can talk about this sober."

"I don't think one full glass is going to impair you."

"I know." Gem smiled. "I am kind of a lightweight, though. I'm good."

"Okay." Austin set the bottle aside.

"So, Christie." Gem met Austin's gaze, read acceptance there. Thankfully not pity or disappointment. "My feelings for Christie were pretty complicated. As I said, she was one of my friends, probably my best friend from freshman year on. She was beautiful, smart, funny, and loyal. I never admitted any kind of attraction to myself, but whenever I wanted to talk or needed to feel understood, she was the one I called. Not Paul."

"Paul must have known she'd be a safe choice, especially if you had reservations."

"Oh, I'm sure that was part of it." Gem grimaced. Paul had been far more perceptive than she'd been when it came to her feelings for Christie. Just another one of her many blind spots. "Whatever else he thought, he was right about that."

"So the three of you..."

"The three of us. Yes. After I told Christie what Paul had suggested, I thought we'd laugh it off. But she didn't laugh. She said she liked the idea, that she'd always wanted to be closer to both of us." Gem rubbed the bridge of her nose, closed her eyes for a second. Why could she still remember the glow in Christie's eyes when she'd said that, long after the excitement she'd felt then had turned to acid? "I remember her saying she could get into the idea, and the strangest feeling came over me. Excitement, different than anything I'd ever known. She said she wanted to be closer to both of us, but what I heard was she wanted to be closer to *me*. And for the first time, I realized that I wanted to be closer to her too."

"And you blame yourself for misreading things?"

"I blame myself for trusting Christie and for letting Paul's needs dictate mine." Gem swallowed the bitterness clawing at her throat. She would not let the past ambush her again. "I don't think twenty-four hours passed before the three of us were…well, I don't think I have to spell that out. I knew the second I kissed her why everything had always seemed just a little bit off with Paul. It wasn't him, it was me after all."

"Gem," Austin said gently, "most of us are raised to think we're heterosexual. Sometimes it takes a while to sort out expectation from desire."

"I know. That's not what bothered me. What bothered me was that I'd gotten myself into that situation because I'd been totally wrong about the man I married. He wanted Christie, not an open relationship with me. Oh, I should probably mention they're married now."

Austin winced. "Sorry."

"I'm not." Divorcing Paul was one of the only things about the whole mess she didn't regret. "I certainly don't want to be married to him and didn't, from about the next morning on. I left him a few days later, after the second or third time we'd all been together. I might've been naïve and ignored all the signals up until that time, but I couldn't ignore what was happening between them. And I couldn't ignore the way I felt physically about being with Christie."

Gem sat back while the waitress deposited their dinners. She drew a deep breath and discovered she felt amazingly good. Pissed-off still, but the anger only fueled her resolve to never take anything or anyone at face value again. She'd learned an important lesson that had kept her life uncomplicated and her heart securely locked away.

"And since then you've been on that even keel you mentioned?" Austin said.

"Let's just say since then I've made it a point not to act on impetuous impulses. Until today."

"That's a pretty good record. What, six or seven years?"

"Seven years, ten months." Gem smiled and broke off a piece of bread from the warm loaf in the breadbasket. "I like to know what I am doing and what I'm getting into before I commit to a course of action. I've been happy, comfortable, living that way. You derailed my train a little bit."

"You've pretty much derailed mine too," Austin admitted.

"Should I apologize?"

"No," Austin said against all her better judgment. "I wouldn't want to change a thing."

Gem glanced out the window. "We'll be there in a few hours, won't we."

"Looks like it."

Gem smiled, weariness setting in. She had every reason to be tired, but she didn't think that was it. The road trip was coming to an end, and she had a secret: she didn't want it to be over.

Chapter Eight

Gem pushed away her half-finished meal, swallowed the dregs of her wine, and placed the glass carefully on the carved wooden coaster decorated with a seashell. She blew out a breath. "I had no idea I was going to go there, and I think I should apologize. It's probably way too much information at any point, but especially when we hardly—"

"No, it's fine. Well, not *fine* fine," Austin said quietly, "but…" She wanted to tread carefully in the unfamiliar waters. Her emotions were rolling around like a buoy on a rough sea, tilting from one side to the other and occasionally going under altogether. Interpersonal revelations weren't exactly her strong point. She didn't think she'd ever had the kind of soul-baring conversation she'd just had with Gem—who in her past would've talked to her of something so deeply personal, so meaningful, so revealing? Not her goal-oriented, action-loving family—not her mother, with her cool, calculating surgeon's brain able to assess any situation and act instantly, no regrets and no second guesses; not her father, the jocular daredevil, who loved to fly into danger and was bored whenever he wasn't, but never talked about what it meant to face death on a daily basis; not her jock of a brother for whom skill, success, and celebrity came easily. If they'd suffered along the way to victory, they kept the pain, if it was there at all, buried even to themselves. And who would she have talked to if not family—certainly not the women with whom she had fleeting relationships, some more than one night, true, but none where a touch of compassion and understanding was valued more than heat and passion. She and Gem had shared one simple kiss and so much more. She was humbled to be trusted with so much, angry for the pain Gem had suffered, and helpless knowing she could do nothing about it. She cleared her throat. "I should confess right now that I'm really bad at this kind of thing."

Gem's smile was a little rueful, a little amused. "This kind of thing being…?"

"Touching when it's not physical."

Gem caught her breath. Yes, that was exactly what had been going on between them most of the day. The kiss aside, they'd been touching, exploring, connecting, even when they hadn't been physically close. No wonder she'd wanted to kiss her. The whole day had been a seduction, and the whole dating scenario had been turned on its head. "I know what you mean. It's a little disconcerting how easy it's been to…be with you."

Austin laughed. "Just a little."

"I know you're going to be busy once you arrive at Rock Hill," Gem said, tentatively feeling her way along an unfamiliar path. "But I suppose you have to eat at some point, get a little fresh air. You do surface now and then, don't you?"

"My schedule is pretty irregular," Austin said. She couldn't make any kind of plans. Best-case scenario, she'd have nothing to do and then she would happily spend a week or so relaxing in some little seaside hotel and getting to know Gem better. Or she could be sitting out on the ocean in a containment ship, getting no sleep and watching an oil spill spread toward land. "But I'd like to see you again, if it's possible. Maybe I could call you?"

"Sure, yes. That's good for now, then." Gem toyed with the empty wineglass. "It would probably be good to slow down and back up a little bit anyhow."

"As long as we don't have to start the drive over again."

Gem laughed, appreciating Austin's attempt to defuse the tension. "I can't say I'll mind getting to the end of this particular road trip. At least in some ways." She touched Austin's hand, remembered she'd just said they needed to back up a little, and pulled away. Mixed messages much? "Although I'm glad we had this day."

"Thanks. Me too." Austin gathered up the bill the waitress left on their table and pulled out a credit card. "I suppose it's time we took advantage of the break in the weather and got going."

"Yes. Give me a minute and I'll be ready." Gem rose and headed toward the rest rooms at the far end of the room.

Austin signaled the waitress and checked her phone. Miracle of miracles, she not only had a signal, she had voice mail. Six of them, all brief and progressively more irritated messages from Eloise. The last being, *Where the hell are you?*

She pressed *call back* on the last one. Even though it was well after seven and the last time they'd spoken had been three in the morning, Eloise picked up her office line on the second ring. Her greeting was terse. "I did stress there was some urgency to this job, didn't I?"

"Have you been watching the weather?"

"Of course I've been watching the weather. Along with maritime reports, satellite projections of the storm's trajectory, and hourly updates from the rig. Not to be repetitious, but where are you?"

"About an hour and a half out. I got grounded in Baltimore and I've been driving all day, basically getting nowhere. Things have cleared here for the moment, so I ought to get in before ten."

"Good. Ray is waiting on the rig for you to call. As of an hour ago, the fog was too heavy for the birds to fly. You ought to be able to reach him by phone, though."

"We have a problem."

"Really?" Eloise's cool voice was laden with sarcasm. She must be tired if she allowed that much emotion to show. "What exactly would that be, other than the obvious?"

Austin signed the credit card slip the waitress left, keeping one eye on the far side of the room for Gem's return. "This wildlife sanctuary isn't just any wildlife sanctuary. It's some pivotal point on the Atlantic Flyway."

"Enlighten me."

"That's a particular route that large numbers of endangered species travel this time of year."

"Why don't I know about this?"

"I don't know," Austin said. "Don't you have people who research these things?"

"I'm supposed to have," Eloise said.

Austin was very glad she wasn't one of those people. "At any rate, it's not only a locus for scientific research, but also tourism and bird watching. And I've never seen a birdwatcher who wasn't a rabid environmentalist."

"How exactly did you get all of this information while you were out of touch? If you couldn't answer my calls, I assume you couldn't search the Internet."

"I'm actually traveling with the lead biologist who's heading up a research team at the sanctuary."

The line went silent, one of the only times Austin had ever experienced Eloise to be wordless.

"How did that happen?"

"By chance. We ended up getting one of the last vehicles out of the airport—that's not really important. What is important is that if we do have a spill, we're going to be under a magnifying glass, even more so than normally."

"Then I'm glad we hired you."

The message was clear—Austin's job was to keep the lens of public scrutiny focused somewhere other than on the company. "Right. What's the status out on the rig?"

"Ray says the breach hasn't widened, and there's no surface contamination at this point."

"So we've still got time."

"We're bringing in the ships just in case. If we have to, we can burn, as long as the surface skim doesn't get away from us."

"We'll have to make a statement before we do that. We're walking the line right now. Someone's going to ask the question sooner or later as to when we first knew about the breach."

"We're not required to report containable leaks."

"I know that's the party line."

"It's more than that, it's the law. We have to accept regulations that aren't always to our benefit, and we ought to be able to use those that are."

"The public doesn't care about the law, Eloise, it's all about perception."

"And that's your job, isn't it?"

Austin watched Gem walking back toward her. Manipulating perception, yes. That was her job, that was her skill. That was her. "I have to go."

❖

Maybe it was the wine or the night closing in around the vehicle that sent Gem to sleep, but the deceleration of the SUV was what roused her. She jolted awake, discovered her head leaning at an awkward angle against the side window, and straightened with a nearly inaudible groan. "Sorry, I flaked out on you."

"Not a problem," Austin said.

"I wasn't snoring, was I?"

"Um…no?"

"Good answer." Gem blinked and peered through the windshield. Fog had rolled in again, but that wasn't uncommon along the shore. It didn't necessarily harbinger another storm, although she estimated this time it did. The town of Rock Hill, more a village really, encompassed barely a mile in length, the main street hugging the shoreline and the residential areas extending from it like tiny bristles on one of those spindly brushes used to clean test tubes. There were no hotels, merely a few dozen bed-and-breakfasts situated along the main drag, and at this time of year, they would be empty except for seasonal events like Thanksgiving, Christmas, New Year's, and of course, the great migration. No Vacancy signs abounded. Fortunately, she didn't have to worry about that. She had a car waiting for her at the tiny airport at the far end of the island. By midnight, she ought to be in her own quiet cabin, warm and dry and…alone. Usually she looked forward to solitude. Tonight her feelings were mixed.

She hadn't spent so many continuous hours with one single person in weeks—possibly months. She didn't really count dinner and an evening spent watching television and then sleeping with Kim in the same way. They talked, of course, shared the events of their recent days, discussed books or movies they'd read or were interested in seeing, and slept companionably until they enacted their choreographed morning routine of moving around one another in the bathroom—hers or Kim's, depending on whose residence they'd spent the night at, before going off to work.

Those nights were pleasant, but not intense. Not like the day she'd just spent with Austin. An exhausting day, an exhilarating day, a day fraught with emotion and excitement. A night alone would be welcome. She needed to think about what had happened, perhaps even make sense of it if she was lucky. Still, she didn't want to say good night. She didn't want to let go of the feeling of being so alive. She never knew where the next conversation would take them, when casual contact would morph into something more, when she'd look across the space between them and be struck by the sensual angle of Austin's jaw or the erotic promise in her hands.

"Which way to the airport?" Austin asked.

"Actually, there's only one way to and from anything in this place. Just keep driving straight and you'll eventually end up at the airport. It's at the very end of the island. I'm sorry to make you play chauffeur now. I'm sure you're beat."

Austin smiled and shook her head. "I'm fine, really. I'm used to crazy travel schedules with no sleep."

Gem frowned. "Really? I got the impression you didn't get out all that much—that you tended to hibernate with your work."

Austin's jaw tightened. "I don't really have any set schedule."

"Okay." Gem sensed the issue was closed although she couldn't quite see why. They rode in silence until Austin turned into the access road to the airport. Five or six small planes, dimly illuminated in the diffuse glow of the halogen lights penetrating the fog, were tied down at the end of the runway beside the small single-story terminal. "It looks like all the flights have been grounded. I'm not surprised."

"I'm sure there were plenty of people who didn't get off the island today if they'd planned on flying." Austin pulled up in front of the terminal. "I'll wait until you get your car so you can transfer your luggage."

"Oh, you don't need to do that."

Austin leaned closer and squeezed her hand. "I want to. It's no trouble."

"Thanks," Gem said. "It shouldn't be long."

She hurried inside and wasn't surprised to find the waiting room empty. Clearly, no flights were leaving here anytime soon. No one was behind the counter, but an open door spilled light from an office in the rear.

"Hello?"

A few seconds later a trim, middle-aged sandy-haired woman in a long-sleeve navy-blue shirt and dark pants emerged. Her name tag read *Peg*. "Hi. Can I help you?"

"Yes," Gem said. "I was supposed to arrive early this morning from Baltimore, but my flight was canceled."

Peg made a face. "Everything's been canceled. I'm not sure we'll fly tomorrow."

"Yes, well, I reserved a car. Can I pick it up here?"

"Sure can." Peg pulled a folder out from under the counter, flipped it open, and scanned a page. "We won't have much of a choice for you, I'm afraid. When news of the storm came in and the weather started turning bad, a lot of folks who were supposed to fly out rented cars. Name?"

Gem told her. "Anything with four wheels and an engine will be perfect."

Peg smiled, gave her some paperwork to fill out, and handed her the keys. "I hope you're not headed too far tonight."

"No, just out to Kramer Point."

"Not tonight you won't be."

"I'm sorry?"

"Not by car. Part of the causeway's washed out. I don't know how bad it is, but last I heard, they've stopped all traffic out to the Point in both directions."

"And the pontoon boats?"

"You mean from Flyers?" Peg chuckled. "Even if you could find someone around to rent you one, only a crazy person would try that at night, and in this weather?" She cocked her head. "You don't exactly look crazy to me."

"Right at this moment, you'd be surprised." Gem sighed and picked up the keys. "Thanks."

As she approached the car, she could see Austin behind the wheel, her head tipped back against the seat. She had to be tired, but she wouldn't admit it. Gem smiled to herself. She understood priding oneself on independence, even sometimes when it wasn't completely to her benefit. She opened the car door as quietly as she could, but Austin was already sitting upright and gazing in her direction when she slid in.

"All set?" Austin asked.

"Yes and no. I've got a car, but I can't get to my cabin tonight. Apparently the road is underwater."

Austin frowned. "You're going to have trouble finding anyplace to stay in town."

"There's got to be one room. I'll make some calls. You should get going. I can't imagine you want anything more than to crawl into bed right now."

Austin grinned. "Well, now that you mention it…"

Gem's face heated. "I guess you're not so tired you can't make trouble."

Austin's grin widened. "Never am."

"I'll just get my bags."

"Wait." Austin grabbed her hand. "Why don't you call around from here, and then I'll follow you to your place. The roads are really bad tonight."

Gem should say no, but she didn't really want to. The parking lot was empty and a little creepy in the fog. Visibility was no more than a few feet. The interior of the SUV was warm, and Austin was there. Gem flicked on the dash light and perused the town's weekly magazine she'd picked up inside that listed all the restaurants, motels, B and Bs, and other businesses. Twenty minutes later, she closed her phone. "Other than going door to door, I think I'm out of options."

"Nothing?"

Gem shook her head. "Well, it won't be the first time I've slept in my car."

Austin laughed. "It's hardly going to come to that."

"I don't plan on sleeping in the airport."

"Of course not. You'll sleep with me."

CHAPTER NINE

"I appreciate the offer," Gem said, "but I'm afraid I can't take you up on it."

"I was kidding about the *with me* part," Austin said. "But not about sharing quarters. I've got a room and you don't. Not much different than me having a car and you being stranded."

"I agree with the logic," Gem said, "but the reality is a little bit different. I know what the rooms are like in these places where space is worth more than gold—if there's three square feet to move around between the bed and the door, I'd be surprised. Which means there's no extra room for an extra body." She took a deep breath. After all, she had been the one to open this particular door, and Austin couldn't be faulted for testing the waters. "And as appealing as the thought might be, I'm not sleeping with you."

"I admit, I'm a little old to be sharing a bed in a purely platonic fashion with a woman I find attractive—summer camp this isn't," Austin said. "But given that we are two adults, we can probably rein in our teenage hormonal impulses for one night."

Gem laughed. Austin was hard to say no to, and what she didn't intend to say was that she was saying no more to herself—okay, completely to herself—than to Austin. She wasn't entirely certain she could rein in those hormones as easily as Austin seemed to think she could. Ordinarily, she wouldn't think twice about bunking with another woman in an emergency. She'd shared close quarters plenty of times out in the field with women she liked, including women she found attractive, theoretically. Unfortunately, her attraction to Austin was already far beyond theoretical. She trusted Austin not to push—she hadn't so far—but she didn't trust herself. She didn't know what her body was doing. Well, she did, she recognized desire after all, but she didn't know *why*. And she needed to. She simply did not have these kind of impulses, but there they were. Even now, desire kindled deep inside. The biologist in her understood the unconscious basis of attraction, the pheromones and hormones that governed physical responses, but she hadn't been motivated by instinct in a long time.

Aware Austin was contemplating her patiently, Gem searched for some rational plan. "Let's do this. Let's make sure you actually have accommodations. I wouldn't be surprised if half the people who had planned to check out today didn't. And in this kind of weather, when it's unlikely that people who had reservations would actually make it, the innkeepers might simply have ignored incoming reservations. We might both be sleeping in the truck."

"I can just about guarantee that's not going to happen," Austin said. "But it's a plan, and it's better than leaving you here at the airport sitting on your luggage. Let me MapQuest this place and you can follow—"

"What's the name of the inn? I know the town well, and new businesses are unusual. Chances are I've been there or at least by it."

Austin thumbed through her emails and found the information from Eloise. "Gulls Inn." She laughed. "Doesn't every town along the shore have one of those?"

"Of course. It's on Bay Street, the main road, all the way at the other end. I'll go first."

"See you there." Austin pulled out behind Gem, the muted red glow of the rental car taillights the only illumination in the fog. She didn't know how long her cell signal would last, but she figured it would be strongest near the airport. She needed to get in touch with Ray Tatum, if only to let him know she was on-site. From what Eloise had said, they weren't in crisis mode yet, and there was nothing she could do out at the rig even if she could get there, which wasn't happening tonight. She'd kept the email from Eloise open and squinted at the message by the greenish light from the dash, picked out the phone number Eloise had included for Ray, and thumbed it to call. He answered on the fourth ring, his brusque, faintly Irish-accented voice staticky.

"Tatum."

"Ray, it's me, Austin. I finally made it to Rock Hill. What's the situation?"

"Fucking storm is killing us," he said.

From experience, she knew something was always killing Ray. She'd worked with him enough times to know his hyperbole masked a hard-nosed bulldog of a personality. He'd do anything necessary to protect the rig, the oil, and by extension, the company. She liked him, but sometimes he was a pain in the ass to keep on a short tether. "Looks like there's a break for a while."

"My fancy-pants PhD meteorologist tells me it's a false calm. Another front will be rolling in tomorrow night or the next day. We've got a small window of clear air starting around ten tomorrow."

"Can you get me out to the rig for a look around?"

"Unless something blows wide open tonight, in which case I can't get you out here by boat or air anyhow, midmorning should be fine. I'll have a bird at the airport for you."

"How do things look?"

"The rig foreman, Paulie Antanole, first noticed the pressure drop at one in the morning," he said. "His boys were right quick about getting the sealer valves engaged. Kept a lid on things, but we haven't stopped the leak."

"Can you plug it?"

"If we can isolate the level, maybe." Tatum sighed. "Hate to kill the well if we don't have to."

Austin didn't have the authority to order Tatum to inactivate the well, and trying to explain to him that GOP would be happier losing a few million in profits from this one rig than having a PR nightmare that would cost far more wasn't worth her breath. Tatum was an oilman—he'd do what he was ordered to do if all else failed, but he'd want to save the well if he could. "But you're not blooming on the surface?"

"One thing the currents are good for in this fucking storm," he growled, "is they're dispersing it before it reaches the surface."

Austin wasn't assured. Dispersion that far from shore was safe, if it was really dispersing. When Deepwater Horizon blew in the Gulf of Mexico, underwater plumes of oil rode the currents as far as the Florida coast, fouling beaches and poisoning sea life. They couldn't let that happen here. "Who's watching currents?"

"Ali Farr."

"He's sure we don't have a collection that's going to get loose?"

"Fuck me if I know. He says we're good so far."

"What's your gut feeling on this, Ray?"

"I don't like it. If we can get the remote underwater vehicles down there and get a seal, we've got a chance. If the fucking storm doesn't hit. Otherwise, my guess is we'll see surface oil in the next thirty-six hours."

So they needed some luck, and hers had been running pretty bad so far. Austin watched Gem's taillights wink in the fog. Less than forty-eight hours and Gem would know the rest of her story. The fragile link between them would be broken.

She blinked the fatigue from her eyes. "I'll check in first thing in the morning if I don't hear anything from you tonight. For now I guess we sit on our hands."

"Been doing that all fucking day," Tatum said. "I hope we dragged your ass out here for nothing."

Austin thought of the hours with Gem that felt more like days, Gem and the scant time left to them. "Not for nothing, Ray. Definitely not for nothing."

❖

Gem kept an eye on her rearview mirror, checking to make sure she didn't lose Austin. Every few seconds, she caught a glimpse of headlights flickering through the soup. Ahead of her, her headlights disappeared in a blurry cone, giving her about twenty feet of visibility. Fortunately, they only had a mile or so to go, and at a cautious crawl, she spotted the sign for Gulls Inn fifteen minutes later. She pulled in to a miniscule parking lot nearly filled with cars. Not a good sign. She found a free space at the end and wedged in with enough room for Austin to park a few seconds later.

"Doesn't look promising," Gem said when Austin joined her. "The place looks full."

The Gulls Inn, a three-story sprawling Victorian with ornate trim, a wraparound porch, and an extension off the back, appeared to have once been a private residence, now converted into a B and B. Most windows were dark. A small lighted sign over a side door read *Office*.

"Let's go find out," Austin said.

The office was little more than a converted foyer bisected by a short, waist-high counter. A door behind that presumably led into the rest of the building. Wall shelves held tourist brochures and maps, a printer, and the usual office accouterments. An old-fashioned bell sat on the counter with a handwritten sign that said *Ring Me*. Austin did. A minute later the interior door opened and an older man in a loose gray cardigan buttoned over a crisp white shirt and baggy black pants walked in. His thinning gray hair matched the color of his sweater. His blue eyes were friendly. "How are you folks doing? Bad night to be out and about."

"Glad to be here. We're about ready to stop driving," Austin said. "I have a reservation under Germaine."

His eyebrows rose. "I'd about given up on you. That reservation came in from—"

"Flights were canceled," Austin said before he could elaborate on whichever of Eloise's minions had made the reservation, probably on the company's account. "We ended up needing to drive."

He'd already pulled a card from a stack in an old-fashioned index box he'd set on top of the counter. "I've got you in the Harbor Room—got a nice view of the bay and a small private balcony." He glanced at Gem. "It says here reservation for one, and it's only got the one bed and bath."

"That'll be fine," Austin said.

"Well then, I'll get you the key and you'll be all set. You're on the third floor, at the back. You can get to it from the outside staircase. You'll see it from the lot. Number five."

When he turned to pull a key off a pegboard, Gem murmured, "I don't think—"

"We'll work it out," Austin said.

Gem decided they could sort things out in private and waited until they were back outside. "Honestly, you've been more than a lifesaver all day long, but—"

Austin stopped abruptly, gripped her shoulders, and kissed her.

Gem's knees went loose and she grabbed Austin's jacket, a flood of desire melting the rest of her sentence and leaving her mind a hot blank. Austin's mouth was soft, sliding over hers, warm and slick and possessive. Gem's breath shortened, her throat tightened, and her lips parted to pull Austin in. No hesitation, no resistance, no brakes at all. Austin's tongue played over the surface of her mouth, barely touching, a teasing invitation of more. More. Yes.

Gem moaned and slid her arms around Austin's waist, pressing hard.

Austin stepped back and braced herself against the SUV. Gem followed, urgent and hungry. Her head swam and the kiss went on and on until she finally pulled away, needing to breathe, needing to…stop. She slid her hands under Austin's jacket, her fingers digging into Austin's back. Her belly was fused to Austin's, her hips nestled between Austin's legs. They fit. Everything fit. That couldn't be right, could it? "I can't think while you're kissing me."

Austin grinned. "Good. We should do more of it."

"This isn't me."

"Yes, it is," Austin murmured, kissing her neck. "Tonight, it is."

Gem tilted her head back, surrendered her throat. "Just for tonight, then."

"All right."

Gem braced her hands against Austin's shoulders and pushed away from her. Her body ached at the loss. She needed to move before she changed her mind. "Let's get our luggage and find the room."

Austin grabbed Gem's hand, held it as if she was afraid she might disappear. "Yeah. Good idea."

Austin pulled the bags from the back one-handed, and Gem found hers. Still holding Austin's hand, she half stumbled, half raced up the winding staircase to the third floor. Number five was the first door they came to. Austin unlocked the door, shoved it open, and tossed her bag in. She took Gem's duffel, threw it in after hers, and tugged Gem inside.

A barely perceptible gray glow streamed into the room through the balcony doors. A foghorn mourned in the distance. Otherwise the night was still and empty. For Gem, time held no meaning. For that moment, she had stepped outside her world. She'd never done anything like this before, not consciously, and she was very conscious of what she was doing. "I…"

"Shh." Austin's finger grazed her mouth. Despite the dim light, the gleam in Austin's eyes was brightly visible as she backed Gem against the closed door. "I wasn't done kissing you."

Gem pushed Austin's jacket down her shoulders. "Then take that off."

Austin jerked her arms free and tossed the jacket somewhere behind them. Gem yanked Austin's shirt from her pants and slid her palms underneath. Austin shuddered at the contact, her back arching.

"Fuck, Gem," Austin gasped.

"Your skin is so hot," Gem muttered, trailing her fingertips down the firm columns of muscles. "Beautiful."

Austin gave a sound like a growl. "Trying to go slow here, but if you keep doing that—"

"Oh, I'm going to keep doing that," Gem whispered. That and more. More. "There's a bed right behind you. I think we should use it."

CHAPTER TEN

The back of Austin's legs hit the edge of the bed, she went down, and Gem followed, straddling her hips with both hands planted on either side of Austin's shoulders. Austin was pinned, a position she rarely assumed and instantly liked. They were body to body, but with way too many clothes between them. She ached for flesh on flesh.

Too late. Too slow. Deft fingers danced down the front of her shirt, and buttons popped open. Her skin prickled in anticipation. Soon now. A touch, a caress, a teasing promise. A visage swam into focus—a blond halo of curls framing a sculpted face with starlit eyes. Austin gasped. A sliver of reason, sharp as a scalpel, sliced through the haze. Gem. This was Gem. Gem touching her, kissing her, and in two seconds they would both be naked and there'd be no turning back. She caught Gem's wrists, forced the words out through a throat thick with desire. "Gem, are you—"

Gem's mouth covered hers, swallowing the question. The kiss was sure and deep and went on and on until Austin's reluctance broke and winged away. Gem drew back, her thumb brushing Austin's mouth. "Don't ask me if I'm sure. I wouldn't have come up here if I wasn't."

"All right," Austin said, trusting Gem to know herself. If Gem knew all the reasons Austin was there, she might have made a different decision, but this moment, this joining, was about who they had been that day—two women stranded in a storm who'd shared a rare connection. Tonight, for one night, they were who they were. Naked and unmasked.

"Do you want to stop?" Gem's husky voice was barely recognizable.

Austin laughed, and the wildness in hers sounded foreign and dangerous. "Hell no."

"Good," Gem murmured. "No more questions."

Austin closed her eyes as Gem popped the last button and pushed her shirt open. At the first soft touch, she let the doubt and the questions and the last fragile tendrils of guilt drift away. Gem's mouth was at her throat, moving down to the hollow between her collarbones and lower. She groaned as Gem cupped her breast, molded her nipple, fit her lips to it. Ripples of pleasure, bright bursts streaming through her blood, racing to her fingertips, between her legs, down her spine, dazzled and dazed her. So different, so surprising, so amazing. She heard a whimper. Recognized distantly it was her. She slipped her fingers into the hair at Gem's nape and held Gem's head to her breast, wordlessly coaxing.

"Good?" Gem whispered.

"Beyond," Austin said.

Gem smiled at the way Austin trembled beneath her. This woman, so sure, so strong, so damn sexy, lay undefended and open, silently inviting her to feast. And, oh, feast she intended to do. If this was to be her only night, she wanted everything, every taste and touch and sound. Austin's body as she undressed her, pale and ethereal in the scant light, was beautiful, muscular and sleek, the skin smooth as silk beneath her hands and her mouth. She eased off the shirt from one arm and then the other and let it fall by the bed. Austin's breasts filled her hands, nipples hard knots against her palms. She spread her fingers, let them drift down the taut planes of Austin's belly, watched her tense and quiver.

"Mmm." She kissed Austin's stomach, teasing her with quick flicks of her tongue until she groaned. Laughing softly, she said, "Chopping wood does great things for a body."

Gem sat back, resting her weight on Austin's thighs, and opened Austin's pants. Austin raised her head and looked down, her expression dazed. When she would've helped, Gem pushed her hands away.

"Let me," Gem said.

"I'm feeling a little useless here," Austin said.

"Oh, believe me, you're anything but." Gem bent forward and swirled her tongue on the soft skin below Austin's navel.

Austin jumped. "Fuck, Gem. You make me crazy."

"There, see? Hardly useless. Now let me finish."

Austin sighed and dropped her hands, her eyes on Gem. Gem watched Austin's jaw clench as she slid down the zipper, tugged the pants down her thighs, and pulled them off. The cords on Austin's neck stood out as she fought to give Gem control. The sight of that surrender kindled a blaze in Gem's depths. Such power as she'd never imagined. At last Austin was naked and Gem slid off the bed and stood beside it, just taking her in. When she couldn't go another second without touching her again, she hurriedly undressed and sat beside her, resting her palm on Austin's middle. "You're amazing."

Austin covered Gem's hand, pressed it harder to her stomach. "I don't know how much longer I can go without touching you."

"Give me a little more time. I want to explore, discover you." Gem traced her fingers down the center of Austin's body, watched her nipples tighten and her abdomen tense. She pressed low on Austin's belly until the muscles under her hand quivered. "Do you mind?"

"Not right now."

"Good. Hold on a little longer." Gem leaned down, kissed Austin's breast, and licked around her nipple until Austin moaned again. She sighed, her mouth skimming Austin's throat. "I could come just from touching you."

"So can I," Austin breathed.

Gem laughed. "Please don't. Not yet anyway."

"Whatever you want."

Whatever you want. Whatever you want. Gem struggled to see through years of denial and avoidance. *Whatever you want.* What was that? She hadn't thought she wanted anything for so long. Oh yes, quiet, comfort, safety, balance. But not this wild pulse in her belly, this consuming hunger in her blood, this scorching fire in her marrow. Never this. Never before. *Whatever you want.* More, that was what she wanted. That was all she could feel. More.

Hungry now, famished, Gem climbed over her, pushed her thighs apart, and knelt between them. Leaning down, she kissed the base of Austin's belly, her breasts, and her mouth. Austin cradled her hips tight between her legs. Surrendering, but still so strong, so sure.

"You," Gem said. "I want you."

"Then take," Austin whispered, her palms sliding over Gem's breasts, down her belly, to her hips. She reared up, wrapped her arms around Gem's waist, and pulled her down until they were face-to-face. She licked along the angle of Gem's jaw, grasped her head, and kissed her hard. The kind of kiss she'd given her outside—demanding, possessive, unbridled.

Gem's heart beat insistently between her thighs. She ached deep inside, a primal drumbeat of desire, the call to join, to fill and be filled. She straddled Austin's thigh and pushed down, the sudden pressure against her clit sending her spiraling to peak. She jerked away, too close.

"God," she gasped. "So good."

"Better than good." Austin winged her hands down Gem's back, cradled her ass, and rocked her thigh between Gem's legs. She could feel how close Gem was with every slide of Gem's slick hot flesh over her skin. She wanted to feel her come apart, come *on* her. She pressed her leg upward, watched Gem throw her head back, knew she could push her over in another minute.

"Do you want me to make you come?" Austin asked.

Gem's eyes were heavy lidded, her smile slow and sensuous. "Oh yes. So very much." She braced her hands on Austin's shoulders, her hair falling down to frame Austin's face. They were close, kissing close, when Gem whispered, "But I want you to come with me."

Austin's clit tensed and the muscles on the insides of her thighs clenched. She didn't give control, didn't come first, but tonight, she'd give anything for the pleasure of pleasing Gem.

"Stroke me," she said.

Gem skimmed one hand down the center of Austin's chest, over her belly, and cupped between her legs. She squeezed and pressed a thumb to the base of Austin's clit until Austin groaned. "Like that?"

"Just like that," Austin said through gritted teeth. She gripped Gem's ass, drew her up and down along her thigh, making her hips hitch and surge. "I'm going to make you come."

"Yes, you are." Gem skated her fingers on either side of Austin's clit, and stroked and pressed, stroked and pressed.

White flame seared Austin's senses. "It feels so good."

"You feel so good." Gem slid inside, her thumb still stroking, circling, pressing.

"*Fuck.*" Austin jerked. "That's going to make me come."

"Oh yes." Gem gasped, rocking back with a startled cry. "Yes." She arched and bucked and drove deeper.

Austin came, her gaze locked on Gem, the image of Gem's release branded on her soul.

Gem shuddered and tumbled down into Austin's arms, her cheek on Austin's shoulder and her face cradled in the curve of Austin's neck. "Oh my God. That was unbelievable."

Austin kissed her temple and wrapped her in a tight embrace. "Second that."

Gem kissed the side of Austin's throat, the wild beat of Austin's pulse racing against her lips. *Whatever you want.* Never had she ever imagined this. She closed her eyes. She hadn't a single thought in her mind, only the sound of Austin's heart beating, defining her world.

❖

Austin woke to the sound of the shower running. The bed beside her was empty, and when she ran her hand over the faint indentation where Gem had lain beside her, the sheets were cool. They'd finally fallen asleep only to awaken a few hours later, turn to one another, and slide into another kiss, another caress, another searching exploration. They'd made love a second time in the dark hours of the night and slept again. But now the heat had dissipated and the empty bed signaled the night was over and a new day had arrived. Their detour from reality had ended. She found her watch on the small bedside table. She couldn't remember having removed it. Seven thirty. Plenty of time to get herself together and out to the airport to meet Tatum's helicopter.

The bathroom door opened, and she rolled onto her side to face the adjoining room. Gem came out, a towel wrapped around her torso, her expression turning to surprise and what looked like chagrin when she saw Austin watching.

"Hi," Gem said.

"Morning."

Gem lifted a hand, waved it toward the room. "I was trying not to wake you, but I couldn't face climbing into my clothes without being clean. I felt like I'd spent a week in the same shirt and pants."

"No problem. You didn't wake me."

"Oh, okay. Good."

Gem busied herself with the duffel on the floor. A zipper slid, and Austin imagined her taking out clean clothes. She didn't have to imagine what she looked like underneath that towel. She had a very precise memory of Gem's full breasts and narrow waist and curvaceous hips and thighs. Gem's body was tight and toned, that of a woman who used her muscles for work, not the slim, almost formless physiques of the gym goddesses Austin most often found herself sharing a bed with. But for all Gem's strength, she was sensuous and quintessentially female as well. And thinking about that right now was only going to lead her down a road she couldn't afford to take. She swallowed against the dryness in her throat.

"Morning-afters aren't really my specialty," Austin said, "so I'll apologize beforehand for being a bit of a clod."

Gem straightened, clean clothes in one hand and the other holding the towel to her body. Her gaze slid down over Austin's chest for a second and back to her face. Austin hitched the sheet a little higher.

"I'm not expecting anything in the way of…morning-after conversation," Gem said with a quirky little smile. "Last night was last night, right?"

"I think that's what we agreed on," Austin said, but that wasn't what she was thinking. She was thinking she didn't want last night to be the last night, the only night, even though she had no way—and no right—to suggest differently.

"So I'm not going to say what you've probably heard so many times you probably don't believe it any longer," Gem said conversationally as she stepped into panties and jeans and somehow managed to get them on while still keeping the towel covering her chest and not showing anything else.

"What do you think that would be?" Austin said, wondering if Gem had any idea she almost never had a conversation worth mentioning, let alone remembering, with women in the morning.

"That I don't usually do that sort of thing." Gem frowned. "Actually, I *never* do that kind of thing."

"It wouldn't matter to me if you had." Austin never really gave any thought to what a woman's past might be when they were only spending a night together, why should she? They owed her no explanations. But this was Gem, and everything she needed to know had already been said. "I know that last night was different."

"Do you?" Gem said quietly.

Austin sat up, letting the sheet fall. Nudity wasn't anything that bothered her and false modesty was ridiculous at this point. "I do. For me too."

Gem took off the wet towel and draped it over the bedpost. She was nude from the waist up, her chest slightly flushed from the heat of the shower still, her breasts uplifted and rose tipped. Austin wanted to groan but suppressed it. The time for that kind of connection had passed.

"Then we understand each other." Gem slipped into a yellow button-down cotton shirt and closed it with steady fingers. She bent, shoved clothing into her duffel, and stood with the bag in hand. "I need to get out to the sanctuary. The storm has probably wreaked havoc with some of the nesting areas. I imagine you want to get settled and get to work too."

Austin slid from the bed, pulled on jeans from the pile of discards on the floor, and shrugged into her shirt. She left it unbuttoned. Work. Yes, she had a lot of that to do. "Be careful out there. It sounds like the roads got pretty rough last night."

Gem nodded. "I will. I…I hope your stay is productive."

Austin ran a hand through her hair. "Thanks."

Gem turned, opened the door, and paused. She looked back. "I won't say good-bye, just in case."

"All right," Austin murmured. "Not good-bye, then."

CHAPTER ELEVEN

The fog had lifted, leaving behind a cold, damp glaze on the railings, stair treads, and surfaces of parked cars. Scattered dryer-sheet wisps of clouds streaked the steel-gray sky. Gem turned up the collar of the denim jacket she'd pulled from her luggage, tossed her duffel into the backseat of her car, and headed down the nearly empty one-way main street. A few locals scurried along walking dogs, and others, bundled up in rain slickers and hunched against the wind, congregated in front of the coffee shop and diner, two of the only places with lights showing. Gem pulled over in front of the coffee shop and put on her emergency flashers. She hurried into the too-warm room, ordered a black eye from the harried teen behind the counter, and grabbed a muffin of nondescript ingredients to eat as she drove. All the things she would do on any ordinary morning, except this was no ordinary morning. She wasn't fanciful enough to believe that a single night could change her life, but something had definitely changed inside her. Everything she valued was still the same—her job, her friends, her family, the satisfaction she found in small, day-to-day things like coffee and muffins—but those things no longer encapsulated her world. Something new had been added, and the solace she had once taken in the sameness of her life had vanished.

Gem sat in the car, sipping coffee and breaking pieces off her muffin, reluctant to drive away and leave the night behind.

Austin had somehow awakened her desire for the unknown.

She hadn't been eager to explore anything beyond the familiar since those last days with Paul and Christie. Those long-ago days had been different from the last twenty-four hours, so very different. She hadn't sought or welcomed the experiences Paul insisted she'd enjoy, even though she'd vaguely acknowledged a desire for something she hadn't been able to name then—a desire to save her marriage because she thought she should, the need to meet Paul's needs, and beneath it all, the simmering unrest that only seemed to ease when she was with Christie. Easy to recognize in hindsight, nearly impossible to sort out from her fragmented emotions at the time. Now she knew that what had driven her to sleep with both of them had really been her desire for Christie, or at least, for a woman.

A tap on her window made her jump. A fresh-faced woman with short, wind-blown sandy hair in a navy flak jacket with an American flag emblem on one sleeve and a Rock Hill Police patch on the other smiled in at her. Gem rolled down the window.

"Morning, I—"

"You okay, ma'am?" The officer couldn't be more than twenty or any cuter if she tried. She had dimples on her dimples. "You've been sitting here with the flashers on and the engine running for about ten minutes."

"Sorry, I was lost in thought."

"No problem. Not much traffic this morning."

Gem finished her coffee and set the empty in the cup holder. "I have to go anyhow—is the causeway open?"

"Ought to be soon. They've been cleaning up out that way since dawn."

"Thanks."

"Sure thing. See you around."

"Right." Gem pulled slowly away, watching the cop saunter back to her patrol car in her rearview mirror. She had a swagger that looked good on her small, tight body. A faint zing of sexual interest shot along her nerve endings, and Gem caught herself up short. Really? Now she was cruising cute young strangers? What had Austin unleashed—or maybe more fairly, what had she been keeping caged? *Not that it matters now. It's over.*

Gem turned off the main street onto the narrow spur leading to the causeway and, beyond that, the wildlife sanctuary. If the airport was functional and the causeway was passable, the other members of the research team ought to be arriving soon and she could get back into the swing of her life. She'd know about the road in a minute. Rock Hill Island was actually a peninsula connected to an island by a quarter-mile causeway with the marshlands on one side and the sound on the other. She rounded a bend and breathed a sigh of relief. The roadway was clear, although the effects of the storm were everywhere. The shoreline on the harbor side of the narrow concrete span was twenty feet narrower than she recalled, the erosion from the heavy surf and pounding rain having left deep trenches in the sand and layers of small rocks along the water's edge. Tide pools collected in the marshes on the opposite side, but the waters had receded enough that the orange police barricades had been pulled aside to allow cars to pass.

She headed across, feeling as she always did that with every rotation of the wheels she was leaving the world behind. Usually that knowledge was accompanied by a feeling of freedom as she shed her daily responsibilities and looked forward to a few weeks of immersion in study and solitude. This morning she was anything but happy to be leaving the world behind. Austin was back in Rock Hill, and she wasn't eager to forget her or what they'd shared.

The night with Austin had reminded her all too forcefully what passion felt like, and she'd rejoiced in it. She'd thought freedom was a quiet place of contemplation, but she'd relearned in the moments of abandoning herself to sensation that freedom was also the wild flight of birds on the wing, soaring above the clouds, diving into the currents, climbing into the heavens. Her skin tingled at the memory. No, she wasn't eager to leave that behind at all.

With a sigh, she turned into the ten-car lot fronting the L-shaped, single-story stucco building housing the tiny visitors' center and sanctuary offices. The long arm of the L extending toward the back had been allocated to the research team while on-site. A red pickup truck and a yellow Volkswagen Beetle with bright red turtle decals along one side were the only other vehicles. Her heart lifted. Emily and Joe had arrived.

Emily Costanzas was a turtle woman who traveled from Michigan every year to study the migratory and reproductive patterns of the freshwater and sea turtles that nested in the marshlands and beaches in late summer. The sea turtle hatchlings would be emerging at any time now, headed to the sea, where they would grow to maturity over the ensuing decades—if they survived. Joe Edelman was a grass man, an ecologist from Maine who studied the impact of migratory birds carrying seeds from distant places and how those transplants affected the biology of the sanctuary. Gem, Emily, and Joe were the three most senior researchers in their group, and they'd worked together for five years. More than colleagues, they were friends.

Gem hurried inside and down the corridor toward the conference room at the end of the building that served as a dining hall and meeting area for the team. Emily and Joe sat at a round Formica table in the center of the room with cups of coffee and a box of doughnuts.

"Hey," Gem called.

Emily bounced to her feet. Small, red haired, and blue eyed, she exuded energy twenty-four hours a day, even when she was sleeping, as Gem had discovered when they'd shared quarters in the past. Emily tended to talk in her sleep.

"Gem." Emily, dressed for fieldwork in tan cargo pants and a T-shirt proclaiming *Love a Sea Turtle* in pastel pink, opened her arms wide and hugged Gem for a long moment. "You made it. I didn't expect to see you until later today, if then."

Joe, a heavyset middle-aged guy with close-cut salt-and-pepper hair and a wide broad face with a slightly off-center nose and a C-shaped scar over his left cheek that betrayed his college boxing days, grinned and waved. "Great to see you."

Gem kissed Emily's cheek and waved back to Joe. "Believe it or not, I drove. Well, I didn't, but I grabbed a ride with someone who did."

"Wow," Emily said, "that must've been one hell of a trip in that storm."

Gem felt her face color and hoped they wouldn't notice. Yes, it'd been one hell of a trip.

❖

Austin sat on the side of the bed with the echo of Gem's fading steps resonating in her thoughts. She'd been there awhile, long after the sound of the car starting and Gem leaving had succumbed to the silence. Her mind was uncomfortably absent the usual whirlwind of ideas and schedules and seething have-tos, the myriad responsibilities that drove her days and kept her from examining the totality of her life. Now she was left with only the memories of the day before—snippets of conversation, the glimmer of amusement in Gem's eyes when she teased, the lift of her breasts and curve of her mouth when she threw her head back in ecstasy. As Austin focused on the images, she realized Gem was all she could think of and all she *wanted* to think of.

Fingers itching, Austin rummaged through her leather satchel, pulled out her pad, and found a drawing pencil in the side pocket. Rapidly she sketched the picture emblazoned on her brain—Gem straddling her, hands gripping Austin's thighs, her torso arched in an elegant C, her neck taut, head thrown back, and hair flying. Gem uncaged, powerful and free and heart-stopping. The lines and shadows came rapidly as her hand raced over the page, driven with the kind of urgency that usually drove her in other ways. What compelled her now was not the need for success, or proving herself, or winning anyone else's approval. This passion was born of gratitude, wonder, and supreme pleasure. When her hand finally stilled, she looked at what she had done and her chest filled. Yes, that was Gem—stunning and surprising and like no other. Austin captioned the drawing *Wonder*, signed and dated it.

No one else would ever see it, the image was too personal, but she wanted her stamp on it in a way she'd wished she'd been able to leave her stamp on Gem. Even now, a flood of possessiveness and desire burned so hot inside her she didn't even have to ask if she'd ever felt that way before. She knew she hadn't. She wasn't done wanting to touch her again, and feared she might never be. Gem set off a storm within her to seek and claim and possess. She never wanted anyone else to see the woman she had drawn. She had no right to feel that way, but there it was. The ache in her depths was as much pleasure as pain, discovery and loss all wrapped up in one.

Carefully, she closed the pad and stored it back in her case, stripped, showered, and dressed in khakis, clean socks, her boots that had finally dried, and a dark-blue cotton polo shirt. She pulled on her windbreaker and carried her duffel down to the car. Half an hour later she took a seat on a stool at the counter in the small diner in the center of town. A blowsy bottle-blonde with teased curls and a wide smile, tight T-shirt cut dangerously low, and tighter jeans sashayed over with the menu in one hand and a pot of coffee in the other.

"Good morning, stranger," the blonde said, pouring coffee without being asked.

"It's not raining, so it must be," Austin said. "I don't need a menu. I'll take the special with bacon, eggs over easy, and wheat toast."

"You got it." The blonde leaned an elbow on the counter, giving Austin a panoramic view down her shirt. "Just get in this morning? Are the planes flying again?"

"I don't know." Austin focused on adding cream to the coffee and avoiding the show, which she wasn't sure wasn't deliberate. She sipped. Hot and strong, just the way she liked it. Which she pointedly did not say. "I got in last night. Drove."

The blonde's eyebrows rose. "You must have some cojones, then."

Austin grinned. What the hell. "They'll do."

"I'll just bet." The blonde chuckled, shouted Austin's order to the fry cook, and swiveled away to refill the cups of the other three people at the counter. The booths along the front windows were empty. Austin found a day-old newspaper in a rack by the door and read it while she ate her breakfast. She didn't really absorb any of the news, but it kept her mind off Gem for a few minutes at a time. In between recaps of the coming storms, local crime stats, and high school sports scores, she'd picture Gem's face when she was about to climax or hear her urgent cries or feel the press of her breasts, and a hard knot twisted in her stomach. Gem had held nothing back, at least in those moments, and neither had she. But she had at other times.

She hadn't lied, but she hadn't admitted the facts she knew would push Gem away. She had reasons for not revealing what had brought her to Rock Hill Island, good reasons for it, but after the night they'd spent together, those rationales echoed hollowly even to her. With a sigh, she left a twenty by her plate, finished the coffee, and headed for the door.

"Stay dry," the blonde called after her.

Austin drove to the airport and arrived twenty minutes early. She made arrangements with the ticket agent—singular—for the airline, who doubled as a representative for the rental agency, to keep the car another week. At 9:55 she walked out behind the terminal to the far end of the runway and waited. At 9:59 the *chop chop chop* of an approaching helicopter signaled the end of her journey with Gem and the beginning of the job. The bird set down, the side door slid open, and a flight jockey she didn't recognize signaled her to come aboard. Austin lowered her head and ran across the tarmac. As she climbed aboard, she carefully relegated the moments spent with Gem to the private vault of forsaken dreams that seemed to grow ever larger with each passing year.

CHAPTER TWELVE

Joe rinsed his coffee cup in the small sink and turned it upside down on the drain board. "I'm going out for a look-see while the weather holds."

"Good idea," Emily said. "The beaches along the causeway really took a beating, and I'm worried about the nesting areas. I ought to head out too." She turned to Gem. "I guess you probably want to get settled after the trip you had getting here."

Gem finished off a powdered-sugar doughnut, eating it more for the energy boost than the taste, and dusted off her hands on a paper napkin. "Actually, I'm pretty keyed up. I wouldn't mind getting a look around myself."

"How about we meet at the Point in half an hour or so? That will give you a chance to get your gear out to your cabin."

"What's the situation with the trails?"

"Everything was underwater last night," Emily said. "I couldn't get out to my place until this morning." She laughed. "You'll probably be okay, but I hope you've got high boots in your gear."

"I'll send up a flare if I get stuck," Gem called as she walked out into a still-rainless morning.

She drove to where the road ended in a makeshift, sandy parking lot, dragged her gear out of the car again, and set off down a winding footpath that ran through the scrub paralleling the shoreline. Off to the right, the wetlands were dotted with small ponds and connecting streams, where freshwater met sea. Her cabin was the farthest in the chain of half a dozen, about a mile's easy hike from the parking area. She had learned to pack very efficiently, with an emphasis on raingear, serviceable shirts and jeans, and plenty of warm socks. The nights would be cold and if the rain continued, which it often did under the best of circumstances, she'd be changing her footwear frequently. She also had her cameras, spotting scopes, laptop, and electronic data bands for tagging fledglings in a waterproof bag in her duffel.

As she walked along, a pleasant sweat breaking on her neck, her thoughts kept returning to Austin—was she already caught up in her work, was she thinking about Gem, had she already forgotten last night? Somehow she couldn't bring herself to believe the night had meant nothing more to Austin than a quick physical encounter. On the surface, it was exactly that, but nothing between them had been on the surface from the beginning. But maybe that was just her. Austin had broken her defenses and slipped inside. She felt her still, the memory a warm thrill brimming just beneath her skin.

A heron flew up with a startled cry, its wings spread wide, gracefully beating on the cold, clear air as it tried to distract her from its nest.

"Don't worry, I won't be disturbing anything." She followed its path for a while, reminded of the fragile balance between man and nature, nowhere more critical than right here. The sanctuary provided a layer of protection to the wildlife and plant species, but nothing could completely safeguard against predators and hapless humans. The conservationists fought a never-ending battle with the wind and sea to prevent erosion of the key areas, fencing vulnerable nesting grounds and routing tourist traffic along paths where they'd do the least damage. She and her fellow researchers did their best not to disrupt any of the life-forms they studied, but their very presence was a disturbance.

She'd always felt at home here, but the deeper she moved into the sanctuary, the more she felt her foreignness. She'd always wanted to be a bird, envied them their grace and freedom. She'd never considered what she wanted to flee from or what she might fly to. She hadn't wanted to flee from Austin, and that's what made the night so hard to forget. So she'd stop trying to forget—what was the harm in reliving such a remarkable experience, just because it was over?

Oddly more settled, she rounded a corner and saw her cabin with a sense of homecoming. The small single-story salt-box sat on a shallow rise surrounded by marsh grasses and sheltered by a few pines. With its weathered gray shingles, unadorned front porch, and split-log railing, the place was simple, efficient, and functional. Her heart lifted at the sight of it. In moments like these, she wondered how she managed to live in the high-rise condo where she spent a good part of her year, as constrained as a bird in a cage.

She did a quick tour of the cabin, found it tight and dry, and switched on the electricity, the water, and the generator. After assuring herself everything was in good working order, she headed back out to take another winding path through the dunes to the shore where Emily was just approaching from farther down the beach. They walked toward each other and halted at the high-tide line. The wind had picked up and Gem's hair blew loose from the band she'd used to hold it back. She settled the navy cap with the USCG logo, a gift from her sister, more firmly on her head. "How are things down your way?"

"Wet," Emily said, frowning down at the sand.

"Jeremy and the kids okay?"

"Mmm," Emily said absently, tracing back and forth over a twenty-square-foot patch of beach.

Gem waited patiently and checked the sky, not expecting much conversation for a while. She knew Emily, and nothing captured Emily's attention like the study of turtles. Now and then the sun would peek out, a little teasing glimpse of heat and light, before the clouds swooped in again. Still no rain.

Emily made another humming sound in her throat, knelt, and gently brushed at the sand ten feet above the high-tide line.

"What?" Gem sidled over, stopping well away from where Emily worked. After a few more moments, Emily had carefully scooped out a shallow bowl in the bottom of which lay an irregular mound of white gelatinous blobs. She grinned up at Gem.

"Green sea turtle eggs. Mature. They ought to be hatching anytime."

"I don't know how you find those nests. Is it some kind of turtle radar?"

"Instinct for kin."

Gem laughed. "I forgot you were a turtle in a previous life."

Emily rose, photographed the clutch, and pulled out a roll of yellow caution tape from the side pocket of her cargo pants. She found a few sticks and taped off the area around the nest. "I'll come back and screen it later."

They walked a mile in both directions, but Emily didn't find any other signs of nesting. While they roamed, Gem took stock of the shorebirds, all of them native to the area. That would change in a day or two when the migrant flocks began arriving. She mentally mapped out sites for her cameras and blinds.

"Come back for some tea," Emily said, interrupting Gem's mental planning.

Gem almost declined, but she was unusually restless, and the thought of rattling around in her cabin or studying flight paths on her computer decided her. "Sure, for a little while. I've got to catch up on my notes and start charting—"

"I know, I know." Emily laughed. "Me too. But let's catch up on us first. We're way behind in emails."

"Deal."

After a short walk in companionable silence, Gem relaxed at the two-person wooden table under the window in Emily's kitchen area, while Emily made tea and set out a box of crackers and a block of cheese.

As they drank and snacked, Gem asked, "So? How's Jeremy?"

"He's great," Emily said. "The kids are great. I love them like crazy, and I'm so happy to be here for the next few weeks I could burst into song."

Gem laughed. "I'll give you six hours before you're Skyping with them."

"Too late, already did that." Emily grinned. "How about you? Still seeing Kim?"

Gem started, the question seeming to recall some former life. She hadn't thought about Kim since—well, since she'd met Austin at the airport. God, what was she going to do about Kim?

Emily cocked her head. "I guess that's not a simple yes-or-no answer."

Gem rubbed her face. "Sorry. My mind's a little slow."

"That's okay. If you don't want to talk about it—"

"No, well…no, not really, but mostly…I don't know." Gem laughed ruefully. "God, I'm a mess. Yes, I'm still seeing her, but it's not really going anywhere."

"Do you want it to?"

"I never really thought about it."

"Maybe that's an answer."

"Yes, maybe you're right." What *had* she been doing with Kim, and what was she going to do now? She hadn't broken any promises by sleeping with Austin, and she wasn't entirely certain Kim would even care, but *she* did. Not because she was guilty, but because she realized she'd been cheating both of them in different ways. She didn't love Kim, and though Kim never complained, she deserved someone who cherished her. And she deserved—well, she wasn't really certain. She wasn't even certain what she wanted any longer.

"I can hear the wheels turning," Emily said.

"Just soul-searching," Gem said.

"Sounds serious."

"I don't know. It might be." Secretly, she knew everything had already changed.

❖

Rig 86, or Red Devil as the 60,000 square-foot semisubmersible rig had been dubbed by its crew, rose from the indigo waters on four bright red pillars like a giant's Erector set. The helipad was a small green hexagon extending over the water from one corner, ringed in white with a big white circle in the middle enclosing a capital *H*, as if the chopper pilot wouldn't know where to set down. Every other square foot of the surface was piled several stories high with containers, cranes, engines, drill heads, pipes, hoses, and the myriad cables and winches that connected the above-sea platform to the underwater pontoons. Red lifeboats resembling children's bath toys swayed from cables along the side of the rig.

Austin thumbed her mic. "Has the crew been evacuated?"

"All but the essentials," the operations team leader responded. The OTL, Brian Reddy, was a sun-bronzed fortysomething guy with flint-gray eyes, a lean clean-shaven face, and a rangy body in a black canvas flight suit and work boots. Austin had seen a dozen like him on oil rigs everywhere: no-nonsense, hard-eyed men and occasionally women, who were responsible for the lives of dozens of platform personnel and drill crews, all sitting on millions of gallons of flammable fuel that, if ignited, could kill them in a heartbeat.

"Where's the command post?" Austin asked. The drill crew would be working the rig, trying to stop the leak, but the geologists, salvage teams, boom crews, and reps from the company would be waiting a safe distance from the rig, just in case, for the signal to start active containment protocols.

"On the lead ship," Reddy responded, pointing out the window. "Set and ready to go if we need them."

As the bird settled onto the LZ, Austin counted four ships ringing the platform. The surface of the sea was deceptively calm after the previous day's storm, five-foot waves breaking indolently against the pylons, no sign of a glimmering oil sheen on the surface.

"Tatum is here with the crew," Reddy added.

No surprise there. No way would Tatum leave the rig, unless it was actively on fire. Reddy slid the door open and gestured for Austin to go ahead. She jumped down and sprinted across the deck to where Tatum waited with a woman. Ray Tatum had the size and temperament of a bantam rooster—five feet six inches of feistiness and proud of it. Austin held out a hand. "Hey, Ray."

"Austin," he said gruffly. He gestured to the brunette, a woman about Austin's age in a black leather jacket, tapered black pants, and low-heeled ankle boots who managed to look stylish and entirely capable. "This is Dr. Claudia Spencer, our weather girl."

Austin raised an eyebrow in Dr. Spencer's direction.

Spencer just grinned and held out her hand in apparent good humor. "Good to meet you, Austin. Ray is a little peeved at me this morning because I haven't been able to predict the weather by gazing at the stars."

Reddy smothered a laugh and Tatum grunted, but Austin caught the tail end of a brief grin on Ray Tatum's grizzled face. So Tatum liked her.

Austin shook her hand. "I'm sure once you get a fix on the sun, you'll be able to do that."

"Undoubtedly."

Claudia Spencer was clearly unflappable and used to dealing with roughnecks who put about as much stock in science as they did in soothsayers. The only things Tatum paid attention to were the direction of the prevailing winds, the color of the sky, and the rock of the pontoons under his feet. He was old school, but smart enough to listen to the rest of his team when things got critical. Hopefully they weren't there yet.

"Well, now that we're all cozy, come on over to the office," Tatum said, "and I'll fill you in. We've got some coffee that you can probably use."

"Thanks," Austin said and followed the trio to a rectangular metal container that served as the rig's operations center. Tatum kicked out a chair at the head of a battered metal table and sat down with a grimy coffee cup while the others grabbed mugs. Austin waved off the coffee when Reddy offered her some. It would be bad, and until she had to, she intended to avoid it.

"I'll make this short and sweet," Tatum said, "because no news is good news, and I don't fucking have any good news."

Austin said nothing. The time for wishing was over. All she could do now was deal with the facts.

"We shut as many valves down as we could to isolate and slow the breach," Tatum said. "We've gotten all the mileage we can out of that."

Reddy said, "We're down to losing maybe 30,000 barrels of oil per day, but at that rate, if we can't slow it down more, we're going to have surface oil, no doubt about it."

"Dispersants won't work?" Austin asked.

"Can't count on it, not this close to shore," Tatum grunted.

"And not if we have the weather I expect," Claudia said. "The waves will make the emulsions unstable and hard to monitor."

"Are you sanding the well yet?" Austin inquired. One of the first things the drill crew would do was pump mud into the well to slow the flow, and if that didn't work, add metal balls to the mix, a crude but effective way of simply blocking the channel that ordinarily allowed oil to flow to the surface. If the flow could be reduced enough, the oil reaching the surface could be burned as it appeared, and kept from encroaching on land.

"We will be today," Tatum said, a muscle the size of a Ping-Pong ball bunching at the angle of his jaw. Fouling the well was a concession he obviously didn't want to make.

"What about drilling relief wells?" If they could take some pressure off the main well through secondary wells nearby, they might be able to contain the breach and preserve the oil.

"The rock boys and girls are looking for the best sites for us to do that," Tatum said, referring to the geologists, "but that's going to take time we don't have. Secondary measure if it gets bad."

Meaning if the flow increased or got away from them and the leak went on for weeks or months. Like it had in the Gulf. That was a nightmare she wasn't ready to contemplate.

Reddy spoke up. "We could skim and burn if it hits the surface. We'll get some air pollution, but that shouldn't provoke too much of a fuss."

"Both of those approaches require low wind and calm seas," Claudia said in a tone so modulated and controlled she ought to be anchoring a network news show. "And even without stargazing, I can tell you neither of those things are likely. A tropical storm is coalescing and headed north. Projections have it reaching us sometime in the next two days, and it's growing in strength every hour."

Tatum made some remark not fit for ordinary mixed company. "Well, if we were a hundred and fifty miles out, I'd be a lot less worried. But we're practically sitting on the fucking shore, and if the currents pick up and the wind starts blowing, we're gonna have oil all up and down the coast. God damn it."

"We need to start laying down the booms," Reddy said.

"Before we do that," Austin said, "we'll have to make a public announcement about the breach. There's no way we can keep that quiet." She glanced at Tatum and Reddy. "How long before we know if you can get the flow substantially reduced by pumping the well?"

"Twelve hours, maybe."

Austin glanced at Spencer. "Ahead of the storm, you think?"

"It'll be close. If you want to deploy the booms, you'll need to do it before the storm rolls in or they won't be effective."

Tatum lifted a shoulder. "We're just gonna do what we do." He speared Austin with a glance. "You and the other desk jockeys can decide what to tell people about it."

Austin didn't take offense, even though she was far from a desk jockey. She didn't blame Tatum for tossing the hot potato in her direction. That's why she was there, after all. "I'll make some calls."

Tatum and Reddy stood up. "We'll get back to work."

The two men left, and Claudia rose to dump her coffee in the sink.

"Did you actually drink that?" Austin asked.

"No, I just faked it. Makes me look like one of the boys." Claudia smiled and cradled her cup between long, slender fingers.

Yep, camera-ready beautiful. It would take more than drinking deadly coffee to make her look anything but gorgeous, but Austin wasn't going to mention that. Spencer leaned against the counter, crossing her long legs at the ankle. She studied Austin frankly, and Austin waited.

"I take it you're the spin doctor in all of this," Claudia finally said.

"More or less. I'm hoping I won't have a lot to do."

"So am I. You do know what's on shore."

"You mean the sanctuary?"

She nodded. "Any shore town is a problem, but this magnifies the difficulties a hundredfold."

"How is it you know about it?"

She laughed, although she didn't appear amused. "My ex was a rabid birdwatcher. I've actually been here a couple of times."

"I'm surprised you're here on the rig. Shouldn't you be on the ship? It's safer there."

"Now you sound like Tatum. You're here, why shouldn't I be?"

"Point taken. But…?"

"I like to see how the weather is affecting the stability of the platform. I can give the company a better read on the potential effects of the wind and current that way."

"Pretty gutsy."

"Oh, I'm not that brave, believe me. I'll be the first one off if things start to deteriorate."

Austin was pretty sure Spencer knew there might not be enough time if that happened, but none of them ever talked about that.

CHAPTER THIRTEEN

G em got back to her cabin late morning, stored her clothes in the narrow four-drawer dresser next to the twin-size bed tucked into an alcove adjoining the bathroom, and set up her computer on the table that served as desk and dining table. Fortunately, the research center had good Internet connections and had installed relay towers two years before, so she had the bandwidth she needed for her satellite and tracking programs. Many of the flocks she followed had adults or fledglings who had been tagged elsewhere in the country. Most naturalist organizations were linked into the national database, and members tagged birds in the watch groups, providing information such as location, estimated age, nesting behavior, and on occasion, deaths. By accessing the national network of data transmissions, she could locate tagged birds within flocks migrating up and down the flyway.

When she first logged in, her computer screen looked like something out of an air-traffic controller's nightmare, with streaming data points that at first glance appeared random and chaotic. However, when she filtered for species and isolated those, discernible pathways became evident, as flocks coalesced and moved en masse along their migratory routes. She filtered for saltmarsh sparrows and anticipated, from the recent logged locations and rate of movement, they would be arriving within the week. She opened another window on her browser and checked the weather forecast. After scanning the first update, a knot of anxiety settled in her midsection. The storm yesterday had been only an advance warning.

A tropical storm was forming off the Bahamas, and forecasts were for northwest movement over the next two to four days. Depending on the trajectory, the heat rise from the ocean, condensation, wind speed, and a host of other factors, the storm could come ashore close to them as a lot of wind and rain or something much more dangerous. The salt marshes along the Eastern Seaboard were already endangered from erosion from rising sea levels, and a storm like this would keep the birds away, or if they'd already descended, would put them in harm's way. The timing couldn't have been worse.

Gem's cell rang and her heart leapt. *Austin.* She caught herself in the next instant and chided herself for the whimsy. Austin didn't even have her phone number, hadn't asked for it, which ought to tell her something about what the night had meant to her. Of course, she hadn't asked for Austin's either.

She checked the readout, still a little hopeful. Alexis. Smiling despite the lingering disappointment, she answered. "Hi."

"Hi, yourself," her sister said. "Where are you?"

"At the sanctuary. I got in this morning."

"I'm surprised you made it with the weather."

"Long story," Gem said, preferring not to recount once again her day with Austin. Even talking about it stirred an ache that she really wanted to avoid. "Where are you?"

Alexis, a commissioned officer and medic in the Coast Guard, was stationed across the sound from the sanctuary as part of the search-and-rescue team.

"On duty. Routine shore patrol right now. Things are pretty quiet. The storm has kept even the fishermen ashore."

"It looks like you're going to be busy pretty soon."

"We're gearing up for it," Alexis said. "If the projections hold, you're going to be right in the path. Are you planning on staying?"

"Of course. We'll be fine here."

"I've seen those cabins you guys sleep in," Alexis said disdainfully. "A good huff and puff, and they're going to be kindling."

Gem laughed. Older sisters were a real pain, especially ones that weren't that much older but liked to act like they were. Alexis had always been protective of her growing up, when she wasn't giving her a hard time. They'd never been particularly competitive about grades or social connections or anything else, but sometimes following in her big sister's successful footsteps had been a challenge all the same, especially since Alexis was naturally the outgoing one. Alex loved excitement and had always been something of a daredevil. She'd always loved the sea—its challenges and dangers—and had chosen her career early and never wavered. Gem was quieter and more contemplative. Hence, she was the landlubber, and the fanciful one.

"You'll be careful, won't you?" Gem didn't have to say out loud what they both knew—Alexis would be the one at risk during the coming storm, answering distress calls from ships that were bound to be caught on the open water no matter how many warnings were issued. Sea rescues in high winds and rolling swells had brought down more than one helicopter. Gem pushed the worry away— Alexis and her team were experts. She'd be fine.

"Always am," Alex said lightly. "You too, okay?"

"Absolutely. And when you get a break, let's do dinner."

"Will do. Love you. Bye."

"Love you," Gem murmured as the connection disappeared. She set her phone aside and sighed. As close as she was to Alexis, she'd never talked to her much about her personal life, another result of bad timing. Alex had always known she was a lesbian and had come out when she was fourteen. When Gem finally realized she and Alex shared the same interest in women, they'd already been living apart for years and had missed the chance to share stories about girlfriends. Plus, Alexis had never liked Paul, had actively tried to dissuade Gem from marrying him, but she hadn't listened. Alexis had been the only one in the family who had objected to him. Everyone else, most especially her parents and brother—who had been Paul's best friend and probably still was—thought the match was perfect as well as destined. Knowing Alexis had been right in warning her away had made it hard for her to talk about what had happened.

For an instant, she wished she'd told her about meeting Austin, but then what would she say? *I met a woman who made me feel things I didn't know I wanted to feel and who made me behave in ways I barely recognize, and I loved every minute of it?*

No, she wouldn't be able to explain that to her sister any more than she could explain it to herself.

❖

Austin peered over Claudia's shoulder at the satellite readouts streaming across the two large monitors connected to Claudia's mega-souped-up laptop. She could read the storm patterns well enough to know they indicated trouble. "Looks like it's picking up speed."

"Mmm, and size." Claudia skimmed the pointer to a dense area behind the swirling configuration that represented the growing tropical storm. "Those vertical updrafts are feeding it."

"So you're saying it's going to be big?"

"Along with the El Niño effect on the ocean temps, this has the makings of a monster." Claudia swiveled in her chair and looked up at Austin. Her eyes weren't really black, but a deep, deep brown, so dense they almost appeared to have no color. Austin didn't think she'd ever seen eyes quite so mesmerizing. "I'm afraid we're going to get thrashed. And we're sitting out here like a rubber duck."

"Not quite that bad. This rig is designed to withstand storms of that magnitude, and with a good coxswain to hold the trim and keep it on balance, it shouldn't be that big a deal."

"Trust me. If things go as I expect, this storm will be a very big deal. We'll be in for a very rough ride."

"Then with what's going on deep underwater, that breach is likely to get a whole lot worse," Austin muttered.

"I'd say so."

"Are you willing to put that in writing?"

Claudia smiled wryly. "Not right at this moment. I don't like to stake my reputation on a gut feeling, although I'm usually right.

Give me ten hours and I will sign my name to a prediction, one way or the other."

"Eloise will want an answer before that."

"She'll have to wait."

Claudia's tone was friendly, but Austin detected steel beneath the easy manner. "Maybe by then Reddy and his team will have the well locked down."

"You don't really believe that, do you?"

"Nine times out of ten, maybe ninety-nine times out of a hundred, these kind of things are contained without any substantial spill."

"If we weren't looking at a perfect storm of conditions here," Claudia said, "I wouldn't be as worried. But given what the situation is on land—well…"

"Yeah, I know. Recipe for a nightmare."

"So what is it," Claudia asked, indicating the control room and the computer monitors and the communications center that right now went unmanned but continued to emit bits of chatter between Reddy and Tatum and the teams working on the well platform, "that you do about all of this?"

"If and when we go public," Austin said, "I'll be the face of the company on-site for the press. All communication will go through me."

"You mean you can actually keep Tatum quiet?" Claudia laughed. "This is the first time I've worked with him, but I'd heard his reputation before. He certainly lives up to it."

"He's really good at what he does, and he's not a bad guy."

"You mean for a chauvinist?"

"I've seen him with female OTLs, not that there's many, and he doesn't even seem to notice they're women."

"That's because they're wearing hard hats, work boots, and coveralls."

"Yeah, maybe." Austin laughed. "And yes, keeping Tatum and any other unauthorized individuals from making statements to the press is my job."

"Including me?" Claudia asked, a teasing glint in her eye.

"Especially you."

Claudia made a humming sound that might have been the equivalent of *you hope*. "Can't they just do all that spinning from headquarters?"

"Oh, somebody above my pay grade will release the sanitized and politically correct statements that will get picked up by the national media, but what's really happening right here on the ground is what we need to control. There'll be reporters everywhere, talking to anyone they can talk to, and GOP wants a technical expert—not a media spokesperson—to direct the message that goes out."

"Sounds like a lot of fun."

"That's the easy part."

"Really? I'm not sure I want to know the bad part."

"That would be dealing with all of the agencies involved in containment if the oil gets away from us. U.S. Fish and Wildlife are the first responders and will be in charge of the operation, but lots of other agencies and even independent organizations get involved. Considering where we are? We'll have a regular circus."

"Couldn't be a worse place or a worse time," Claudia said.

"No," Austin said, thinking of Gem and the sanctuary, "it couldn't be."

"So what now?"

"We wait," Austin said, "until the leak stops, the well blows, or you tell us the storm is going to tear the rig out of the water."

"Lovely," Claudia muttered.

Austin's cell rang and she checked it. "And now I do the other part of my job." She answered Eloise's call. "Good morning."

"Is it? What have you got for me?"

"Nothing new. They haven't stopped the leak, but they slowed it. They're still working on it, and we'll know more by nightfall."

"That's not what I wanted to hear."

"I know," Austin said, "but that's what we've got."

"No, what we've got is a big-ass storm headed right for you and a gathering of some of the nation's premier wildlife scientists fifty miles away on shore."

"Really? I didn't realize—"

"Apparently, your passenger didn't explain to you exactly what a big deal this project is. It's federally funded at a very high level and has every tree hugger and green agency supporting it. Add to that the recent outbreak of avian flu in the Midwest and the concern for human crossover, and even the damn CDC is involved."

Austin tried to adjust the picture she'd had of Gem's role at the sanctuary, remembering Gem had told her she was a virologist studying the association between wild bird flu and domestic flocks. "I guess I didn't realize—"

"What's your passenger's name?"

"Gem…Gillian Martin. She's a—"

"PhD virologist from Yale. That's wonderful." Eloise sounded as if she was chewing bits of broken glass. "She's the lead researcher and her work is funded by the CDC and the NIH and half a dozen other places with acronyms I could give you, but that wouldn't mean anything. We're talking international reputation here. Could you have possibly picked up anyone more likely to shoot us down in flames?"

Eloise's researchers had been busy. "I really didn't have any way of knowing that, and besides—"

"Well, now that you do"—Eloise actually paused for breath— "you can put that knowledge to good use."

"I don't think I follow."

"You have a direct pipeline inside the sanctuary. Make contact, find out what the status is there after yesterday's storm. If the conditions are already compromised, we can't be blamed as much for anything that happens if we have problems with the rig. Just take a look around. Test the waters."

Austin unclenched her jaw. "You mean spy?"

"No," Eloise said coolly, "I mean gather information. Information is essential where communication management is concerned, and you are the communications specialist. It's all in a day's work."

"I don't see how anything we learn now would really be of benefit," Austin said. Communication management was Eloise-speak for keeping a lid on bad press, which Austin would do, up to a point. The point being lying—or spying. No way was she going to pump Gem for information, not after what they'd shared. Gem wasn't a source—she was…well, that was kind of ill-defined, but she was special, and that's all that mattered.

"At least get boots on the ground and take a look at what the situation requires if we have to institute protective measures. Advance knowledge will allow us to plan and deploy more efficiently."

Eloise was an expert at manipulation, and Austin knew it. But she couldn't argue when she made sense. The more Austin and the company knew about the exact nature of the sanctuary, the better they could design the protocols they would need to protect it.

"I'll see what I can find out, but I'm not going to lie about who I am."

"Of course not," Eloise said, "but there's no need to advertise it until necessary, is there?"

Austin sighed. Rock and hard place. She could keep on protesting, but part of her job was to assess the logistics and personalities she might have to work with, and beyond that, she couldn't keep pretending she didn't want to see Gem again.

CHAPTER FOURTEEN

A lexis scanned the water ahead of the cutter, checking for smaller vessels, solitary sea forms, and other flotsam and jetsam that didn't show on sonar or radar. Air temps were warmer than usual for this time of year, and she wore only a light flight jacket, cap, and gloves. On the one hand, it was nice to be able to stand on deck while patrolling without being lacerated by frigid winds, but the high temperatures were a deceptive gift whose price was steep. The unseasonably warm Gulf winds were harbingers of virulent and unpredictable storms that were forecast to be more plentiful and extend later into the fall than during other years.

Tropical storm Norma was thundering down upon them now, big, fast, and threatening major damage, and Alexis couldn't do anything but wait while trying to secure the sea, shores, and inhabitants before it arrived. Seafaring traffic was down, but not absent. After the high winds and heavy rains of the previous day and a half, commercial fishing boats had started to put out to sea in hopes of making up for their lost catches, and despite the maritime weather warnings, she'd spotted a few intrepid pleasure sailors and touring boats as well. The onboard radar screen at her console beeped rhythmically, and she scanned it reflexively every few minutes. On the last sweep, she picked up four new blips just emerging on the upper left-hand corner of her field, about twenty nautical miles northeast. She didn't have to check the map to know that put the ships in the waters off the oil rig, nothing unusual in and of itself, but the timing was strange given the storm warnings. The oil rig was a common destination for tankers offloading oil from the rig, transport ships delivering equipment, and other vessels. Ordinarily, she didn't pay much attention to the traffic, as their patrol range was considerably closer to shore. This morning, though, any activity on the seas caught her notice.

She would have expected the rig to ramp down production until the weather cleared. The oil platform sat out in the ocean like an apple in a barrel. Considerably more stable, but all the same, a speck compared to the vastness of the sea. A speck that housed dozens of vulnerable human beings as well as an underwater threat to the entire coastline.

She calculated the directional adjustment and thumbed her radio to contact the helmsman. "Lieutenant, course change. Let's go see what's going on out at the rig."

"Aye, aye, Commander."

She gave him the coordinates, and the patrol boat made a sweeping curve and headed farther out to sea. Thirty minutes later, they came in visual range of Rig 86 and the four big ships riding the waves in a semicircle a half mile away. She switched to an open channel and hailed the rig.

"This is Coast Guard Cutter Hayes Adams, hailing Rig 86. Come in."

A moment later, a female voice, deep and steady, replied, "Coast Guard Cutter Hayes Adams, this is Rig 86. Morning to you. Over."

"Permission to come aboard, over," Alexis said, although she didn't really need permission. As federal law enforcement agents, coastguardsmen could board any oceangoing vessel in territorial waters, and the rig was technically a ship since the platform was anchored to a stationary underwater hull. All the same, she was making a routine check and extended the courtesy of a request.

"Permission granted. Use the south side dock."

"Affirmed, Rig 86."

Alexis directed the helmsman to the south side of the platform, where he brought it smoothly in to the ocean-level dock and idled as the crew threw down for temporary anchor. Alexis climbed down the ladder, crossed the dock, and rode up in the crane-operated lift to the rig platform two stories above the water. A woman with short dark hair, average height, early thirties, in the usual uniform of windbreaker, boots, and serviceable pants awaited her with a friendly smile. Alexis didn't recognize her, and she thought she'd met most of the crew leaders at one time or another. She held out her hand. "Commander Alexis Martin. Good to meet you."

Alexis thought she saw a flicker of surprise in the woman's eyes, but the smile didn't falter, and the hand that closed around hers was firm. "Austin Germaine. Welcome aboard, Commander."

❖

Austin led the Coast Guard officer through the warren of containers and equipment to the command center, mentally evaluating. Martin. Had to be a coincidence the officer shared Gem's last name. Her luck couldn't possibly be that bad. She searched for some physical resemblance to Gem and tried to tell herself the shape of the officer's sea-green eyes, the particular golden hue of her hair, and the subtle squareness to her chin weren't really similar to Gem's remarkable features. Her artist's eye disagreed, however. The likeness was subtle, but it was there. God damn it.

As she opened the door to the command center, Austin said, "Come on in and make yourself at home. We've got some decent coffee. The OTL is out with the drill crew, but I can get him up here if you need him. I'm acting sub right now."

"Thanks," Alexis said, unzipping her jacket and stowing her gloves in the pockets, "but I'm just doing a drop-by to check on storm preparedness. No need to call the OTL. I'm good without coffee, but appreciate it." She glanced around the room. The usually crowded command center was oddly empty. The only other occupant was a woman who sat at a nearby workstation in front of two huge computer monitors showing satellite graphics and a variety of charts.

"Dr. Claudia Spencer is our oceanographer and meteorologist," Austin said, apparently following Alexis's gaze.

Claudia glanced over her shoulder and smiled in Alexis's direction.

Alexis straightened. Claudia Spencer was gorgeous. Ordinarily, the sight of a beautiful woman didn't give her a little charge, but this one did. Her hair and eyes were the color of a starless sky, deep black and endless; her elegant features and pale skin as flawless as polished ivory; her sensuous mouth wide and full, and at the moment, lifting in a deliberate smile. Alexis cleared her throat. "Ma'am."

The stunning brunette laughed. "Hardly. Commander, is it?"

"Yes, ma'am, Alexis Martin."

"Very nice to meet you, Commander." Claudia's voice was throaty and warm, as rich as dark honey. She held Alexis's gaze for another few seconds and then turned back to her computer screen.

Alexis dragged her attention back to Austin. "How's the rig riding out the weather?"

"So far so good. As you can see," Austin indicated Claudia's screens, "we're keeping an eye on what's coming, but as I'm sure you know, these semisubmersibles have incredible stability, even in big storms."

"I know, but we don't want a replay of what happened with the Petrobras."

Austin winced. Petrobras 36 was the world's biggest semisubmersible rig until it exploded and sank in bad weather off the coast of Brazil. "Believe me, neither do we."

"I noticed you've got a convoy out there. Transport?"

"Potentially. We're keeping our nonessentials off the rig," Austin said, carefully keeping to the truth. She wasn't about to lie to anyone, but particularly not to a Coast Guard officer whose duty it was to protect all of them.

"Good idea," Alexis said. "How's your storage level on the rig?"

"We've offloaded most of our fuel already," Austin said, again sticking to the facts.

"You have everything at the ready to evacuate the rig if there are problems?"

"We have protocols in place. Ray Tatum will contact the company to make the call if the situation changes." Austin indicated Claudia with a tilt of her head. "Dr. Spencer's keeping a close eye on the storm as well as evaluating the stability of the rig. We won't take any chances."

"I doubted you would." Alexis glanced toward Claudia Spencer again. The brunette didn't turn around, and Alexis hid her disappointment. Everything sounded in order, and she had no reason to stay. She pulled her gloves from her pocket and slapped them against her thigh. "Good enough. I'll let you get back to it, then."

"I'll walk you out," Austin said.

Claudia turned and caught Alexis's eyes. "Safe seas, Commander."

Alexis nodded. "And to you, Doctor."

Alexis walked with Austin to the far side of the deck and swung her leg over the side of the railing into the cage. "Make sure you institute those protocols with plenty of time. This one is going to be tough to call." The wind whipped her hair, the sting bringing tears to the corners of her eyes. "No matter how good your meteorologist might be."

"You've got my word on that, Commander."

Alexis nodded and disappeared as the cage rapidly descended to the dock below.

Austin gripped the rail and watched the cutter glide away in a rapid curve, headed toward the convoy riding easily on the horizon at the moment. The last thing she wanted was to put anyone in danger, and if they didn't make the right call at the right time, it wasn't just their crew they'd put at risk. Claudia wanted ten hours to make a firm prediction. They had six left, and every one hung over her head like the sword of Damocles.

❖

Gem set out when the sun finally broke through the clouds for a few precious moments. The weather report suggested they might have scattered clouds with a bit of sun for the rest of the afternoon, and she intended to make the most of it. She wanted to get her cameras situated and temporary blinds set up where she could view and record the various migrants en route through the sanctuary. With her backpack full of equipment and a water bottle tucked into the pocket of her cargo pants, she followed the main trail away from her cabin into the marsh for a quarter of a mile, using her GPS to map her route and mark observation locations. Then she left the trail and headed into the undeveloped areas where tourists had no access, taking care not to disturb the native vegetation that provided not only cover, but food for the birds. The type and plentifulness of the reeds, grasses, and other ground cover constituted two of the prime determinants of which birds nested in which part of the sanctuary. She stopped at intervals and set her infrared-capable video cameras to cover areas she anticipated would be prime nesting spots and attached extended battery packs. Some of the birds would only rest for a day or less, others might remain for several. She would make a twice-daily circuit, downloading the camera readouts and changing batteries.

She didn't have to make the trip every day, let alone twice a day. She could just as easily monitor the cameras from her cabin's computer, but she preferred to do it manually. A camera could only see where its lens was pointed, but her human senses could follow the trill of birdsong, catch the flicker of wings on the air, spy a flash of color in a way a still camera never could. And besides that, she was a field researcher. She didn't want to sit in a warm room in front of a computer monitor. She wanted her boots on the ground, no matter how muddy, and the wind in her hair, and the beauty around her warming her spirit.

In a couple of hours she'd completed her preliminary route, which she'd modify as the flocks arrived, and was only a twenty-minute fast walk from the center. Hopefully some of the other team members had arrived. She could use a little company to divert her attention. Activity seemed to be the only panacea to thoughts of Austin. Some of those thoughts were immensely enjoyable, but beneath the pleasant memories was a tide of sadness threatening to rise. She needed to call Kim too, and she'd been putting it off.

Funny, now that she thought of it, that Kim hadn't called her or even requested when they'd parted that Gem call her when she arrived. She hadn't thought to wonder what Kim's schedule was either. How long had they been in that stagnant place, both of them going through the motions because it was easier than admitting they had only the barest of connections any longer? They were friends, but she was closer to Emily, who she only saw in person a couple of times a year. Her night with Austin aside, it was time for her and Kim to move on, and the weeks of separation while she was in the field would be a natural time to make the break. She sighed. So she'd call—as soon as she got back to the cabin.

The visitors' center's main area was empty except for a twentysomething brown-haired boy in a pressed plaid shirt and jeans, who looked up eagerly when she walked in.

"Hi," he said in a high soft tenor, "welcome to the Rock Hill Island sanctuary. Can I help you?"

"Hi." Gem held out her hand. "I'm Gem Martin. I'm part of the research team."

Disappointment flickered across his features and then he smiled again. "Oh, hi. I'm Paul."

The name used to give Gem a start, even recently, but today she had no reaction at all. Paul was long gone and would not steal a moment of her time, now or ever. "I don't imagine you're getting much in the way of visitors today."

"No. It's deadly quiet." He brightened again. "But tomorrow's Friday, so the weekend ought to be busy. If the storm doesn't keep everyone away."

"You know birdwatchers. They'll be here."

"I hope so. This is one of the biggest weeks of the year for us. The donations really help."

"Well, stay warm and dry, Paul," Gem said and went on down the hall to the canteen. To her disappointment, the small dining area was empty. Emily and Joe must still be out in the field somewhere, and the other team members either hadn't arrived or were getting settled into their cabins. She checked the coffeepot, found it nearly full, sniffed, and decided it was fresh enough to drink. She poured a cup and turned at the sound of footsteps behind her. Maybe Emily or Joe—

She caught her breath, and her heart actually raced in her chest.

"The guy out front said I should come back," Austin said from the doorway. "I hope it's okay."

CHAPTER FIFTEEN

Gem couldn't quite believe Austin was real. She'd been thinking about her so much since leaving her in what felt like another world, and yet here she was, somehow right in the middle of hers. She set her coffee cup down. "Stay right there for a minute."

Austin raised a brow but stood still and silent, a glint in her eyes that dared Gem to do her worst. Gem closed the distance and lightly kissed her on the mouth. "Yup. Warm and breathing."

Austin laughed; a rush of pleasure and something else, something light and bright and beautiful that after a few seconds she recognized as happiness, rushed through her. "I guess I should ask, is there some particular reason you thought I might not be alive?"

"Honestly, I wasn't sure I'd see you again, and this is the last place I would've imagined you to turn up. So I just wanted to make sure you were actually flesh and blood."

At the rate her heart was pounding, Austin wasn't certain she was actually going to remain that way much longer. "Oh, I'm very much alive. But feel free to check anytime you find it necessary."

"I can see that you're quite well and functioning normally." Gem gestured to the coffeepot. "I was about to have some coffee, which I could probably do without, but if you're interested—"

"None for me," Austin said. "I'm pretty much running on rocket fuel at this point."

"Mmm, me too," Gem said. Too much caffeine must be the source of her sudden case of the trembles. The swirling tides in her midsection couldn't have anything to do with Austin. Just to prove her point, she leaned a hip against the counter and indulged herself with a long look. Austin wore plain dark pants, an equally plain, serviceable blue work shirt under a light black jacket, and work boots. Just as she thought—Austin looked amazing. She was every bit as good as the memories Gem had been conjuring all morning. Better in person, even. Her dark eyes glittered with attention and energy. Her hair was windblown, carelessly framing her bold face, giving her a piratical air. She was every inch sexy. Gem feigned a calm she didn't feel. "Now that we've established your vital status, what are you doing here?"

"I wanted to get out of the motel," Austin said, again true but not altogether so, "considering the sun is shining and I'm not sure how long that's going to last, and…I wanted to see you again. I've been thinking about how I was going to manage that since the minute you walked out this morning."

And thank you, Eloise, for giving me the excuse to be here.

Gem's breath left her in a rush, along with most of her reasoning faculties. Austin had a way of sweeping her off her metaphorical feet—she was always a little off balance around her. She hadn't been the object of true interest, real passion, for a decade. Maybe longer than that. By the time she and Paul had married, they were more friends than lovers, having been dating exclusively since they were fifteen. Her attraction to Christie had been obsession, in retrospect, and completely one-sided. She had long ago come to terms with the hard knowledge that Christie's attraction to her had been nothing more than Christie's desire for a conduit to Paul. Austin's interest was unmistakable, and being on the receiving end of that attraction left her light-headed and excited. "I'm glad you're here."

"I know I'm probably interrupting your work," Austin said. "It's the first day and all, so I just took a chance. Listen, I don't mean to keep you, but maybe—"

"No," Gem said quickly, before Austin had a chance to disappear or she *did* awaken and find this a dream, "this is actually a great time. The full team isn't here yet, and I've just finished most of what I needed to do today, at least in terms of fieldwork. I can finish up what I need to do online anytime tonight."

"Okay, then how about the nickel tour?"

Gem laughed. "You really want to take a look at a basic research facility?"

"I'd like to see your digs," Austin said, "and since I've never been to the sanctuary, and it isn't raining, I wouldn't mind a walk around."

"Done. This place won't take but ten minutes to see and then we can get outside."

"You sure you don't mind?"

"Not at all." Gem more than didn't mind. She looked forward to showing Austin the sanctuary, something she'd never shared with Kim or anyone close to her other than Alex, who stopped by from time to time when Gem was in residence. But the wonders of a coastal marshland were as familiar to Alex as a city street was to most other people. She still appreciated the wonder of it, but there was little Gem could show her that she didn't already know about. Gem lightly took Austin's arm and pointed down the hall. "We've commandeered a few rooms down this wing where we run some of the basic analyses on samples that might deteriorate in shipping. Our botanist, Joe Edelman, routinely does water samples, bacterial cultures and counts, that kind of thing, looking at the composition of the freshwater pools, algae counts, and quite a few other things that if you were absolutely dying to know, I'm sure Joe could spend hours explaining to you."

Austin laughed. "I think I get the picture. What about you? What do you do here?"

"This is going to sound exceedingly unsexy, I'm afraid," Gem said, opening the next door down the hall and revealing a standard laboratory setup—several benches running lengthwise down the center of the room, an isolation hood against one wall, incubators, racks of test tubes, Petri dishes, pipettes, beakers, all the things Austin remembered from biology and chemistry labs in high school and college and never thought she'd have to think about again.

"Gem," Austin murmured, "everything about you is sexy."

Gem halted and the lab disappeared from her awareness. She caught Austin's scent—fresh air, the sea, and a subtle hint of spice. Gem resisted the urge to press her face to Austin's neck, to breathe her in, to lick her. Lick her? What was happening to her? Whatever it was, she wasn't in the mood to fight it. It felt too good. "You might want to reserve that line for dinner some night, when I'm not wearing mud-caked boots and shapeless clothes."

"I don't see why." Austin captured Gem's hand. "You'd be beautiful in anything you were wearing, and at the risk of being crass, I already know how beautiful you are when you're not wearing anything at all."

Gem freed her hand and slapped it to Austin's chest, keeping two feet of distance between them. "Ground rules. You are not to say anything provocative, suggestive, or seductive for the rest of the afternoon."

Austin's smile widened. "And why is that?"

"Because I'm trying to maintain some degree of maturity and decorum. And every time you flirt with me, all I can think about is being in bed with you."

"Would that being-in-bed be past tense, present, or future?"

"All of the above." Gem was breathing quickly, her palms were slightly damp, and desire churned in her middle. Austin was the sexiest woman she'd ever seen and just being near her scalded her, inside and out. Some ferocious, all-consuming lust had been released the night before and the short leash Gem'd kept it on all morning had snapped. She wanted to kiss Austin again, right here in the lab.

"I can read your thoughts," Austin said softly.

"You cannot." Gem closed her hand on the front of Austin's shirt, tugged her a little closer. "At least, I sincerely hope you can't." She kissed Austin for the second time that afternoon, but this time it wasn't light and it wasn't fleeting. She nibbled Austin's lower lip, sucked it lightly between her teeth, tasted her, probed and teased.

Austin groaned and gripped Gem's hips, drawing her close until they were touching everywhere. She made a sound at the base of her throat, a soft growl, and Gem turned liquid inside. She wound her arms around Austin's shoulders, angled her mouth to take her deeper, her fingers gliding through Austin's hair, her breasts pressing hard to Austin's.

Distantly, she heard a squeak and "Oops. Sorry."

Gem peered over Austin's shoulder. Emily stared wide-eyed from the doorway. Gem pulled away but kept her arms on Austin's shoulders. "Hey, Em."

Emily slid both hands into her back pockets, faint spots of color high on her cheeks, her blue eyes sparkling with amusement and undisguised interest. "Well, I'd say I'm sorry again, but really, I'm not. You could just carry on—"

Austin laughed and turned in Emily's direction. "Hi. I'm a friend of Gem's."

"Oh, I figured that out," Emily said lightly, holding out her hand. "Emily Costanzas."

"Austin Germaine. Nice to meet you."

Emily gave Gem a pointed look. "You are in so much trouble."

Gem swept her hand down Austin's back. "I know, I know."

Emily backed out into the hall and waved. "Well, I'd love to continue the observation—I mean, conversation, but you know—"

"Bye, Em!" Gem called after her.

Laughter followed as Emily disappeared.

"Sorry about that," Austin said.

"Really?"

Austin grinned. "No, not really. I'm sorry we were interrupted, though."

"Ah, probably just as well."

"It's not a problem, is it?"

"What, Emily? No. We're all adults, after all."

Austin's dark eyes trapped hers. "She's not a special friend?"

"You mean girlfriend?"

"Yeah, that's what I mean."

"No, Emily's a good friend, a colleague. But not an intimate friend." Gem hesitated. "We didn't talk about any of that last night. It didn't seem that there was any reason to."

"We both agreed what last night was," Austin said. "Last night was a thing unto itself."

"And today?"

Austin cupped her face, kissed her gently. "Today is a new day."

"Then perhaps we should take that walk."

"We should. Okay. But first, you were going to tell me what you do in this place."

"Part of what I do is study the possible transmission of pathogens from wild to domestic birds."

"Right, like bird flu."

"Yes. So when I come across a sick or, occasionally, dying bird, I'll do the necropsy in here and culture various organs, isolate blood specimens, and sample other biological tissues for organisms."

"Like a mini morgue."

"Yes."

"That's fascinating."

"Sometimes it's the most routine things that lead us to a breakthrough." Gem rarely discussed the specifics of her work, and almost never that part of it. Most people, Kim being one of them, did not like to hear about the less picturesque side of things. Austin's interest, however, was clearly genuine, and Gem warmed to the praise. "I enjoy the methodical routine of it all."

"So the sanctuary is really your laboratory—not just this room, but all of it."

"Yes, in a way. Would you like to see it?"

Austin grabbed Gem's hand. "Very much."

❖

Austin almost hadn't come, but Eloise's mandate had given her the excuse to see Gem again, and she wanted to. She'd wanted to see her as soon as she'd disappeared that morning. If she'd been able to banish the storm and cancel her job and abandon her responsibilities, she would've spent the day in bed with Gem, naked and absorbed in her. Exploring, savoring, reveling in the pure pleasure of being with her. Walking beside her down a narrow trail through knee-high marsh grass and evergreens dripping rainwater in tiny droplets fractured by sunlight into millions of miniscule rainbows was almost as satisfying as those moments she'd spent entwined with her. Gem's enthusiasm, her clear love of nature and her work, suffused her with an ethereal beauty Austin itched to draw. She despaired at being able to capture the passion and energy in her eyes, but she ached to try. They spent an hour wandering through the marsh, with Gem pointing out where she'd set up cameras and planned to watch the birds as they arrived. They finally emerged on the far end of the island and walked back along the shore. Once or twice they passed sandy patches isolated with yellow caution tape.

"Nesting areas?" Austin asked.

"Yes, but not for the birds. Turtles." Gem pointed to the screens covering sections of the beach. "Emily's been busy already, setting screens to protect the buried clutches from predators. Once the babies emerge, most of them under unprotected conditions will never make it to the sea. They'll be eaten by birds or crabs. Sometimes out of a clutch of a hundred and fifty eggs, not a single baby makes it to the sea."

"No wonder they're endangered." Austin gazed out over the ocean. Right now, the rig was invisible, fifty miles out, but she could see it as clearly as if it floated just offshore. The sea was clear and calm with low waves breaking intimately against the beach and running in frothy rivulets back to the water's edge. Despite the placid surf, the signs of yesterday's storm were everywhere, with deep gullies cut into the sandy beach leaving nothing but chains of rocks in furrowed trenches. "It looks like this stretch took quite a beating."

Gem pushed strands of hair away from her face as the wind picked up. The sky darkened and a bank of clouds drifted across the sun. "Yes, all along the coastline, really. If we get another round like yesterday, we're going to lose a lot of this beach."

"What about the turtles?"

"It depends on when they hatch. Once they get to the sea, they'll head for deep water, and if a larger predator doesn't get them, they'll spend years alone, just growing to maturity before they mate. It's late in the season, but a few species do hatch this time of year. If we get hit hard before they hatch, Emily's going to be sitting out here with an umbrella, if I know her."

"You're kidding about that, right?" Austin frowned. "We're talking about a big storm, Gem. Possible hurricane intensity, and projections have it headed right for you. All of you ought to vacate here."

Gem frowned and gave her an odd look. "Don't you mean all of us? You're not planning on staying in town if things get bad, are you?"

Austin hedged. "I'm not sitting on a little spit of land with the ocean a couple hundred yards away."

"I don't think any of us will be leaving. We've ridden out plenty of storms here before."

Austin took in the shoreline in both directions. The inland sanctuary areas Gem had shown her were only a few hundred yards away. An oil spill, if it reached this far, would endanger everything in the sanctuary. They couldn't let that happen. She'd seen it now. She'd fulfilled Eloise's orders. She had no reason to stay, and she'd already said too much to Gem. "I should let you get back to work."

Gem studied her, as if trying to decipher the sudden distance. "You probably have work to do too."

"I do." Austin smiled, thinking about the work she truly enjoyed. "Ciri is about to wage an epic battle, and the future of the universe hinges on her vanquishing Charos."

Gem laughed. "Oh really? And if she fails?"

"Then the door to the underworld will blow open, and Charos's forces will pour forth to wreak havoc and terror on the unsuspecting populace."

"And I don't suppose we'll find out the outcome of the battle in the next volume, will we?"

"Well…" Austin shrugged, grinning. The wind picked up more and she zipped her jacket against the chill. "That wouldn't be the best marketing plan."

"Do you storyboard it, or do you do one panel at a time?"

"You do know your graphic novels, don't you?"

"I told you I was a fan."

"Some brief sketches, but mostly I go panel by panel."

"You still haven't invited me up to see your…sketches yet."

"Will you come?" Austin had no right to open these doors, but she couldn't stop. Didn't want to stop.

"Absolutely."

"Then as soon as I can, I will." She didn't know when that might be or how she would manage it, but she would. She wanted to share that with Gem. She wanted Gem to see what mattered to her. "So I guess I should go."

"How about something warm for the road? My cabin's not too far."

She didn't have much time. The window of clear weather was closing and decisions had to be made. She had a bird to catch back out to the rig. She checked her watch. "If I told you I only had an hour—"

"Then I'd say we should hurry."

CHAPTER SIXTEEN

Austin took Gem's hand and followed her along the winding path from the shore back into the sanctuary. Stiff, damp cattails, four feet high, growing up to the edges of the narrow trail, brushed her pants and soaked the material below her knees. Occasional tufts of wispy material from the dark brown seed cones drifted off and stuck to her skin.

"These reeds," Gem said as they walked, "are prime habitat for the birds and lots of other wildlife. They also keep the shore erosion down." She laughed, her face radiant with pleasure. "They're hell on clothes, though."

"I'm having a hard time seeing you in a lab," Austin said. "You must feel pretty cooped up."

Gem's mouth twisted and she nodded. "Sometimes I do, but the other part of my work is valuable and feeds other needs, so I just look forward to the times I can escape."

Escape. Austin never considered that a possibility. She'd carved out two separate lives for herself—the one her family and, if she was honest, she considered worthy of the family image, and the other a private one, the one that fed her secret self. Choices she'd made. "I'm glad. I'd hate thinking of you trapped inside when you didn't want to be."

Gem squeezed her hand. "Thank you."

The way Gem said it made Austin think she'd done something special, and she warmed inside even as the skin on the back of her neck and hands grew clammy with the tendrils of fog that skirted through the rushes and closed in around them. The clouds had coalesced into a thick gray blanket, blotting out what little sunshine there'd been just moments before. She ought to get back to the airport and let Tatum know she was ready for a lift back to the rig, but she'd always been a gambler, and the stakes were high this time. She might not see Gem again for days, and when she did, it wouldn't be like this. They wouldn't be holding hands and walking along in silent communion.

She didn't need to study the odds or the weather-satellite images to know the storm was on its way, and the company couldn't wait any longer. If, when she returned, Tatum and Reddy didn't have a far more positive report than they'd had that morning, she'd have to push Eloise to go public. The turning point was upon them, from both PR and ethical positions. When she saw Gem again, they'd likely be on opposite sides of the problem—at least that had always been her experience when dealing with the environmentalists. She could overcome that initial animosity almost every time, with patience and logic and good-faith cooperation on the part of the company. But the personal had never entered into it, and everything about her interaction with Gem so far had been personal. Very, very personal.

If she continued down this path, they'd get even more complicated.

Gem slowed and Austin drew up beside her. A weathered cabin squatted in a small clearing surrounded by trees and more marsh grass. Austin saw nothing else in either direction except more wild, dense terrain.

"This is it," Gem said, "home."

"I see you're not much for neighbors."

Gem smiled wryly. "You know, I was thinking something like that this morning. Back in the city, I've got neighbors everywhere, although they're really strangers who just happen to live nearby. Out here, there's just me."

"And you're good with that."

"Most of the time." Gem tugged her hand. "Although not right this moment. Come inside."

Austin could say no—she had one last chance to keep things less complicated. The heat of Gem's hand penetrated the fog reaching out like ghostly fingers, and she followed Gem onto the small porch, through the narrow door, and into the cabin. Gem lit a couple of lamps and the space brightened with a warm glow, chasing the chill away.

In a quick glance, Austin took in the one room. Someone had done a good job of designing the space—everything necessary was there: microwave, small fridge, equally small range, a table/work area, a small sitting area with a love seat and matching chair to relax in, and just visible in an alcove jutting off the rear, a bed. The bathroom must be back there too.

"Looks pretty cozy," Austin said.

"It is." Gem glanced around. "Sometimes I feel like I'm in a cave, but that doesn't bother me."

"My place isn't a whole lot bigger." Austin laughed. "I've probably got a room more than I need. When I'm working, I don't care if I never move, so all I really need is a desk and a chair. Well, that and maybe cinnamon buns."

Gem grinned. "Is that your weakness?"

"I might have more than one of those." Austin leaned against the closed front door, waiting for Gem to set the ground rules. She couldn't get any farther away from Gem physically, and if she got any closer, she was going to put her hands on her. Her heart pounded so hard it must be audible.

Gem's blue eyes flashed, then smoldered to an even deeper indigo. She took a step forward and stopped an arm's length away. "Is that right. Not just cinnamon buns, huh?"

Austin shook her head, swallowing around the lust that clamped her throat in a vise.

"Should I guess?" Gem took another step.

"I think you might have a pretty good idea."

Gem gripped the edges of Austin's jacket, pushed it off her shoulders, and kissed her neck. "I seem to recall a few. My memory's a little hazy, though."

The touch of Gem's lips spread over Austin's skin like burning honey. Austin tossed aside the jacket, let her head fall back against the door, and closed her eyes. She shuddered. "This might not be the best of ideas."

"Why?" Gem kissed her throat again, moved up, nipped the undersurface of the angle of her jaw, and leaned into her, body pressing everywhere. "Are you married?"

"No," Austin rasped. She slid both hands down Gem's back and cradled her hips, opening her thighs to pull Gem between her legs.

"Good." Gem unbuttoned the top button of Austin's shirt, peeled back the fabric, and kissed her chest. "Engaged?"

Austin shook her head, her lids slipping closed, the flames reaching deeper, igniting her darkest reaches. "No. No one."

"So hard to believe," Gem murmured, opening another button, baring the inner curves of Austin's breasts. She kissed first one then the other and rubbed her cheek over the swell of warm, firm flesh. Another button and her hand was inside Austin's shirt, cupping her breast through the thin silk tank she'd worn underneath it. "Why aren't you taken? God, you're beautiful."

"Gem," Austin moaned.

"Hmm? Why not?" Gem teased a nipple beneath sheer black promise.

"I never fell."

Gem squeezed and the tender nipple peaked. "In love, you mean?"

"Yes. God, yes."

"I wouldn't recommend it. It really is some kind of insanity. This is ever so much nicer."

Austin gripped Gem's wrist before the last of her reason dissolved. She couldn't tell her everything, but she had to be sure. "Wait."

Gem stilled. "What, what is it? Oh—you mean me?"

"No—but—"

"I'm not married, I'm not engaged." Gem took a breath, tried to find the truth. "There's a woman, we've been seeing each other almost two years now. We're not committed."

"Why not?"

"I don't love her." The words were a shock and Gem jerked. "I mean, I do, but not—not in the way I need to if I'm going to make promises."

"I thought you didn't believe in love?"

"I don't, or maybe I should just say I don't trust it." Gem caressed Austin's jaw, kissed her slowly until the heat flared again. "This has nothing to do with anyone, anything, but us."

Austin cradled Gem's face, brushed her thumbs over the graceful arches of her cheeks. "You don't know me."

"You don't know me either."

Austin smiled. "It feels like I do, in so many ways."

Gem caught Austin's thumb in her teeth and bit lightly. "Then believe me if I say the same."

"I do."

"Then good. That's enough."

Gem's voice was far away and Austin's grip on caution drifted off with it. She wanted, a hard hot ache drawing tighter in her depths. More than pleasure, more than sex. Need, touch, knowing. Gem. "Don't stop."

"Oh no, not hardly." Gem opened another button on Austin's shirt, pulled the tails free from her pants, and finished exposing her down the middle. She pushed up the thin tank, trailed her fingers up and down the center of Austin's abdomen. "I love your body. I can't get enough."

Austin shuddered. "Take…all you want."

All you want. Gem laughed, feeling wild and wanton and not caring that she didn't have any idea what she was doing. All she knew was she wanted more. Had she ever wanted so much? So simple, so astounding. The taste and touch of her, the sound of her pleasure was flame to oil. She popped the top button of Austin's pants, knelt, and kissed Austin's stomach. Austin's fingers came into her hair, a possessive gesture that thrilled her, turning her liquid and hot inside. She grasped the waistband of Austin's pants. "Say no now or—"

"Yes," Austin said, her voice a harsh whisper.

Gem unzipped her, grasped the layers of clothing, and pulled them down. "Your damn boots."

"Laces."

"I know, I know," Gem muttered, finding the leather and pulling them loose. Austin kicked them off and Gem pressed her shoulders between Austin's thighs.

"God," Austin groaned.

"No, not hardly," Gem whispered, caressing Austin's thighs, running her hands down her legs and up the outer thighs. She couldn't wait any longer. Gripping her hips, she covered her with her mouth. Austin arched and met her with a slow languid thrust. Gem hummed in the back of her throat and tasted her, stroking and exploring with her tongue and her lips. Austin's thighs trembled, and she took more.

"Go slow if you don't—" Austin cradled Gem's head in her hands and rocked into her mouth, the rhythm as easy and natural as waves on the shore. Gem's mouth was a sea of pleasure, and Austin rode the crest higher and higher. Sunlight, burning away the mist, flared behind her eyelids, a blaze of passion and promise. "I'm going to come."

Gem's grip tightened and she coaxed Austin to the brink.

Austin jerked, a cry wrenched from her chest, and she lost the rhythm, lost control, lost the tenuous fragments of awareness that held her anchored to the earth. She soared until her mind blanked and she tumbled from the clouds.

Gem broke her fall, steady and strong. "Right here, baby."

"Sorry." Austin looped her arms around Gem's waist and leaned hard. "I—don't have my legs under me just yet."

Gem laughed and stroked the back of her neck. "Kick off the rest of your clothes. The bed isn't far. One good thing about a small cabin."

"The bed is pretty small too."

"We'll manage," Gem murmured.

A minute later, Gem was naked and Austin stretched out facing her on top of the bed. The little alcove was shadowy, a secret hollow untouched by the world. Austin brushed her fingers through Gem's hair and kissed her. "You're incredible."

"Oh, that was all you."

"I don't know who that was," Austin said. "You just kind of turned me upside down."

"Did I?" Gem kissed her, sliding one leg over Austin's hip, pressing her center to Austin's thigh. The pressure against her sensitive, swollen sex was wonderful and insanity-provoking. "How is that?"

"I'm usually not so…easy."

"Really? Easy, huh." Gem laughed. "I like that."

"So do I." More than she'd ever imagined. Austin kissed her, brushing her fingers over Gem's neck, down her chest, and over her breast. She clasped her gently, teased a nipple with her thumb.

Gem arched, pulled Austin on top of her, and wrapped a leg around Austin's thigh. "How about you show me what you're usually like."

"I would, but…" Austin braced herself on an elbow and rocked against Gem's center until Gem moaned. Slipping a hand between them, she cupped her and slid inside. "There's nothing usual about being with you."

Austin dipped her head and caught Gem's earlobe between her teeth, tugged it just enough to make Gem jerk. Gem tightened around her inside, and Austin pressed her thumb over her clitoris as she stroked. "Nothing usual about this."

Gem's eyes flew open, and she searched Austin's face, her gaze hazy and undone. "You're about to make me come."

"Go ahead. I'm not done."

"I can't—"

Gem's fingers dug into Austin's shoulders as she bore down, riding Austin through a fast hard orgasm and slipping into a rocking rhythm that signaled there was more. Austin kept pace, stroking and pressing, harder and higher, until Gem cried out, a shocked, exultant cry, and came again.

Austin stilled until the pulsations stopped and Gem let out a long sigh. Gently, Austin eased down beside her, wrapped her arm around Gem's shoulders, and cradled her head against her chest. "No, nothing usual at all. Like the first time ever."

"I know. How can that be?" Gem nuzzled Austin's throat. "I don't know what to make of it."

"Maybe we don't have to know any more than this," Austin murmured, hoping desperately that would be true.

CHAPTER SEVENTEEN

Gem's brain finally went back online and reality cut through the lazy haze of satisfaction. Reality was so much more vivid than it had been just a short time before, like a black-and-white image suddenly suffused with color. Austin's heart beating beneath her cheek was real. The scent of spice and sea was real. The lassitude and lingering pleasure in her loins was real. And so, too, was the certainty of the end drawing closer.

She wasn't sure how much time had passed, but she knew it was running out. Usually she could tell the time without a watch to within a minute or so, but apparently great sex derailed her inner compass. Austin had declared she'd only had an hour, without explaining why. Gem hadn't asked. It hadn't been important then. Maybe Austin was one of those people who worked on a specific schedule and never deviated. Gem didn't know, but then she didn't know a lot of things about her. That hadn't seemed important then and still didn't.

She *did* know her touch, more intimately than that of the man she'd been married to or the woman she'd been making love with for the last two years. She knew her body and what caused her to tighten with anticipation and explode with satisfaction. She knew the heat of her gaze and the intensity of her attention. She knew things on some primal, fundamental level that had nothing to do with all the daily tasks of living that usually consumed her time. In another minute or five, Austin would disappear again, possibly never to return, and she'd known that too. Gem pressed a kiss to the inner curve of Austin's breast where her heart beat so close to the surface. "You have to go, don't you?"

Austin stroked Gem's hair slowly, letting strands sift through her fingers. Fog climbed up the small window next to the bed, an ever-thickening shroud heralding danger. "I do. I'm sorry."

Gem rose up and kissed her before meeting her eye to eye. "No apologies are necessary. I knew this would be brief." She grinned. "And I must say, it didn't feel fast, it just felt...amazing."

Austin cupped her jaw, kissed her back. "Such an ordinary word for something extraordinary. But yes, amazing."

Gem sat up and swung over the side of the bed before the fire surging in her depths made her try to keep Austin from leaving. "We should get some clothes on. I'll walk you back."

Austin skimmed a hand down the center of Gem's spine, imprinting the firmness of muscles and the delicacy of fine bones beneath ivory skin. "No need. It's going to be ugly out there."

"All the more reason I should go check in at the center. I want to make sure the team members we expected actually got in today. And that everyone else is settled."

"All right then. You'll be careful, won't you, if you stay?"

Gem turned back, leaned down to kiss her. "I will. And you, the same. You're sure you don't want to get out ahead of the storm? I'm afraid it's not going to be very restful around here for the next few weeks. If it's peace and quiet you need for your work, you might not get it."

"I'll be here."

"I'm glad, then." Gem brushed her fingers through the dark lock of hair slashing across Austin's forehead. "I hope I see you again."

"I do too."

Gem dressed quickly, used to being fast in a cold cabin in the morning, and Austin moved just as efficiently. Outside the fog lay a foot thick over the marshes, but she knew the trail by heart and led Austin back to the center as evening threatened to come early. Only three cars dotted the small parking lot, and she recognized Austin's rental next to her own. She stopped beside Austin's, resisting the urge to grip Austin's jacket and hold her in place for just another minute or two. "Would you mind texting me when you get back to your B and B? Just so I know you're all right."

"As soon as I'm settled," Austin said after a moment. She handed Gem her phone. "Put your number in there. Then you'll have mine when I text you."

"Are you sure? I know it might be a little too persona—"

Austin slid a hand beneath her hair and cupped her neck, drawing her closer, tilting her head up. She kissed her, a deep, possessive kiss. "I'm sure. Very. I'll let you know."

Gem slid her arms around Austin's neck, pressed close, took her mouth again. She drank her in as deeply as she could, feasting on her heat and the dark promise of her mouth. When she drew back, her heart was pounding and her breath was short. "Well. That will hold me for a little while."

"Not long enough for me," Austin muttered.

"Be careful." Gem backpedaled, watching until Austin slid into the driver's seat, started the SUV, and pulled away. The fog quickly swallowed her headlights and Gem finally turned and went inside.

Paul was just zipping up his backpack. "I'm going to close early. There's no one around, and the weather really sucks."

"I don't blame you. Go on ahead. Is anyone in the back?"

"Emily's there. A couple of other people stopped in earlier and then went to their cabins. Joe left about fifteen minutes ago."

"Thanks. Take care on your way home."

"Will do. I'm walking. It's not that far." He headed out the door, his bright orange backpack slung over one shoulder.

"'Night," Gem called after him and went down the hall to the canteen.

Emily was the only one there, nursing a hot cup of instant soup.

"Hey." Gem pulled another packet of soup out of the box that sat on the counter, ran water into a mug, and emptied the packet. After she put it in the microwave, she turned to find Emily studying her with an unmistakable smirk. Heat rushed to her face. "What?"

"How is it you failed to mention the hottie?"

Gem laughed. "Hottie?"

Emily made a sizzling sound. "Like, if I didn't have a thing for a certain type of appendage, I could almost see myself getting all sweaty and—"

Gem held up a hand. "Okay, let's not go there. A picture is worth a thousand words and all."

"Pfft," Emily said. "Seriously, where were you hiding her?"

The microwave dinged, saving Gem for a moment. She took out the soup, stirred it until the lumps on the surface disappeared, and sat down across from Emily. Confession time. "I didn't mention her because I just met her yesterday."

"Whoa." Emily sat up straighter, her expression sharpening. "Yesterday and already—wow. Who knew?"

"Will you stop," Gem said, laughing again self-consciously. "You make me sound like a...I don't know what."

"Woman with hidden depths? Dark passions? Secret desires?" Emily lowered her voice and drew out the words as if she was introducing an X-rated movie.

"You're really going to make me suffer, aren't you?"

"Damn straight. I don't get to hear very many interesting sex stories. All my friends are married and have been for so long that it's babies and diapers and bills. So spill."

Gem blew on her soup and took a cautious sip. It was too salty, too chickeny, and tasted delicious. She realized she hadn't had anything to eat since the muffin about ten years ago, which might explain part of the appeal. And she really couldn't stall any longer. "We met at the airport and ended up sharing a ride out here. She's the one I told you about."

Emily made a come-along gesture with her hand. "And?"

"And, well, we really connected, and then last night we—"

Emily's mouth dropped open. "Are you kidding me? You slept with her and you didn't even mention her when I was asking you what's new? Like, you know, anything exciting happening in your life such as you met this really hot woman and just happened to fall into bed with her, like, a few hours before?"

"Because it sounds crazy," Gem said, protesting. "It sounds crazy when you say it, and it would've sounded crazier when I said it. I don't do that sort of thing."

"Well, apparently you do. More than once."

"How did you know—"

"Are you telling me…" Emily slapped her forehead. "Oh my God. You are in trouble now. Really? Today?"

Gem covered her face with her hands. "I'm not talking about this."

"You so are. So who seduced who?"

"There wasn't any seduction."

Emily's eyebrows rose. "Really? How does that work, then? I mean, do you just have a conversation where you discuss the possibility of having sex and come to some kind of decision as to who should take their clothes off first—"

"That's not what I meant. It's just that it wasn't like that." Gem pushed a hand through her hair. "It wasn't like anything I've ever experienced. It was just…meant to be, I guess."

"Oh," Emily said softly. "That's just…kind of incredible. Good for you."

The tension ebbed from Gem's shoulders. "You think? I mean, you don't think I'm crazy?"

Emily guffawed. "Are you kidding me? Of course not. The last time I looked, you were well over twenty-one. And if you met somebody you really connect with and she's hot—and boy, she really is hot—then why not?"

"I do sort of have a girlfriend."

"I never got the impression you two had made any long-term plans. Am I wrong on that?"

Gem shook her head. "No, we never have. We've just kind of gone along. We've never talked about living together or making anything more formal. And if it did come up, I would've said no. I think she would have too."

"If you didn't make any plans or promises about monogamy and such, I'm not even sure it's something you have to tell her. Except if it changes things."

Gem drank some more of her soup. "Oh, it changes things. It changed me."

"Are you going to see Austin again?"

"I don't know. We didn't make any specific plans. It's almost as if we're both waiting."

"For what?"

Gem sighed. "I don't know."

❖

"You fucking waited long enough to call," Tatum snarled over the shortwave when Austin finally reached him. "It's fucking soup out here. How do you expect the bird to fly in this?"

"Look, I'm sorry," Austin said. "The weather moved in faster than I expected. I can stay here tonight, and we can try again—"

"Hell no. We want you out here to take the heat with us. I've got a bird on its way right now. Fortunately for you, it's a short trip, but I'd put on a life jacket when you climb aboard."

"I'm really sorry, Ray, I—"

"Forget it. It's good practice for these boys. They sit on their asses most of the time drinking coffee and reading girly magazines. Even the girls."

Austin laughed. "Sure and why not. I'll check in with you, soon as I arrive."

"You do that."

The bird arrived ten minutes later. She climbed aboard and took the seat opposite the pilot. When she pulled on her headgear and connected her mic, she said, "I'm Austin. Sorry to drag you out in this."

"Benny," the pilot, a woman Austin didn't know, said with a shrug as she lifted off. "No problem. I could find my way back to the rig with my eyes closed."

"Well, thanks for the lift, Benny."

"Happy to oblige. I'd read all the skin mags anyhow."

Austin grinned. Ray Tatum knew how to hold a crew together, and they'd need that glue before this was all over.

Benny was a fast, accomplished pilot and she set the bird down without a single bump thirty minutes later. The landing lights on the helipad were barely visible through the heavy fog, but the red beacon on the central tower shone above the layer of mist like a blinking red eye. As the rotor slowed, Austin jumped out and jogged across the platform to the command trailer. The air temperature had dropped twenty degrees, but it was still unseasonably warm outside. She shed her jacket as she walked in and dropped it over the back of a chair.

Tatum, Reddy, and Claudia stood in front of the largest satellite monitor, studying the patches of green and black swirling across the screen.

"How does it look?" Austin said.

"The front's coalescing," Claudia said, glancing over her shoulder at Austin with a worried frown. "This isn't going to be a tropical storm. It's going to come ashore a hurricane, category two, at least."

"Well, fuck me," Tatum said.

"I'll second that," Austin muttered. "What's the situation with the well?"

Reddy shot her a dark look. "We're still leaking. Slow, but we can't stop it. We're containing it, but just barely."

"And if the rig starts rocking in the storm? What's your best guess then?"

"We'll double our rate of loss, best case."

Austin glanced at Ray. "Ray? You agree?"

"Fuck me," he repeated. "We can't be sure of that, but it's a possibility."

"Right then." Austin punched in Eloise's number.

"Tell me something I want to hear," Eloise said.

"I take it you've seen the weather reports?"

"I'm getting the same information from Dr. Spencer that you are, along with updates from a dozen other meteorologists sitting in stations up and down the coast."

"Then you know we're going to get hit hard."

"The rig is built to take it. What's the situation with the leak?"

"Still slow, but not slowing," Austin said. "In my opinion, the risk of an uncontained spill warrants preventative measures now. We should alert Fish and Wildlife so we can begin containment procedures. We want to get out in front of this on the record before we bring in the booms."

"Can't you buy us any more time? We can start drilling secondaries—"

"No, not with the storm headed our way. Everything is going to slow down—roads will close, flights will be canceled. People and equipment are going to have difficulty even getting here, which means everyone is going to be short staffed. Multiply our usual response time by three, and we'll be lucky to have enough manpower and equipment to protect the shore if we do have a spill. If we don't move now, we're going to look negligent."

The silence over the line spoke volumes as to how much Eloise did not like that word. Austin had used it intentionally to underscore the gravity of the situation. She needed Eloise to pull the trigger on going public.

"You're pushing me to a place I don't like to go," Eloise said, "considering we don't have any visible signs of a leak at the surface or, if I'm getting the correct information from your Dr. Spencer, in any underwater currents."

"We don't, *yet*," Austin said, "but I don't think anyone in this room will bet against that happening soon. And when it does, we have to be able to show appropriate intervention and full disclosure well ahead of the spill."

"Very well," Eloise said, her fury a cold and lethal blade. "I'll contact the authorities. Be prepared to coordinate. Hopefully the storm will at least keep the reporters away for a while longer."

"I'll need to contact the Coast Guard and the research team at the sanctuary."

"First let me handle it at our level. Then you can contact the locals."

Austin gritted her teeth. Translation: Eloise would deal with the bureaucrats, because that's where the political pressure would come from. The individuals on the front line would have to wait. "Let me know as soon as you've made your statement. Then I'll set up a joint briefing here."

"I'll leave that to you," Eloise said. "Expect my call within the next few hours."

"Right." Austin disconnected and faced the others. Tatum and Reddy looked weary, Claudia contemplative. "We've got about an hour or two before the fat hits the fire."

Claudia tilted her head and gave her a long look. "I don't think you made her very happy. She would've liked it if you had tried to buy her a little more time."

Austin shrugged. "There isn't any more time."

"Tough call," Tatum said, "but it's done now." He glanced at Reddy. "Let's go back to work."

"Let me know if the situation changes," Austin said.

"You'll be the first to know."

The men disappeared, and Claudia settled back into her chair in front of the monitors. She continued looking at Austin, a crease between her perfectly arched brows. "If Eloise is inclined to shoot the messenger, your job could be on the line."

"If it is, it is." Austin was used to being the messenger bearing bad news and had taken more than a few arrows in similar situations. She wasn't worried about Eloise—she had no control over what she might do. If Eloise wanted to fire her for the call she'd made, she didn't really care. She was a lot more concerned about Gem—who was right in the path of a potentially major oil spill, not to mention a hurricane.

CHAPTER EIGHTEEN

G em woke to the thrum of her cell phone vibrating on the straight-backed wooden chair she'd placed next to her bed to use as a nightstand. She fumbled for it in the otherworldly darkness of the cabin. Her eyes were open but they might as well have been closed. With no moonlight coming through the window, the blackness was absolute. Her sister's name flashed almost too brightly across the screen and, blinking, she thumbed *accept.* "God, what time is it?"

"Half past the witching hour," Alex grumbled. "Were you sleeping?"

"Of course I was sleeping. It's the middle of the night and I got almost no sleep last night."

"Why not?"

"Because—" Gem caught herself. Oh no, she wasn't going there with Alex. No way was she discussing having sex with a stranger, even if Austin didn't feel like a stranger, with her sister. Or any kind of sex, for that matter. That ship had sailed along with Paul. "What's wrong? Are you all right?"

"I was about to ask you the same thing."

Gem tamped down her impatience. One thing her sister was not was a drama queen. If she was calling in the middle of the night, something was happening. "Alex, you're not making any sense."

"We just got an all-sector alert. Everyone is on standby readiness, but we don't know why."

"That's not normal, I guess."

"Not without a briefing, no."

"And you're calling me because?"

"Our sector commander ordered me to head the incident-response team."

"And that's a problem?"

"No, I've headed up emergency responses countless times. But something's not right about this one."

"I know you're speaking English, but your sentences don't make any sense to me. What's off about all of this?"

"When I asked my CO for the mission details, he said we would be briefed ASAP, but that other notifications had to go out, and a task force would be assembled and read-in all at once. He mentioned he wanted me to lead the team because I knew the sanctuary."

"What about the sanctuary?" Gem was awake now and sat up on the narrow bed. "Is this something related to the storm, do you think?"

"I don't know, it could be. Projections are now for hurricane category."

Gem's heart thudded. The sanctuary could be devastated by a storm of that magnitude. "That's disaster enough as far as I'm concerned. We'll have to start making provisions to secure the shoreline. I'm glad you called. We hadn't gotten that word yet."

"There's something more going on, Gem, or we would have gotten more information. You haven't heard anything? No one has called you?"

Gem checked her phone for missed calls. "No, nothing, but sometimes the service here hiccups. Are you sure your CO wasn't just making some tangential comment because the sanctuary is in your sector?"

"I don't think so. You'll let me know if you hear anything?"

"Of course, and you too. You'll be careful, won't you, no matter what it's about?"

"We've got a hurricane coming. It's going to be a hell of a few days." Alex sounded a lot more excited than anxious. "I'll be fine, don't worry."

"Of course I'll worry. Love you."

"Love you too. Talk soon."

After Alex disconnected, Gem stared into the dark, trying to make sense of her sister's message. If something critical was about to impact the sanctuary, the Coast Guard would definitely be alerted. They were charged with securing the shoreline, not just from illegal activities like drugs and human smuggling, but physically, as in the case of hurricanes. If the coming storm had escalated to hurricane levels, the station responsible for that sector would be involved in the preparations and recovery. That was probably all that was happening.

But why hadn't she heard anything?

She scanned her messages. A text blinked that hadn't been there when she'd gone to sleep, and she tapped it.

Sorry. Couldn't get a signal. All is good. Talk soon. A

The message was completely impersonal, friendly, and no more. But she smiled as her heart fluttered. She'd thought Austin had forgotten to text her—or hadn't wanted to. She saved the message and added the phone number to her contacts, typing in *Austin Germaine* along with the number. Somehow doing that made the last few days with Austin seem a little more solid and real. She almost texted back but stopped when she remembered the time. First thing in the morning, she'd send a short message. Just to say hello. That ought to be safe enough.

❖

Austin sat in front of a desk piled with folders, stacks of loose, fingerprint-smudged papers, and a few coffee cups with dregs growing things she'd rather not think about. She crossed her left ankle over her right knee, balanced a pad of drafting paper she'd found in one of the piles on her leg, and sketched facial studies— Gem in various poses—thoughtful, excited, serious, and playful. She longed to capture her face suffused with passion again, but she'd wait until she was alone for that. No rush—she wasn't about to forget. Her body still burned with hunger for more.

"Those are really good," Claudia said from behind her. "She's beautiful."

"Yes." Austin smiled and casually flipped over the page.

"You could make a living doing that."

"I might have to, seeing how this is coming down."

Claudia rested a hip on the only spare inch of the corner of the desk. "I thought we'd have heard something from the company a long time ago. Weren't we looking at a timetable of a few hours?"

Austin stood, turned the pad facedown on the counter, and stretched. Some of the soreness was due to inactivity, but not all of it. Some was from the hours she'd spent in Gem's bed. She tamped down the images of Gem in her arms before they destroyed her focus. "I think Eloise misjudged the rate at which attorneys move, particularly late on a Friday night going into a Saturday morning when half the country is obsessed with watching the news of the impending hurricane."

"Ah," Claudia said musingly. "The attorneys. I'd forgotten about those."

"Lucky you. I seem to live with them shadowing my shoulder."

"Well, that's the nature of your beast, isn't it? You only get called out in a crisis, and where there's a corporate crisis, there's an attorney or twenty."

Austin laughed. "You're absolutely right. Once they've discussed the wording of the formal statement, and the appropriate federal bureaus and agencies have been advised, Eloise will—"

Austin's phone rang and she pulled it from her pocket. "And that would be her now," she said to Claudia as she answered. "Germaine."

"The Department of Fish and Wildlife has been advised, we have a statement ready to release to the Associated Press, and your name has been provided as the on-site incident commander," Eloise snapped out. "Coast Guard command at the regional level has been alerted, but not given any details. We haven't yet contacted the people at the sanctuary, mostly because we're still going through channels and their exact directorship is a labyrinth."

"I know who is in charge," Austin said, hearing the flatness in her voice.

"I am aware of that, and I suggest you set something up for early in the morning. You'll have to wake a few people up."

"I understand." If Eloise thought her orders put Austin in an uncomfortable position, she gave no sign of it. And Austin had no room to complain. She'd been the one to complicate the situation, and now she'd have to pay the price. "I'll contact them as soon as we finish."

"Good. Our meteorologists tell us you will have at least thirty-six hours before significant winds and water impact the shoreline."

"That means we have twenty-four hours, maybe a little longer, to contain any oil that makes it to the surface or gets caught up in the currents."

"That's our estimation, yes."

"Then I need to get to shore."

"You need to set up your command center on shore, but I want you overseeing the work on the rig," Eloise said.

"Tatum can—"

"Not Tatum—I want a direct line, and I want you on the other end of it."

"Right. I'll split my time."

"I'm sure you'll manage."

"Thanks." Austin wasn't at all sure she'd be able to manage anything once Gem discovered who she was and why she was here. But she'd know very soon. She checked her phone for messages. There were none, but she had Gem's number. She glanced at Claudia. "You got the gist of that?"

"Enough. I guess it's time for you to stir up a storm," Claudia said quietly.

"Past time," Austin murmured and tapped Gem's number.

❖

Gem couldn't sleep and it was a few more hours until sunrise. Finally she gave up trying, got up, and lit a lamp in the center of the table. The cabin was chilly, and she heated water for tea. While the water boiled, she made toast and checked the cabinets for peanut butter. Hallelujah, someone had left a jar. She needed to stock in some supplies first thing in the morning.

Fortified with caffeine and protein, she settled into a chair at the table and powered up her laptop. She'd bookmarked the NOAA site and studied the latest forecasts. The projected cone of the storm's movement predicted landfall somewhere along the coast within fifty miles of the sanctuary if the storm kept on course at its current speed. That was close enough to be a direct hit, and even if it wasn't, the high winds and storm surge would strip coastal trees, erode the shoreline, and flood the coastal marshes with enough sediment to destroy habitats and waterways. The resident wildlife and migratory populations would be decimated. If they acted quickly, they could sandbag the high-tide line and at least limit erosion beyond that point. That kind of mobilization took days, though, and they might not have that long. Someone in DC should have warned her—their team reported directly to a division at the NIH, but bureaucrats being who they were, no one probably thought to take responsibility. It was done now and her complaints wouldn't change anything. She rubbed her eyes and thought about calling Emily, but there was no point in both of them losing sleep.

She had the number of her liaison at the NIH. She'd just have to wake him up and get him to contact FEMA and approve funding for the people and equipment she'd need. They could get the trucks and FEMA personnel moving before daylight, hopefully out of Baltimore. Until then, they'd just have to—

Her phone rang and, expecting it to be Alex, she thumbed it on and said, "Have you heard anything else?"

"Gem?"

She recognized the voice but it took her a moment to grasp Austin was calling her at three a.m. "Austin?"

"Yes, sorry. I woke you."

"No," she said, confused and pleased at the same time. "Is everything all right?"

"I'm afraid it isn't."

Austin sounded different—formal and distant. Gem's heart beat a rapid tattoo against the inside of her rib cage. "Are you hurt?"

"No, I'm sorry. Let me explain why I'm calling. There's a developing situation that may involve the sanctuary. I'd like you to gather your people for a briefing at seven a.m. I'll be able to explain then to everyone at once exactly what's going on."

"I'm not following," Gem said quietly. "What are you talking about?"

"All I can say at this time is we have some problems that may impact the sanctuary. It's best if everyone hears the details at one time."

"And you want me to get the team together at seven a.m.?" Gem parroted Austin's request while trying to assimilate the impossible. Why was Austin involved in anything to do with the sanctuary? "Can you at least tell me—"

"I'm sorry, I can't. I know this all seems cryptic, but if you could just hold your questions until the briefing—"

Everyone kept mentioning a briefing, but no one was giving any details. Gem's temper flared. "At seven a.m. at the sanctuary."

"Yes, the sanctuary visitors' center would be fine for now."

"Austin—"

"I'm sorry, Gem, I'll explain everything in a few hours."

"I don't understand what's going on, but I don't seem to have any choice," Gem said, hearing the ice in her voice.

"I really am sorry." Austin sounded weary. "I'll talk to you soon."

"Good night, then," Gem said, understanding on some fundamental level that everything she thought she knew about Austin and what they'd shared had suddenly changed. She redialed Alex with a steady hand, but her insides roiled like rough surf.

"Martin," Alex said almost immediately.

"I just got the strangest call—"

"About what?"

"About a meeting—"

"Hold on for a second, Gem…" Alex's voice faded. "What is it?"

Gem could make out Alex talking to someone nearby, her tone raised in question and a low male voice replying.

"Vice Admiral? Sir, this is Commander Martin," Alex's muffled voice came through to Gem.

Gem waited while minutes passed, trying and failing to put Austin from her mind.

"Gem?"

"Yes, I'm here."

"It looks like I'm going to be seeing you in the morning," Alex said. "Zero-seven-hundred, to be precise."

"That's what I was about to tell you. I got a call also. What's going on?"

"I don't know," Alex said, a hard bite to her voice. "I still haven't been briefed."

Her sister was not happy, and Gem didn't blame her. She didn't like being kept in the dark either.

"Why is this all so cloak-and-dagger?" Gem said.

"I'm not sure, but I've got a pretty good guess—that was Vice Admiral Moorhouse just now, informing us we'd be meeting with someone by the name of Austin Germaine, and not only that, we'd apparently be sharing incident command responsibility with her team—whatever that might be."

A cold hand fisted in Gem's middle. "I'm sorry? Are you sure about that name?"

"Very sure. In fact, I met her yesterday out at Rig 86."

"The offshore oil installation?"

"Yeah—I was doing a routine check about storm preparedness and talked to her then."

"That can't be right," Gem murmured more to herself than Alex. "Austin wouldn't have any reason to be out there."

"About thirty, average height, beyond average looks although not my type—on the rugged, adventurous side with the required dashing dark hair and intense eyes."

"That—could be her." Gem had thought of Austin as a pirate, and maybe she'd been more right than she knew.

"You know her?" Alex asked.

"No," Gem said, the chill spreading through her. "No, I don't know her at all."

CHAPTER NINETEEN

Austin pulled into the lot in front of the sanctuary at 6:50. She cut the engine and turned to Claudia. "There's a possibility our reception is going to be less than friendly."

Claudia had changed into a pale champagne business suit with a tailored emerald-green shirt with French cuffs and diamond links that glittered at her wrists, and low black heels. Her hair was swept back in a simple gold clasp. She sat, hands lightly clasped in her lap, looking coolly elegant and professional. She definitely didn't look as if she'd spent the last few days nearly sleepless on an oil rig fifty miles out in the ocean. Under other circumstances, she would have been just the type of woman Austin would seek out for an evening's entertainment, but that was before. Before she'd met Gem and awakened to the true pleasures of an intimate encounter. She rubbed a hand over her face, feeling the fatigue tearing at the edges of her mind. Way too early in the game for that.

Claudia gave Austin an appraising glance. "You mean something beyond the usual initial suspicion and distrust?"

"It's possible." Austin grimaced. "I'm…acquainted with one of the senior researchers here. Something of an unusual circumstance. Maybe a bit of miscommunication."

"An unusual circumstance and miscommunication." Claudia nodded as if she understood all that Austin had *not* said.

Claudia couldn't know the depths of the complications unless she were psychic, and even then it would be a stretch. Austin blew out a breath. "Just don't be surprised if we get an icy reception. My fault. I should have handled a few things differently."

"I suspect once all the facts are laid out and the timetable is presented, everyone is going to be too busy worrying too much about what's coming to dwell on should've-beens."

"I hope you're right," Austin muttered.

Claudia squeezed her arm, a welcome show of sympathy Austin knew she didn't deserve, and said, "Let's go find out."

The small foyer was empty, but the lights in the hall where Gem had taken her less than twenty-four hours before were on, and the faint rumble of indistinguishable voices came from that direction.

"This way," Austin said.

"I take it you've been here before."

"Yes." Austin steeled herself for the first glimpse of Gem. By now, Gem would probably know why she was here, and even if she didn't, she'd be confused and likely angry about the subterfuge surrounding the meeting. Even knowing her reception would be a cold one, she looked forward to seeing her again. Being near her in any way at all was infinitely better than the void her absence created.

Austin paused in the doorway of the common room to let Claudia precede her. The room looked different than it had when she'd come upon Gem making a cup of coffee the first time she'd been there. Two tables had been pushed together in the center of the room. Several half-full pots of coffee sat on the automatic coffeemaker next to a stack of paper cups. The space wasn't large and, with six people already in it, felt a little crowded. Alex Martin, in uniform, stood near the head of the table with a young male coastguardsman who looked like an enlisted man, possibly her aide. They stopped talking when Austin and Claudia appeared.

Gem stood where she had the morning before, leaning against the counter with a cup of coffee in her hands. Emily and a tall, burly middle-aged man flanked her. The sixth man Austin didn't know, but she knew what he did. His expensive three-piece suit, monogrammed briefcase, and five-hundred-dollar haircut advertised that well enough, even if she hadn't worked with plenty like him before. He was an attorney for the company, here to document the proceedings and ensure that, as the company's representative, Austin presented all the appropriate recommendations and handled negotiations in a way that would stand up to legal scrutiny.

Gem's gaze met Austin's across the room, cool, detached, completely impersonal. The twenty feet between them felt like two thousand miles, and a chill rolled down Austin's spine. She waited for Gem to acknowledge her, to say something, anything, although she didn't expect a confrontation in front of a roomful of strangers. Gem was far too experienced and professional for that. Gem's gaze cut away as if *they* were strangers. Austin absorbed the sting of the rebuke without flinching. She needed to keep this meeting on track, and in order to do that, she had to put her personal feelings aside. She could do it, she'd had a lot of practice, but it hurt more this time than anything she'd done in a long time.

Silence spread through the room and Austin stepped a little away from Claudia, drawing all eyes to her. "Thanks, everyone, for getting here so promptly. I'm Austin Germaine, and I represent Global Oil Productions." She gestured to Claudia. "This is Dr. Claudia Spencer, a meteorologist who works with us. Most of you already know each other, I gather." Now that she saw Alex and Gem in the same room, there was no doubt their shared last name was also shared genetics. They had to be sisters. She held out her hand to the attorney. "We haven't met."

"Robert Cramer," he said in a polished Boston accent. "Also here for Global Oil."

"Perhaps we could all sit down and I'll explain why we're here," Austin said.

Alex said stiffly, "Perhaps you can explain why you seem to be in charge but none of us know who you are or why we're here to serve at your pleasure."

"Actually," Austin said, "we're hoping this will be a joint venture, because everyone's cooperation is going to be necessary." She pulled out a chair at the end of the table opposite where Alex stood, acutely aware of Gem watching her motionlessly. Was she ever going to speak to her again? "Please, if everyone will sit, we'll get started."

Reluctantly, Alex and the other coastguardsman took seats. Cramer took a position midway down one side of the group of tables in neutral territory. Claudia sat at Austin's right and Gem ended up sitting on her left. If Austin stretched out her hand on the table, their fingers would touch. She ached for just an instant's contact, but when she glanced at Gem, Gem shifted subtly in her chair, breaking eye contact.

Austin squared her shoulders and scanned the faces watching her. She'd done this enough times to know the way to keep control was to lay out the problem and the solution before dissenters could gain a foothold. "As all of you are aware, Rig 86 is a semisubmersible drilling platform operated by GOP about fifty miles offshore. We have a slow but containable leak in the main drill shaft, and we're concerned the approaching storm may cause an escalation of oil loss. To be on the safe side, we are proactively instituting emergency procedures to ensure the integrity of the shoreline and waters."

Alex Martin's eyes glinted. "Why are we just hearing about this?"

"Because at this point," Austin said smoothly, "we don't have any evidence of oil on the surface or tracking underwater, but the effect of the storm is a variable we can't predict. GOP is naturally desirous to do everything possible to prevent damage to the coastline and wildlife."

"Naturally," Gem said, the first word she'd uttered, quiet but sharp-edged with sarcasm. "How long have you been watching the well?"

"The wells are under constant surveillance, as I'm sure you know," Austin said just as quietly, carefully keeping any direct reference to the timeline off the record. Of course Gem would do the math and deduce Austin must have known of the problem days before.

"I've been asked," Claudia interjected, drawing attention away from Austin and giving her a chance to breathe, "to consult on the impact of the storm on the rig and the potential for escalating leaks. Right now, as Dr. Germaine noted, the situation is stable and under control, but Norma's tracking directly for us, and growing in speed and dimension hourly." She turned to Gem as if knowing she was the other true power in the room. "This is going to be a large, powerful storm when it comes ashore. I suspect the governor will order evacuation of the island and neighboring areas sometime today."

"We're not going anywhere." Emily, her chin thrust forward belligerently. She glanced at Gem as if for affirmation.

"Dr. Costanzas is right," Gem said. "We are not leaving the sanctuary. I've been in contact with FEMA and we have teams on their way to help fortify the shoreline against the surge. There's not much we can do about the trees if we get hurricane-force winds, but we'll be prepared for the reparations if nothing else." She looked at Austin. "How likely is it we're going to get oil coming ashore?"

Gem's gaze was direct and hard, her tone evenly modulated. Austin couldn't tell if she was furious, unmoved, or had already simply dismissed her. "My guess—"

Cramer cleared his throat. "Actually, Dr. Martin," he said to Gem in an officious tone, "it's really not possible for Dr. Germaine to make that kind of assessment. We're here because Global Oil—"

"Dr. Germaine," Gem said as if the attorney hadn't spoken, "your opinion is?"

"I think we'll have oil headed toward shore along with the storm surge," Austin said, ignoring the annoyed sigh from Cramer, "which is why we plan on deploying booms this morning to buffer the coastline and prevent that from happening. We'll also be instituting all the usual protocols in advance of the leak surfacing."

"I'll want details," Gem said.

"Of course."

Alex Martin spoke up. "What about the four ships at anchor off the rig? You need to get your people off the sea before the storm hits."

"We'll commence transporting all nonessential personnel out of the area within the next twelve hours," Austin said. "The ships will remain deployed as long as possible to assist in the containment procedures."

"How many people on the rig now?" Alex asked.

"Just six members of the drill team, three pilots, the incident commander, the OTL, and me. Dr. Spencer will remain he—"

"I'll be returning to the rig," Claudia said, "for the time being. It's the best way to judge the stability of the platform. The on-site readings are far more accurate than anything—"

"Once the storm tracks as far as the rig," Alex said, "we may not be able to fly. Evacuation will be nearly impossible."

"We'll see that the rig is evacuated before that," Austin said.

"I'll make sure you do," Alex said.

"So what now?" Gem said. "It will still be hours before the FEMA teams arrive."

Austin focused on Gem, happy that Gem held her gaze even if her eyes were shuttered and unreadable. "I'll coordinate with Commander Martin regarding the containment procedures at sea. It makes the most sense for you to take charge of the landside of things. You know the sanctuary, the critical areas that will need protection, and the location of wildlife at risk if the spill gets past the booms."

"How much oil are we talking about?"

Cramer interrupted hastily. "There is *no* oil at this point, I'd like to remind everyone. Under other circumstances, we wouldn't even be having this conversation. GOP has instituted the appropriate and required procedures to control the slow escape from the drill site, but unfortunately, with the weather—"

"I think we all understand the situation," Gem said abruptly, never looking away from Austin. "How much oil, Dr. Germaine?"

"I don't know," Austin said. "We've got nothing on the surface yet but there's a potential for major contamination if the rig founders in the storm. Then the integrity of the drill shaft is at risk."

"Then we need to prepare for the worst."

"That would be my advice," Austin said.

"I think we all know what we have to do, then." Gem rose and walked out.

"I need to brief my CO," Alex said. "Then I'd like to sit down with you, Dr. Germaine—"

"Austin, please," Austin said, straining to follow the sound of Gem's footsteps down the hall.

"Austin," Alex said, "and get a precise accounting of the ships, manpower, and their allocation. Then we'll talk about evacuation procedures."

Cramer stood and closed his briefcase. "I am staying in town tonight, but I plan on leaving first thing tomorrow morning. You can reach me after that by phone or through the company offices."

"Fine." Austin pushed back from the table. "If you'll excuse me."

Cramer shook his head. "Lousy time for a hurricane."

Claudia smiled faintly at Alex as he shrugged into his Armani raincoat, lifted his briefcase, and strode out. "Is there ever a good time for a hurricane?"

Alex shook her head, a quick grin softening the sharp angles of her face, before turning to her aide. "Get the car, Seaman. I'll be right there."

"Yes, ma'am," the coastguardsman said and nodded to Claudia on his way out. "Ma'am."

Claudia laughed softly. "I think I might be starting to get used to that, and I'm not certain that's an altogether good thing."

Alex smiled. She hadn't expected to see Dr. Claudia Spencer again, but she was glad that she had. She'd worked with all kinds of teams when disasters struck: federal, state, private, and environmental. She'd been deployed to northern New Jersey after Hurricane Sandy. She liked to think she didn't have any preconceived biases. She especially didn't want an adversarial relationship with Claudia Spencer. "How long you been out at the rig?"

Claudia considered her answer carefully. She knew the laws requiring a corporation to reveal a potential contamination situation, and she agreed with Austin and Eloise that they hadn't quite reached that point. All the same, as a representative of the company, she had to be careful. "Not long before you came aboard."

"I understand chain of command. I respect it. We're on the same side in this."

"I'm glad." Claudia relaxed, realizing just how much she hadn't wanted a conflict with the very handsome Coast Guard officer. "I don't think your—sister, is it?—feels the same way."

Alex's expression darkened. "Gem is worried about the sanctuary. This place…these birds and animals and every blade of grass…is precious to her. She's been through this kind of thing before. She knows what to do, and there's no one better at it than her."

"I don't doubt it." Alex was loyal, that was to be expected, but she also seemed to be aware, as was Claudia, more was happening here than either understood. Austin had alluded to complications, and after Claudia had met Gem Martin, she'd gotten a clue as to just what those issues might be. Gem was the woman in the sketches Austin had drawn. Their studious avoidance of each other was another clue something had gone wrong. She sighed. "The next few days are going to be hard for everyone, and not just because of the storm and the oil."

Alex moved down to a seat next to Claudia. "You really should reconsider going back out to the rig."

"I was hired to do a job," Claudia said, momentarily distracted by the subtle scent of spice and sandalwood. Alex's eyes were as dark as her sister's were blue, and right now they focused on Claudia with laser-like intensity. "But I appreciate your concern."

"I don't have to tell you how quickly things can change out there if the storm picks up speed or the front expands. We might be looking at hours instead of days."

"I'm aware," Claudia said, "just as I'm aware that you and your team will be out on the seas through all of it."

"We're trained for it."

"The crews on the rigs are trained for emergencies too. And I promise, I'm no swashbuckler." Claudia lightly touched Alex's hand to relay her appreciation. "I'll get to land in plenty of time."

"I'll take you at your word," Alex said.

"Good. Now I need to get back to work." Claudia stood. "I hope I see you again under less hectic conditions."

"I hope so too."

❖

Gem walked out through the front door into a dank gray morning, with no trace of sun and a cold wet wind blowing in from the sea. A morning not unlike many others this time of year, but today the ominous atmosphere settled heavily in her heart. She strode a few steps into the parking lot and stopped, taking a deep breath to settle her nerves and regroup. Of all the scenarios she'd fabricated between Austin's late-night call and this early-morning meeting, the truth had been nowhere on her radar. Austin Germaine wasn't Ace Gardner, the graphic artist who had sketched a superhero with bold unerring strokes on the back of a place mat in some small coastal restaurant while a storm lashed the windows and they shared intimacies of their lives. She wasn't the woman who'd knelt in the rain changing a tire, or poured a glass of wine while listening to Gem talk about some of her most private experiences. Austin was a troubleshooter for an oil company, a fixer of some kind, undoubtedly very intelligent, and a spinner of webs.

"Gem," Austin said from behind her.

"I don't think this is a good time to talk," Gem said without turning around.

"There isn't going to be a better time," Austin said. "I couldn't tell you earlier."

"I kept thinking we weren't strangers, but I couldn't have been more wrong. I knew I was not myself, but I somehow talked myself into believing I was acting so out of character because something unique had happened between us." She shook her head and laughed brutally. "I thought I had gotten over telling myself lies a long time ago."

"Gem," Austin said wearily. She wanted to touch her, wanted to reach out and stroke the stiff anger from her back, ease the disillusionment from her jaw. "It wasn't a lie. It was real."

Gem turned, her eyes glacially cold. "No, it wasn't real. It was a fantasy. I didn't know you. I still don't know you. And you know what? I don't want to."

Austin couldn't argue that Gem's feelings weren't valid. She had every right to be hurt and angry. "I'm sorry. I didn't know the situation here, and I couldn't—"

Gem shook her head. "We have nothing to discuss except what needs to be done to prevent the destruction of this sanctuary. If the oil reaches the shore, I can't even begin to calculate the enormity of the loss. I don't care what it takes, we can't let that happen."

"We won't. I promise."

Gem smiled bitterly. "I don't want your promises. Or your assurances. But you must be good, very good, at what you do, or you wouldn't be here. So the only thing I want from you, Dr. Germaine, is your expertise. Now, if you'll excuse me, I have work to do."

"We have work to do." Austin reached for her arm to keep her near and drew back at the last instant. Her touch would not be welcome and knowing that was a knife in her depths. "I want to go over the site maps with you before we deploy the booms. You can tell me where we need to concentrate them."

"Fine. How soon?"

"An hour ago."

Gem's smile was brittle. "Don't you really mean three days ago?"

Austin sighed. "I didn't—"

"Never mind. I understand you can't implicate GOP in any way. That's your real job, isn't it? To protect GOP at any cost?"

Austin reined in her temper. She'd heard these accusations before too. Coming from Gem it hurt, but attempting to explain there were limits to the lengths she would go for the company would only make the situation worse now. She'd have to prove she cared what happened to the environment. "Where would you like to meet to review the topos?"

"I have an office next to the lab I showed you yesterday. I'll meet you there in thirty minutes. Right now I'm going for a walk."

Austin stuffed her hands in her pockets and watched her walk away. She'd known this was coming, known she would lose, but she hadn't imagined how much it would hurt. Not even close.

CHAPTER TWENTY

Gem took the first trail she came to behind the visitors' center and strode rapidly away from the building, the parking lot, the people, civilization. If she could, she'd keep walking until the wild grasses swallowed her, absorbing her inconsequential existence into the natural ebb and flow of life as it had persisted for eons, governed by nothing beyond the laws of nature. Not passion, not desire, not fantasy. No illusion, no delusions, only the beauty and violence of unadorned life. After ten mindless minutes, she slowed enough to look at the darkening sky, register the impact of the rising wind on her neck, and note the heavy weight of moisture in the air. The storm—no, the hurricane—was reality too, and she had choices to make.

She could tell her team to evacuate, get into her rental car, and be off the island and back to the safety of the mainland before it hit, leaving the fate of the sanctuary to the whims of nature as she had just imagined she preferred for herself. But she wouldn't leave, couldn't leave, and believed without doubt she was as much a part of the natural cycle as the coming storm. If she could save the habitat and creatures of the sanctuary, she must. And to do that, she needed to work with Austin Germaine.

Austin. Still so hard to absorb that the woman she'd spent days with, dreamed of, slept with, was so much a part of this and she hadn't known. Gem tried to step back, to imagine what her impression would have been if today had been the first moment she'd met Austin. Would she work with her? Of course. She'd have to. Would she trust her? Unknown. Austin seemed forthright, concerned, and knowledgeable. But there was no mistaking her allegiance, either. She worked for GOP, and while Gem didn't doubt the company and, by extension, Austin, cared what happened to the coastal environment, they undoubtedly cared a great deal more about the image and financial status of the company. Would she like her? In all likelihood, she wouldn't have given Austin more than professional attention, and that did not require liking or disliking.

None of that mattered now. She couldn't be objective. Anger at being forced into a powerless position resurfaced. Austin had lied to her. All right, not exactly, but close enough to make Gem feel discounted and manipulated, something she'd sworn she'd never be again. Austin had kept something back, something enormous, something she knew would have a major impact on Gem's work, on her responsibilities, and on her relationship with Austin.

So many questions she couldn't answer after the fact. Would she have slept with Austin if she had known Austin's real purpose for traveling to the island? Would she have gotten involved with her if she'd known she'd have to work with her in a matter of days?

Gem thought the answer to both questions was no. She would have kept her distance. She would have maintained professional boundaries. She would never have looked at Austin and seen the intense, focused, attentive woman who had drawn her out and set her on fire.

And damn it, she couldn't quite bring herself to be sorry for that.

Frustrated and confused, Gem checked her watch. She'd been gone at least fifteen minutes and she needed to return to the sanctuary. She couldn't, wouldn't, run from Austin or her responsibilities. She'd work with her and relegate the intimate moments they'd spent together to the past, where those moments belonged and where they would stay. The ache of loss would eventually disappear. She knew that from experience.

As she crossed the parking lot, Alex called her name. She slowed as Alex jogged over.

"Hey," Alex said, "I've been looking for you. I'm headed back to the station and then out to patrol. Are you sure you want to stay here?"

"You know I have to," Gem said. "It won't be my first storm, and I'm the logical one to assess the damage and coordinate recovery."

"You're not looking at just a storm," Alex said. "You might be looking at a major oil spill too."

"God, I hope not." Gem balled her fists in the pockets of her windbreaker. "Even more reason for me to stay and organize the various crews. FEMA and the GOP people don't know this environment the way I do."

"Germaine and the rest of them seem to know what they're doing."

"You were out there on the rig, weren't you? How did things look?"

"Yeah." Alex grimaced. "And I didn't see anything amiss, but I probably should have questioned why there were so few people on the rig. They'd already pulled some of their crew."

Gem's stomach plummeted. "So Austin knew there was a spill—"

"No, I think Germaine was telling it to us straight. There's nothing out there, at least visibly, that points to a major spill. Leaks happen a lot more often than you'd realize."

"I'm glad of that," Gem said. "Do you think we'll be all right, then?"

Alex sighed. "We have only their reports as to how bad things are in the deep. Currents can carry underwater oil accumulations for hundreds, thousands of miles. And if the hurricane hits here? Who knows."

"We don't have much time."

"No." Alex studied her, frown lines creasing her brow. "You know her, right? Before this, I mean."

Gem laughed, the sound bitter to her ears. "Yes. A really strange set of coincidences. I rode in with her from the airport."

"I take it she didn't mention anything about what was happening out there."

"No, she didn't." Gem wanted to believe Austin wouldn't

have kept the situation quiet if there were a real threat of a major environmental disaster, but how could she know that? It all came down to her not knowing Austin at all.

"Is there something else going on?" Alex asked.

"What? No," Gem said quickly.

"Then why do you look like you're hurting?"

"Just worried about the sanctuary." Gem smiled thinly and grasped Alex's arm. "And about you, for that matter, out there in what's coming."

"You know we do it all the time. It's not that, but you don't have to tell me if you don't want to."

"What do you think of her...Austin?"

Alex blinked at the sudden change of subject. "I think she's being as straightforward as she can be. She's walking a line, you know how it is. The information she gave me was completely accurate and honest, if not totally inclusive. Within the letter of the law."

Gem blew out a breath. "I'm not sure that's enough."

"Why does it matter so much what she says?"

Heat climbed into Gem's face. She was giving away far too much. "It doesn't, I guess. I just like to know who I'm working with."

"Well, don't worry about it too much. I'll have your back."

Impulsively, Gem hugged her. "I know. Just promise me you'll be careful."

"Always."

Gem watched her sister climb into the Coast Guard SUV and pull out of the lot. She had no choice now but to meet with Austin. She couldn't avoid her, as much as she wanted to. And as much as she wanted to avoid her, she wanted to see her again too. Torn between desire and disillusion, she strode determinedly inside.

Not quite ready to cross swords with Austin without fortification, she detoured to the canteen for coffee, silently chiding herself for delaying. Avoidance wasn't her usual modus operandi. Everything about her relationship with Austin was unlike her. She needed to find her balance, her perspective. How she was going to do that in the midst of a crisis was anybody's guess, but she'd have to find a way.

Emily, the only one remaining from the morning's meeting, pulled a cup of steaming hot chocolate from the microwave and gestured to Gem. "Want one?"

"Chocolate might be just the thing. I've got a minute or two before I meet with Austin." There, she'd said her name without the slightest hitch and only the faintest skip of her heart.

Emily blew on the steam coming out of her cup, sipped, and nodded. "I'll fix one for you."

"Thanks." Gem dropped into one of the chairs at a table someone had pushed back to its normal spot and closed her eyes. She hadn't slept after the calls from first her sister and then Austin. She'd spent part of the time Googling Austin, something else she didn't ordinarily do. Somehow, the whole idea seemed like such an invasion of privacy, but after the strange call from Austin, she had to learn more about her. Unfortunately, she hadn't learned much at all.

Austin Germaine didn't have a Facebook page or a Twitter account or a website, and apparently hadn't authored any articles after a dozen or so on some technical mechanics of deepwater drilling half a dozen years before. Googling Ace Grand brought up all the usual references to her graphic novel titles and awards, but no photos, only a rare interview, and no calendar of personal appearances. Austin aka Ace had managed to keep an extremely low profile on social media. Finally, she found a YouTube clip of a news video from a site in Alaska where an oil transport ship had gone aground and lost its cargo. If she hadn't really been digging she never would have found it. She wondered if GOP had some sort of process where they scrubbed those kinds of things from the Internet. At any rate, Austin had been as well-spoken and had looked as good on camera as the reporter interviewing her. None of it told her anything about the woman behind the image.

Gem gave a little jump when Emily set a steaming cup of hot cocoa in front of her. "Thanks," she said again.

Emily sat beside her. "When do you think the FEMA team will get here?"

"Late morning, I hope. They're quick to mobilize, and I'm sure they want to get here before the storm hits."

"They'll likely set up headquarters on the mainland, don't you think?"

"Probably. Especially if the governor calls for evacuation."

"Just as well. Too many cooks—" Emily shook her head. "We certainly seem to have a lot of those all of a sudden."

"I know, but it's always this way with multijurisdictional situations. Fish and Wildlife, FEMA, the Coast Guard, and, of course, all the privates get involved."

"I caught a newscast just now," Emily said, gesturing to the small TV on the counter whose sound was currently muted. "Just a fifteen-second sound bite on the local news about Rig 86 and a small leak, already contained and of no major consequence."

Gem tasted the chocolate and let the heat and sweetness soothe the rough anger in her throat. "That's GOP's first volley to control the situation. I'm sure we'll hear a lot more if things escalate."

"Hopefully they're not going to." Emily glanced toward the door as if making sure they were alone. "Austin sounded credible. I don't think we've got a major spill yet."

Gem heard the tentativeness in her tone. "Austin didn't mention anything about this to me before. I don't know whether to believe her or not."

"What do your instincts say?" Emily asked gently.

"I'm not sure I can separate my instincts from my wishes, and I'm not sure I trust either one at this point."

"I think your instincts are just fine," Emily said. "I don't see you sleeping with her if you hadn't sensed something exceptional about her."

Gem laughed entirely without humor. "Oh, there's plenty exceptional about her. She's talented and gorgeous and has a way of making a woman feel special. God, I sound ridiculous."

"No, you don't. Define special—besides, you know, the obvious parts where you feel like a sexual goddess."

Gem grinned, a flicker of true humor slicing through the gloom that had descended over her. "I wouldn't use quite that term, but she certainly woke up something in me. It wasn't just the sex, although that was damn nice. I felt understood, as if when I told her things, I didn't have to explain myself. As if she cared."

"I can't believe you would have felt that way if it wasn't true."

The ice settled around Gem's heart again. "Well, there certainly were some major gaps in our connection. While I was blithely recounting God knows how many personal details, she was holding back a huge part of hers."

"I'm not going to defend her. I don't know her at all, and you're one of my best friends," Emily said staunchly, "but it's a big tangle, and the only thing I know for sure is that you are a good judge of your own feelings. So I'd trust them."

"I'll try." Gem sighed and finished the last of her chocolate. She carried the cup to the sink, carefully rinsed it, and set it upside down on the drain board. She squared her shoulders. "I guess it's time to put that to the test."

CHAPTER TWENTY-ONE

Thirty minutes had never felt so long. Austin wanted to go after Gem to continue to plead her case, to say something, anything, that would drive the distance from Gem's eyes and bring some warmth back into her smile. But she didn't have enough time, and this wasn't the time or the place. Her words weren't welcome. She'd run out of time, as she'd known she would, and if she'd listened to the voice of caution she never would have let the situation go so far. She hadn't been fair to Gem or herself, but she couldn't quite bring herself to regret a single moment. She hadn't wanted to be cautious, and she hadn't wanted to listen to reason. She hadn't wanted to push aside what her heart demanded yet again. She'd been ruled by the dictates and desires of others most of her life, until she convinced herself what she was doing was what she wanted. Oh, she'd charted her own course—she couldn't blame anyone else if she wasn't completely satisfied with her life. She'd broken away from the family tradition of risk-taking and adventure and high-profile excitement, but she'd somehow ended up on the edge of danger all the same. And blood had won out. When she'd stood on the precipice facing Gem across a chasm that logic and reason dictated she avoid, she jumped, not caring that she might fall. The risk had been worth it, and she hadn't fallen, at least not right away.

"You need me to stay for this?" Claudia asked.

Austin jerked at the sound of Claudia's voice. She'd actually forgotten she wasn't alone in the room Gem used as an office. The windowless ten- by ten-foot space was sparsely furnished with a serviceable plain wooden desk, a trio of metal filing cabinets, and a round table with four chairs that appeared to serve as a work space and conference area. She and Claudia had settled there to wait for Gem, and instead of reviewing plans for the containment procedures, she'd forgotten everything except the look of hurt and disdain in Gem's eyes.

Time to get a grip. She couldn't afford to forget anything now. A slip of attention or lapse in concentration could mean disaster not just for her, but for those who depended on her. She shook her head. "You're welcome to stay, but if you're really intent on going back to the rig, you should probably grab a lift before the weather gets any worse."

"What about you?"

"I want to stay here until I get a fix on the most-at-risk areas, and I want to be sure the ground team has everything they need."

"Your call." Claudia paused. "I thought you might need reinforcements."

"You noticed." Austin winced. "I don't expect open warfare, maybe just a cold war for a little while."

Claudia glanced over her shoulder, then pulled her chair closer. "It's absolutely none of my business, but I couldn't help noticing that one of the Sisters Martin bore a striking resemblance to the woman you were sketching. They're quite a fascinating pair."

"They are. I met Gem on the drive in. We spent most of a day in a car together, and we..." Austin shook her head. "It was a hell of a trip."

"I take it she didn't know about the rig or your job out there."

"I didn't know what I was going to be facing, and even if I had, I wouldn't have discussed it with anyone. You know the situation."

"Oh, indeed I do. I signed the same forms you did." She pushed back a whisper of hair that had fallen free from the clasp, an unconsciously graceful movement that elicited absolutely no reaction from Austin other than a distant appreciation.

"We'll sort things out," Austin said with more confidence than she felt. Somehow she had to sort things out, or she'd be walking around with a hole in her middle forever.

"I'm always good for backup." Claudia gave her a sympathetic smile and squeezed her hand. "Call me anytime."

Call me anytime.

Gem halted in the doorway to her office, a hot rush of annoyance and something that couldn't possibly be jealousy streaking through her. An instant ago she'd been ready to face Austin in a cool, professional manner, determined not to let the past hinder their working relationship. Now that hard-earned calm boiled away. "Am I early for our meeting?"

Austin's head jerked up. "No, I'm ready when you are."

"I can see that."

Claudia slowly drew her hand from Austin's and turned toward Gem. She smiled, a neutral professional smile. "I was about to head back to the rig. I'm sure we'll meet again before this is over."

Gem gave her a thin smile. "Maybe we'll be lucky and the storm will change course." And she could get back to her life without the unsettling presence of Austin Germaine and her own treacherous desires.

"I hope you're right." Claudia rose, saying to Austin, "I'll call you with an update as soon as I get to the rig."

"Thanks. Be careful."

"Of course." Claudia nodded to Gem and disappeared.

Gem took the seat Claudia had just vacated, edging the chair back a few inches from Austin, who was far too close. So close Gem could smell the spice and sandalwood, the same scent that clung to her pillow. Her throat ached even as her pulse quickened. Annoyed, aroused, she asked sharply, "What is it you need from me?"

Austin couldn't begin to answer that, not when Gem looked at her as if they'd never touched. So she'd start at the beginning, where she should have before she'd let her heart lead her head. "Since you and I will be the primary coordinators, I wanted to give you some perspective on my role."

"I thought you already did that," Gem said.

"The briefing was mostly a sit rep to establish the task force."

"What else is there?"

"I hope there's more."

"A little late for introductions," Gem said without a flicker of a lash, "but go ahead."

Austin tamped down a rejoinder. Gem wasn't going to make it easy for her. Fair enough. "You already know that I'm the point man for GOP in the developing situation out at the rig."

"How long have you been doing it?" Gem hadn't planned on asking any personal questions, but she couldn't help herself. She wanted to know more about Austin. She wanted to know something about her that she could believe—facts, not feelings.

"About five years," Austin said. "I started out as an engineering consultant, but it turns out I'm pretty good at interfacing with the media too."

"So you're not just a good-looking mouthpiece."

Austin let out a sigh. "I'd say thanks but I don't think there's a compliment in there. No, I'm not a PR person—in cases like this the media want to talk to the people on the ground, the ones with oil on their hands. I fit that bill."

Gem pounced. "So why are you here if there's no spill?"

"Are you also an attorney along with your other degrees?" Austin thought she saw a fleeting smile.

"No, that's my brother," Gem said.

"We don't have a spill, but we do have a leak."

"Fine distinction."

"An important one." Austin took her through the early response actions Tatum and Reddy had instituted.

"And Spencer?"

"The rig is a big float, more or less. They don't tip if carefully balanced and adjusted for dynamic ocean conditions—with the storm surge, the best information will come from assessing the situation right at sea level," Austin said. "Plus Claudia will liaise with the federal and state scientific support teams, when and if we get to that point."

"How bad is the leak?"

"Manageable, possibly containable under other circumstances, but as I told you and the others earlier, I don't think we can get out of this without some tangible spill."

"I don't have much experience with this stage of things," Gem said. "I was in the Gulf after Deepwater Horizon, but only during the rescue phase." Even now she could remember the bone-weary hours and mind-numbing devastation. The weeks she'd spent attempting to save the hundreds of birds trapped in the oil spills had been heartbreaking work. So many they hadn't been able to save. "There was oil everywhere."

"We're not going to let that happen here," Austin said determinedly. "We're ahead of things now, because with Deepwater, they didn't have any warning and they couldn't get booms and floats in place fast enough. We can."

Gem had seen the huge lines of floats and the skimmers vacuuming oil from the surface of the water, and she'd seen the coastline drenched in oil that drowned the sea life, starved the waterfowl, and ravaged the ecosystem for decades to come. "What if it gets past the booms? Can we keep it offshore?"

Austin felt Gem's probing gaze, knew Gem was looking for truth, and she had to convince her she was capable of it, for more reasons than the job. "We're hoping it won't even get that far. The booms are backup. Our first choice is to burn it right on the surface when it emerges."

"Isn't it dangerous—burning so close to your rig?"

"We've had plenty of experience with it."

Gem knew it couldn't be that simple. "How likely are you to be able to do all this with the hurricane coming?"

"The burn may be enough. Even the storm isn't likely to extinguish it."

The edge of Gem's anger and resentment dulled as she envisioned Austin and the others on a floating platform miles out in the ocean, corralling a burning oil slick with the hurricane bearing down on them. "That sounds insane."

Austin grinned thinly. "The whole idea of sinking a twelve-inch drill shaft miles down into the surface of the earth from a floating platform is pretty crazy too. But believe it or not, the safety record is pretty damn good. The crews are the best."

Of course Austin was going to say that, but Gem couldn't help imagining the risk. A frisson of fear skittered down her spine. "I suppose you have to be out there during all of this."

Austin lifted a shoulder. "As you said, I'm not just a mouthpiece."

Gem pressed her fingers to her eyes. "I'm sorry, that was uncalled for. I'm a little off balance. Things have been moving so quickly."

"I know," Austin murmured, aching to touch her, aching even more to know she wasn't welcome. "In more ways than one. Gem, I'm sorry you found all this out this way."

Gem leaned back in her chair and let out a long breath. Austin didn't deserve her bitterness, not when a big part of her anger was directed at herself. She'd gone willingly into Austin's arms, and looking at her now, so close, so damn electrifying, she wanted to again. "Why don't we agree to set our personal issues aside. I don't want you out there thinking about anything except what you're doing. And Lord knows, I'm going to have enough to think about here."

"I'd agree with you," Austin said, "but I don't really think I can do that. I haven't stopped thinking about you since the minute we met."

"Don't," Gem said softly.

"Don't what? Tell you the truth? Isn't that why you're angry, because you think I didn't?"

"Partly," Gem admitted. "But only partly. I'm just as angry at myself for falling into something for completely irrational reasons."

"Don't you mean falling into bed with me?"

"Not just falling into bed," Gem murmured, afraid to admit and unable to deny her feelings were much more than just sexual attraction. She couldn't use chemistry as an excuse. Her attraction to Austin had always been more than physical, and time didn't seem to be of any consequence. Their connection had been deep and terribly, wonderfully personal from the beginning. Heaven help her, she'd been falling in love with her since the minute she'd met her. "This isn't the time for this."

"It's never been time—it's just been right," Austin said, finally taking a chance. She slid her hand across the table and rested her fingertips on the top of Gem's balled fist. "I know you're angry and you don't trust me. But just believe this one thing—when I touched you, when you touched me, it was real. Everything you felt and you sensed from me was real."

"I can't think about that right now," Gem whispered.

Austin nodded, rewarded by the softening in Gem's eyes. "All right, then we'll work."

"Let me see your maps," Gem said, slowly pulling her hand away.

Austin turned her laptop toward Gem and pulled up the aerials of the coastline. "We don't have a lot of time, so I want to optimize our positioning of the booms." She pointed a finger. "These show the projected direction of currents and the way the oil is likely to flow if it escapes the burn. Where are the key areas we need to blockade?"

Gem pointed to several places on the map. "These are estuaries leading into the sanctuary. They feed much of the salt marsh, which is critical as both habitat and feeding ground. Contamination here is likely to destroy much of the essential vegetation and trap a great many of the birds."

"Where will you stage the recovery operations, if necessary?"

"Initially at the sanctuary, until we can set up mobile decontamination stations."

"How many people?"

Gem winced. "As many as we can muster. It takes about an hour per bird to wash the oil clear, get them rehydrated and fed, prior to relocation."

"That's a lot of man-hours."

"We lose a lot because we just can't get to them in time."

Austin would do anything to drive the clouds from Gem's eyes. "We'll seed the water between the booms and the shoreline with emulsifiers and chemical solvents if anything gets past the blockades. With the storm surge, though, our best hope is for the oil never to get this far."

"So we're back to the burn again," Gem said.

Austin nodded. "Best case. I need to get back out to the rig."

Gem's stomach tightened. "I'm going to be busy organizing the ground teams, but you'll…keep in touch?"

"Of course."

Gem struggled with the line between personal and professional, a line she'd crossed unwittingly once. She knew better now, crossing it willingly as she reached for Austin's hand. "You'll be careful, won't you."

Austin closed her fingers around Gem's, the link easing the pain in her chest. "I will. You too."

"I'm not the one sitting on top of the powder keg."

CHAPTER TWENTY-TWO

Gem found Emily where she expected her to be, kneeling in the sand on the beach, a baseball cap pulled low over her brow, her red hair flying in the wind, gently applying tiny tracking sensors with acrylic compound to the shells of the baby turtles breaking free of their eggs. The rain held off, but the sky was an angry blanket of gray. She imagined she could feel the storm at her back, thought of the oil rig bobbing on the vast sea, isolated and vulnerable, and how small and defenseless its human inhabitants. Pushing worries about Austin to the back of her mind did nothing to quell the twist of anxiety that coiled in her middle. Gritting her teeth, she knelt in the sand next to Emily. "What can I do?"

"Keep an eye out for stragglers and try to direct them toward the water." Emily's face was fierce, the muscles along her jaw tight and strained. "We're going to lose a lot of them if I can't get the unhatched eggs out in time."

"Can you incubate them in the center?"

"For a while, if we hold power and the whole damn place doesn't blow away." She pushed a strand of damp hair away from her cheek. "Damn it, why now?"

Gem gently redirected a half-dollar sized turtle down the slope toward the water and watched it make its staggering way into the frothy sea. Under ordinary circumstances, most would die before they ever reached the sanctuary of the water. Even if they did find their way to the safety of the sea with a little help from her and Emily, the majority would succumb to larger predators before they ever reached adulthood. Still, more would have a chance to survive with their help, and she didn't feel the least bit guilty thwarting the natural cycle of things, considering how much humans had done to destroy the habitat of these creatures. She'd never be able to even the score.

"There are three more clutches in this area alone," Emily said. "Who knows what might be elsewhere along the coast, and—"

"We can't get to them all," Gem said gently. "But we can look after the ones here."

Emily blew out a breath and sat back on her heels, glancing out to sea. "I've never been through one up close. Have you?"

"No. Some pretty heavy tropical storms, and lots of the aftermath." Gem watched a golf-ball-sized eggshell fracture and a miniscule head pop out. "At least we've got some time to prepare. Where's the rest of your help?"

"I sent them to help Joe board up the cabin windows and lock down the center." Emily balanced a solar-powered tracker on her fingertip and applied the glue, her attention on the emerging hatchling. "Where do you figure we'll ride this out?"

"Once we know for sure it's coming, and when, we'll set up a command center in the village, on high ground. I called the town supervisor right before I came out, and he's promised us a couple of rooms at town hall. Hopefully, we won't need them for long."

"I guess we can always relocate to the FEMA trailers."

Gem grimaced. "Not my first choice. I want to get back into the center as soon as we can."

"I'm with you." As Emily talked, she adroitly caught, tagged, and released the turtle and sent it on its way. Answering some innate imperative, a stream of the hatchlings straggled down the beach toward the surf. An occasional gull swooped low, hoping for an easy catch, but a shout and a wave of the arm from Emily or Gem was enough to dissuade them. Once the hatchlings reached the water and headed out to the protection of the plankton patches, they were on their own.

"I'll grab a couple more hands for you," Gem said, "so you can get the other clutches extracted and stored."

"Thanks."

"You sure you want to stay through the storm?"

"Jeremy's not too happy about it, but he'll cope." Emily grinned. "The kids are really annoyed they're missing all the fun. I don't plan on going anywhere."

Gem squeezed her shoulder. "Thanks."

The *thump-thump-thump* of a helicopter caught her attention and she glanced up to watch it turn course out over the ocean. She wondered if Austin was aboard. *I haven't stopped thinking about you since the minute we met.* A dark thrill raced through her, remembering the heavy-lidded languor in Austin's eyes when they'd lain together naked, caressing, enticing, seducing. No, she hadn't stopped thinking about her either, even when she'd tried. And now every thought was undercut with fear.

"I guess the GOP people have headed back out," Emily said with her uncanny ability to read Gem's mind.

"Yes."

"Talk about a perfect storm."

"Ironic term for it," Gem muttered.

"How is it, working with Austin?" Emily rose and brushed sand from the knees of her cargo pants. "Here, carry this."

Gem grabbed the backpack filled with equipment and followed Emily down the beach. "It's fine. We've both got jobs to do, and we agreed to keep things professional."

"Aha, professional. Very mature." Emily cut her a glance and carefully stepped over the yellow tape surrounding another square of beach. "Really, Gem? From the looks of things, the two of you were on fire. Now you're going to be cool and professional?"

"Damn it, what choice do I have." Gem hunkered down with her back to the rising wind. "It's not like we'd been dating or anything, more like—hell, I don't know what we've been doing."

"Well, if it was me, I'd kick her ass."

Gem grinned.

"Hand me that spade," Emily said, knowing with some sixth sense exactly where the clutch was located. Gem played first assistant as Emily worked.

"It's not as if she's completely responsible," Gem said. "There were two of us in that bed, you know."

Emily looked up, quirked a brow. "Uh-huh. I got that part. Don't tell me you're not steamed about her keeping a whopper of a secret."

Secrets. They'd always been her undoing. Paul's secret fantasies, Christie's secret desires, even her own. For years, she'd been a secret to herself, unable or unwilling to recognize her true needs. She'd promised herself never to fall victim to secrets again, and at the first surge of passion she'd fallen. "I haven't forgotten."

"I like the way she looks at you," Emily said matter-of-factly.

"I'm sorry?"

"She looks at you like she's hungry."

Heat flashed through Gem's chest and into her throat. For an instant, she was straddling Austin's hips, leaning over her, face-to-face, lost in her eyes, consumed by her hunger. Desire coiled in her depths. She should've been embarrassed that Emily had seen that craving, but she couldn't be, not when she hungered herself. "There's more to life than lust."

Emily laughed. "I can't believe you just said that. Go ahead, keep trying to convince yourself you don't want it, but I think it would be easier to just make her suffer. And then find a way to set things right."

Make things right. She wasn't even sure she wanted to, even if it was possible. She didn't trust herself or what she felt, and right now, she wasn't sure she wanted to trust Austin either.

Benny set the bird down on the helipad, and Austin released her seat belt. "When are you and Rio taking the birds to the mainland?"

Removing her headset, Benny rifled a hand through her short-cropped hair. She cut the engine and the rotors slowed, but the sound of the wind rushing past the cockpit made it sound as if they were still flying. "No word on that yet."

Austin frowned. If the storm came up quickly, the helicopters would be stranded on the rig. Benny and Rio were the last two pilots remaining, since they had the most experience flying in bad weather. All the same, they needed to leave while it was still safe to do so. "Dr. Spencer will need a lift back later today. You and Rio should plan on evac-ing all nonessentials then and grounding your birds until the weather clears."

Benny jumped out and came around to join her as they trotted across the platform. "How do the rest of you plan to get off of here?"

"We'll grab a lift with one of the ships after they deploy the booms."

"Roger that. I'll give Rio the word," Benny said and angled off in the direction of the pilots' ready room.

Tatum was just coming into the command center when Austin arrived. Claudia was packing up some of her equipment.

"Any new developments?" Austin said.

"Good news and bad," Tatum said, but for the first time, his expression was slightly less than sour.

"Progress?" They were about at the eleventh hour, but at this point, Austin would take any scrap of good news.

"We got the fucking leak isolated, and Reddy thinks his boys can plug it just above, slowing it down to a manageable trickle until we can get the remotes down there to patch it."

Austin frowned. "The remotes won't function in these kinds of seas."

"You're fucking right about that," Tatum said. "So we need to buy some time."

"That puts us about where we've been all along," Austin said, the bubble of optimism shrinking.

"Not exactly," Tatum said. "Reddy thinks he can get a container shaft down the outside and funnel the oil up the shaft."

"They tried that on Deepwater Horizon," Austin said.

"Yeah, and it didn't work," Tatum said, "but that was then and this is now. We're way ahead of the game." He grinned. "And we're better."

"How long?"

"Too long. We'll have to feed the exterior shaft down in sections and hook them together, which wouldn't take all that long if we had a full crew under perfect conditions, but we fucking don't have any of those things working for us. A couple of days, at least."

Claudia moved over to join the conversation. "But if you can do it, you can contain the leak?"

"That's the idea, and keep the well functioning." Tatum's eyes sparkled as he spoke.

"What about the oil that's leaking now?" Claudia asked, looking from Austin to Tatum.

"We'll burn it," Austin said. "If and when it surfaces."

"We'll start sliding the sheath down now, but it will be slow going with a small crew," Tatum said. "Given a day or two and if the creek don't rise, we got a chance."

Claudia sighed. "I hate to tell you this, but the creek's about to rise. The latest projections have the storm making landfall by midday tomorrow."

"Twenty-four hours," Austin murmured. Her phone rang and she grimaced. She really didn't want to have to tell Eloise they'd have to abandon the rig, ride out the storm, and hope the spill didn't get worse before it was over. "Germaine."

"Linda Kane and NBC News are headed your way."

"How did that happen so quickly? We don't even have oil on the surface yet," Austin said.

"I think she slept with everyone at FEMA down in New Orleans," Eloise snarled. "Someone tipped her off."

"Okay." Austin grabbed her jacket. "I'll head her off before she finds someone to fly her out here."

"That's all we need is her on the rig. Don't let that happen."

"Believe me, I won't."

❖

Gem's phone rang just as Emily was uncovering the third and next to the last clutch. The readout indicated an unknown caller. "This is Gillian Martin."

"Bill Peabody with FEMA. We got ten people in your parking

lot right now, and a half dozen trucks of sand coming in behind us pretty quick. Where do you want us?"

"Stay right there. I'm ten minutes away." She disconnected and turned to Emily. "I'll get a couple of interns out here to help you finish up. FEMA is here."

"Time to start sandbagging. Oh, what fun." Emily grinned. "Keep the interns. I can handle this myself. If you see Joe, send him out and he can help me carry the clutches back."

"I'll find him for you."

As Gem jogged back, she called Joe's number and gave him Emily's location. "As soon as you're done securing the buildings, can you give her a hand?"

"Sure. You know there's a bunch of people out front, right?"

"I'm on it."

"All right then," he said, sounding a little skeptical. "Good luck."

Gem tucked her phone back into her pants pocket. She came around the back of the center and realized she had more company than she expected. A news van with antennae bristling and a satellite dish mounted to the rear sat idling in the middle of the parking lot. A gaggle of people with equipment surrounded another group with microphones out thrust. Great, the press had arrived.

As Gem strode toward the congregation, Austin pulled in, hopped out of her SUV, and cut into their midst ahead of her. Gem edged up to the group, close enough to hear.

"Linda," Austin said with a friendly smile as she extended her hand. "Austin Germaine. We met in Port Arthur after the last big blow down there."

The busty redhead smiled and tilted her head at what Gem figured was a perfect camera-worthy angle. She practically preened, and Gem had an urge to ruffle her own feathers more than a little bit. She pushed a little closer.

"Austin, yes," the reporter purred, "how can I possibly forget? You certainly got here in a hurry, or have you been here for a while?"

Gem tensed. She didn't like the redhead one little bit, a snap judgment totally unlike her. It couldn't possibly be because the redhead was both flirtatious and baiting Austin at the same time. As if Austin could be trapped so easily. All the same, Gem's skin prickled uneasily.

"I just flew in from the rig," Austin said. "I'm afraid we don't have much of a story for you at this point. Unless you're here to cover the hurricane. I can't tell you much about that you don't already know."

"I understand you've got a spill, and it's headed this way." Smiling, Linda waved a hand toward the trucks that were boldly marked with FEMA. "Really, why else?"

Gem stepped forward. "I can answer that, since I called them."

Linda Kane swiveled toward Gem, a boldly arched auburn eyebrow rising. "Really. And who would you be?"

"Gillian Martin. I'm head of the research team here at the sanctuary. This is a protected area and with the storm coming, we need to secure the coastline." She nodded toward the FEMA trucks. "Standard procedure under these conditions."

"And of course, with the oil spill—"

"At this point," Gem said, "we're a lot more worried about the storm than something that might happen. The hurricane is not theoretical."

"I guess we'll all find out about that together, then," Linda said jauntily, as if they were all going to the same cocktail party that evening.

"If you'll excuse us," Gem said, "I need to get these people organized." She turned her back on the reporter and headed toward the lead FEMA van. "Bill?"

A slender, handsome young African American stepped forward, hand outstretched. "That would be me. Our command vehicles are setting up in town. Where do you want the sand?"

"There's an access road behind the building," Gem said, returning his handshake. "Take that down toward the beach. I'll meet you there and we can get started."

"Good enough." He herded his people back to their trucks. "Saddle up, everybody."

Within a minute, the parking lot was empty except for the news van. Gem ignored them as she strode after the FEMA vehicles.

Austin caught up with her on the path. "Thanks for having my back."

"I wasn't. I just wanted to keep the record straight."

"Well, I appreciate it, all the same."

"You're welcome," Gem said, cutting her a glance. "What are you doing here?"

"I thought I'd make myself useful and fill some sandbags."

"I think that's a little below your pay grade, isn't it?"

"I want to help, and right now it's a waiting game out on the rig. There's nothing I can do out there. So if it's all right with you, I'd like to stay."

Gem let out a breath. "All right, as long as you promise to keep those news people out of our hair."

"You don't ask for much, do you?"

"Actually," Gem said, thinking back on all the things she'd once wanted from a lover and never thought to have, "I think I'm finally beginning to."

CHAPTER TWENTY-THREE

Gem dragged a bag of sand to the barricade and heaved it on top. Pressing a hand to the small of her back and stretching her shoulders, she squinted down the beach to survey their progress. The mountain of sand dumped from the FEMA truck still looked like a mountain, but it must be smaller, because the line of sandbags stretching along the high-tide line was higher. She couldn't fool herself into thinking it would be enough if the surge came ashore ten feet high, but even then the wall would be a deterrent to the coastal washout and the overwhelming flooding in the marshes. A quick look at her watch told her they'd been at it much longer than she'd realized—in another hour they'd be working under floodlights. Some of the FEMA crew were rigging them now. As long as they had power, they'd be able to keep erecting their puny physical barrier in the face of one of nature's most violent ambassadors.

She grabbed another empty bag, hefted her shovel, and started back to the sand hill. Halfway there she made the mistake of looking where she had been trying not to look for the past few hours, and a glimpse was enough to stop her in her tracks.

Fifteen feet away, Austin stared out to sea as she talked on her phone. She'd shed her jacket and stood, legs spread, in rolled-up shirtsleeves, dark hair blowing in the wind, one arm resting on the handle of her upright shovel. She might've been standing on the quarterdeck of a three-masted sailing ship, for she looked like nothing less than a pirate captain, with an aura of loosely chained power warning she could spring into action at any moment. She certainly didn't look like anyone's mouthpiece or any of the slick talking heads who so often handled PR at times like this.

Austin didn't have to be out here in the driving winds with a shovel, bagging sand. There were no cameras, at least not this close, and none of the dozen volunteers filling bags paid any attention to her beyond an appreciative glance now and then from a woman or man. She wasn't bending her back for good PR, but she was earning it from Gem all the same. Just watching her made Gem want to touch her, and a whole hell of a lot of other things she couldn't think about now.

Gem should have turned away when Austin tucked the phone into her pants pocket, but she was too slow. They hadn't spoken since they'd reached the beach and started work, and when Austin caught her gaze and held it, Gem couldn't look away. They might've been alone on the windswept coast. When Austin shouldered her shovel and strode toward her, a wave of longing as potent as pain unfurled deep inside her.

Gem forced a casual smile and ignored the sudden tremor in her legs. "Any news?"

"That was Tatum—he's the incident commander on the rig." Austin ran her fingers through her hair, leaving it sexily disheveled. "He's making some progress running an exterior column down the well shaft to contain the oil."

Gem tilted her chin toward the two large ships and a smattering of smaller ones that had been moving up and down along the coast for the past few hours. "But you're going ahead with the booms all the same."

"We have to, considering the storm coming. If we wait until we see oil, we'll be too late."

"That has to be costly for your bosses."

Austin shrugged. "Not nearly as costly as the oil reaching shore."

"In more ways than one," Gem muttered, thinking of the news vans that had set up residence behind the line of FEMA trucks. The camera crews had shot some footage of the sandbag operation and then headed back to the cover of their vehicles. They were here for the oil story, not what happened to the refuge.

"How are things looking from your end?" Austin asked.

"We could use a few dozen more people, but if we keep going as long as we can, we'll make a difference."

"When will you evac to the mainland?"

"My team isn't leaving. We can't risk being cut off from the island. Time is critical in rescue operations, and if we end up dealing with oil on top of storm damage, we'll already be behind."

"Three days of heavy rain closed the causeway before," Austin said. "You might not be able to get back out here even if you stay."

"The Coast Guard will get us here." Gem grinned. "I've got an in with them."

"You'll be in for a rough ride," Austin said, her tone cautious.

"This coming from someone who spends her time on top of oil wells out in the middle of the ocean."

Austin grinned, her rakish expression making Gem's stomach tighten. "It's a little like riding a bucking horse. You just hold on and go with it."

Hold on and go with it. Could anything in life really be that simple? Climbing aboard the roller coaster, strapping into the rocket ship, setting sail without a map? Gem had made a choice to ride the whirlwind when she'd kissed Austin first, when she'd taken her hand and led her upstairs, knowing they'd end up in bed, when she'd abandoned her self-imposed exile from passion. She had followed her desires, and she had surely ended up at sea without a chart. "I made a choice."

Austin regarded her intently, that dark probing gaze gliding over her face in a silent invitation Gem was finding harder and harder to resist. "What was it?"

"To acknowledge my attraction to you...my *desire* for you. I wanted to feel what you make me feel. I was a willing partner."

"I should have stopped you," Austin said, "but I couldn't. I wanted you then. I want you now."

The familiar heat erupted in Gem's chest, flooded her throat, and rolled lower in a liquid rush of desire and need. "This is the wrong time, the wrong place—just about everything is wrong."

"Maybe after this is all over—" Austin said instantly.

"Maybe," Gem said, hesitating while every instinct urged her to abandon caution. She might have, if her feelings hadn't been so intense, so much larger and more frightening than anything she'd experienced in her life.

Austin must have sensed her uncertainty and smiled wryly. "Not like we have any choice." She hefted the shovel. "We seem destined to spend our time together in the middle of a storm."

Gem laughed. No calm center when Austin was involved. Being near her was like standing on the shore in the heart of the hurricane, buffeted by lashing winds and driving rain while lightning flashed across the sky. The wild unbridled beauty filled her, and she had no desire to escape to where it was safe and warm and ultimately passionless. "I don't mind a little weather."

"I'm glad."

"Me too," Gem said, almost ready to dare the whirlwind again. "When—"

"Hey," Emily called, jogging down the beach toward them.

Gem sent Austin a wry look and turned away. "Hi, Em. How's it going?"

"I posted the evac roster as requested. Everybody knows where they need to be and what they need to do."

"Thanks."

"You ought to take a break while you can," Emily said. "By my count, you've been out here six hours. Did you have any lunch?"

"I'm fine."

"It's going to be a long couple of weeks." Emily propped her hands on her hips, her tone gentle but unyielding. "That means everyone has to take care of themselves, but especially you. Go. Get something hot to drink, some food."

Gem knew she was right. She'd skipped lunch, and breakfast had been coffee and a bagel at the center at seven that morning. The early briefing with Austin seemed like it'd been days ago. "All right, I'll take a lunch break."

"Make it a long one. I know where to find you." Emily glanced at Austin. "You should go with her. You've been out here as long as anyone."

"I'm—"

"The FEMA guys have a food truck just over that rise." She made shooing motions. "Go. Go. Both of you."

Gem stowed her empty sandbag and shovel and gestured for Austin to join her. "She's right. Come on."

"If you're sure—"

Gem laughed. "I can't remember the last time I was sure of anything."

"Then maybe I—"

"Come on," Gem said, heading up the slope. "It's only lunch."

❖

The windows on Gem's cabin were boarded up, making the interior dark and cave-like. Feeling awkward, Austin halted just inside the door while Gem lit lamps. She glimpsed the alcove and the bed, remembering lying naked there with Gem, a million years ago. Before everything had changed. She stuffed her hands into her pockets. "If I told you why I was coming in the car that day—"

Gem turned, resting her hips against the counter in the tiny kitchenette. "I get why you didn't. At least, I'm assuming GOP doesn't want any press around incidents like this unless it's absolutely necessary."

"That's pretty much right."

"And who decides when it's necessary?"

"There are laws that spell out at what point notification is required and other agencies get involved."

"And that's when you get to take the stage."

Austin grimaced. "I'd rather not be onstage at all, but it's part of my job, yes. The other part is to coordinate, like I've been doing here. And the company likes to have a direct line to what's going on in the field. That's me too."

"Quite a lot of hats to wear. How do you find time to work on your comics?"

"Fortunately, emergencies at the level where I'm required aren't all that frequent." Austin rubbed her face with both hands. "Although lately, they seem to be. The more global drilling expands"—she shrugged—"the more ground we need to cover."

"I think we've established your reasons for holding back why you were coming. We don't need to go over that ground again."

The remote chill in Gem's tone made it pretty clear the issue wasn't really over, at least not to Austin's satisfaction. Apologies had been made, and accepted. She got that. But a chasm still yawned between them, wide and dark and echoing hollowly in the center of her chest. "If you'd known, would any of this"—she gestured toward the bed—"have happened?"

Gem turned, opened the boxed lunches they'd grabbed from the FEMA truck, carried them to the tiny table, and set them in front of the two chairs. She sat down and opened hers. "Probably not."

Austin joined her and pulled out a sandwich she had no appetite for. Unwrapping it, she took a bite and chased it with lukewarm bottled water. "Then I'm not sorry I didn't tell you, even though I wish we were at a different place right now. I'm not sorry about what we've shared."

Gem studied her sandwich as if it were the most interesting thing in the world. She raised it as if to take a bite and then set it down with a sigh. "I don't regret sleeping with you. I couldn't, it was too damn enjoyable."

Austin grinned. "You have a knack for understatement."

A flicker of a smile grazed Gem's lips. "All right, exceptionally enjoyable."

"That's closer."

"But here's the thing," Gem said. "What happened between us was something almost completely out of my experience. The only time I've ever done anything so…atypical…it was a disaster. And this feels a lot like that."

Austin clamped down on the pulse of temper. "I'm not your husband, who must have been insane to look at another woman when he had you, and I'm not the friend who betrayed you with him." Austin caught Gem's hand, slid their fingers together. "I'm the woman who's been falling in love with you since I turned around and saw you in the airport."

Gem's breath caught. "Just like that?"

"Just exactly like that," Austin said, tightening her grip on Gem's hand when she tried to pull away. "I can't speak for what's right for you, but I can tell you nothing about this is typical for me either. But everything is right. It's probably one of the truest things I've ever done."

Color flushed Gem's throat. "You do like taking risks, don't you?"

"All my life, I've been pushed to take risks. It's the currency my family values most. Most of the time, I think I did it just to prove to them I was worthy." Austin angled her chair until the table was no longer separating them, resisting the urge to pull Gem closer. That was a space Gem would have to cross herself. "But being with you didn't feel like a risk. Falling in love with you feels like the safest thing I've ever done."

"I'm not an impetuous person," Gem said slowly. "I...I need time to absorb what's happened, to think about it, to know if it's right or even if it's anything I want to do again."

Austin could give her time, but she wasn't going to just sit by and do nothing. "I don't mind taking my time with something I want."

"You must admit," Gem said, trying for lightness, "we haven't exactly had a typical relationship. I've never gone to bed with anyone before at least having half a dozen dates. Actually, more like a couple dozen dates."

"Oh, I don't know, I'd say we've had a few dates." Austin released Gem's hand and leaned back in her chair. "Let's see, the first couple hours in the car, exchanging names, a little bit about what we did, where we were from, where we were going counts as the getting-to-know-you date. And then at least two dinner dates, well, one was kind of breakfast, but same difference. I believe we even had candlelight—"

"That's because there was no electricity for a while at the diner."

Austin laughed. "Right."

"We've had an afternoon at the beach," Gem said playfully, welcoming the surge of pleasure that chased away some of the ache she'd carried for the last few days, "and bird-watching."

"Absolutely. And then there's the romantic getaway at the beachside resort—"

Gem snorted. "Tell me you're not counting the Gulls Inn—"

"But of course, that was definitely romantic." Austin grinned. "I'd say we've at least hit your six-date requirement."

"It feels like we have," Gem said softly. Pretending they hadn't shared intimacies, emotional and physical, was impossible. "I don't want you to think it wasn't special, and what you just said…" She drew a long breath, wanting to embrace the desire, afraid of the intensity of her own needs. "I think I just need a little time to catch up."

"Then we'll take time."

"You don't strike me as being a particularly patient woman."

"I can be, when there's something I really want. And I really want you."

The undertow of desire caught Gem so quickly and pulled her under so fast, Gem couldn't escape. In the next breath she went willingly, shifting into Austin's lap to kiss her. "Thank you."

Austin wrapped both arms around her and kissed her throat. "Don't thank me, when I'm the one who's feeling lucky right now."

Gem laughed, surprised by the tremor in Austin's voice and the swell of joy in her heart. A simple kiss from Austin could undo her in a way nothing else ever had. "I've never actually believed in chemistry before, but just touching you does something to me. I'm tingling everywhere."

Austin groaned, running both hands up and down Gem's back. "You can't ask me to be patient and then tell me something like—"

Gem silenced her with another kiss, angling her head to take the kiss deeper, welcoming the heat and the hunger. When she sensed herself falling into the taste of her, seduced by the hard possessive grip of her hands, she pulled away. "You have to be patient. We have to get ba—"

Austin's phone rang and she jerked it from her pocket, her dark eyes swirling with such hunger Gem bit her lip to keep back a moan.

Holding her gaze, Austin snapped, "Germaine." She listened for a second, then said, "I'll need twenty…All right. Tell her to follow the lights." She closed the phone and buried her face against Gem's throat, her breathing still uneven. "I have to go."

Gem's throat tightened. "What is it?"

"We've got oil on the surface."

"God." Gem stood to let Austin up. "It's the middle of the night with a hurricane right around the corner. Can you really do anything now?"

Austin framed Gem's face and kissed her slowly, as if imprinting the taste and feel of her. "We'll start the burn as soon as we can get the projected area of spill."

"I'm the last one to suggest maybe you should rely on the booms closer to shore to contain it," Gem said, grabbing a fistful of Austin's shirt as if to keep her in place, "but this can't be safe."

"We're not letting it get to shore."

Gem slipped her hand inside the collar of Austin's shirt, needing flesh to flesh. "Promise not to do anything risky."

Austin laughed softly and kissed her again. "I promise…where the job is concerned."

Wordlessly, Gem let her go and they started back to the beach. Night had fallen and the wind had kicked up a few knots. The marsh grasses bent and fluttered, emitting a sorrowful sigh. By the time they reached the shore, the blinking lights of the helicopter marked its descent.

Austin jogged toward it, shouting, "I'll see you soon."

"Remember, you promised me," Gem called after her, feeling her words pulled away on the wind.

CHAPTER TWENTY-FOUR

Linda Kane came trotting down the beach, trailing a cable and a cameraman. Despite the wind and mist, her hair appeared perfectly coiffed and her designer brand rain slicker looked to be tailor-made to accentuate her voluptuous figure. She wore sporty black pants and boots with low heels that sank into the sand with every step. Nevertheless, she covered the ground with alacrity.

"Where's the helicopter going?" Linda asked of Gem, a microphone boom thrust into the space over their heads. The soundman braced his legs to hold it steady as the wind gusted offshore.

"Back to the rig," Gem said.

"That seems rather unexpected," Linda said, "especially since it required an emergency helicopter pickup from the beach."

"I really don't know anything about that," Gem said. "Helicopter landings are not something I have time to worry about." She gestured down the beach to the long line of FEMA personnel and volunteers spotlighted in the glow of the halogens standing on stalks like alien praying mantises with single glaring eyes and spindly metal limbs. Hoping to get some public support for the sanctuary, Gem continued, "As you can see, this stretch of coastline borders the Rock Hill marshlands, a section of the wildlife sanctuary along the Atlantic Flyway. That's—"

"I'm sure everything here will be well taken care of, now FEMA's here and in charge," Linda said, facing the camera with a wide bright smile. She made a swift cutting motion below the apparent sight line of the viewfinder. Turning her back to Gem, she said to her assistant, "Call Larry. We need to get up in the air."

Gem watched them rush back down the beach and disappear over the rise where their van must be parked. Emily, who'd been lurking nearby, joined her.

"Did I just hear her say they're going up in the air?"

"Yes, I gather she's chasing the oil story. She sure doesn't care about the sanctuary."

"Bad time to be heading out there," Emily said, pulling up the hood of her windbreaker and cinching it down. "But I guess that's how they get the scoops."

"Apparently." Gem sighed. "And they're going to get a good one. Austin just got word there's oil on the surface. They're going to try to burn it off."

Emily caught her breath. "Damn. Well. I guess that means we're going to need more sandbags."

"Maybe not. Apparently burning is very effective, so I guess there's still hope."

Emily squeezed her arm. "Hey, Austin's an expert, right? So we've got more than hope on our side."

Gem nodded, searching the sky for a single sign that the cloud cover might be breaking. If the moon was out there, she couldn't see it.

❖

Austin keyed her mic and gripped the ceiling strap with one hand as the bird rocked from side to side. "Getting rough up here."

"Wind's picked up and shifts direction every couple of minutes. Air pockets pretty much everywhere."

As if on schedule, the bird bucked and dropped ten feet inside a second. Austin's stomach lurched as Benny pulled up. "I thought you and Rio were getting your birds back to the mainland."

"We plan to, but we've still got crew on the platform."

"As soon as we land, round everybody up. I want everyone gone ASAP."

Benny glanced at her. "Roger that. You're heading to the ships?"

"As soon as we get everything coordinated with the burn crews."

"Just don't wait too long. Getting a launch off the platform might be tricky on these seas."

"I hear you."

Benny set down with a jolt and the helicopter skidded a dozen yards as a blast of air lifted the undercarriage. "I'll have to tie her down until we get ready to leave."

"Make it fast."

"You need to get your meteorologist out here too," Benny said.

Austin shoved her door open, and the wind tried to shove it back. She braced it with an arm. "She's still here?"

"Yeah."

Mentally cursing, Austin said, "I'll see to it," and tugged off her headset. She forced her way out onto the platform, leaning into the wind and pushing toward the office.

Claudia was the only one inside. She stood at the counter, a laptop by her right hand, a chart spread out by her left, and an aerial with a tiny red dot denoting the rig projected on the monitor in front of her.

"You're supposed to be gone," Austin said abruptly.

Claudia didn't look around. "With oil on the surface, I need to do current projections so we can chart the direction of the drift for the ships to set the booms."

Under ordinary circumstances, Austin would've agreed. Two containment ships would isolate the oil within a U of fire-resistant booms, congregating the oil into a thick layer for an optimal burn, and tow it away from the rig. If the oil drifted too fast, it escaped the burn. If it thinned out too much, it wouldn't burn at all. The ships followed courses predicted by a marine meteorologist like Claudia who mapped the currents, the wind speed, the wave height, and a host of other variables. In a lot of ways, this was Claudia's game right now.

"We'll be lucky to get even a few hours' burn with the weather we've got. You've done all you can do. You need to evac."

Claudia looked over her shoulder, an annoyed crease between her brows. "Really? Aren't you being just a little bit chauvinistic here? Reddy and Tatum aren't going anywhere."

"You can track the situation from land," Austin said, smothering a grin. Claudia was probably a little bit right, but she was a desk jockey, not a roughneck. "Whatever happened to 'I'll be the first one off'?"

"I'm still going to be the first one off. And if you'd be quiet and let me work, I'll be off a lot sooner."

"As soon as you send your projections, pack up your gear. The birds are getting ready to leave. Everybody's going with them."

Claudia finally turned to face her. "All of us?"

Austin lifted a shoulder. "Everyone except Tatum, Reddy, and me. We'll deploy to the ships as soon as the evac here is complete."

"And how exactly are you going to do that?"

"We'll take the shuttle launch."

"On this sea?"

Austin waved a hand. "We'll be fine. Would you please get ready to go."

"All right, all right. I'm packing." Claudia finished typing a message and began shutting down her computer with one hand while gathering papers from the counter with the other.

Satisfied, Austin said, "You should make it off the island in plenty of time."

"Where are you going to be?" Claudia pushed folders and a pile of papers into her briefcase.

"I'll stay ashore so we can get back out here ASAP when the storm passes."

"Then I'm staying too. Where can I get a room?"

"Don't you already have one?"

Claudia winced. "Unfortunately, yes, I do, it's in container number thirty-nine on the far end of the platform. However, that's not going to work out any longer."

Austin squeezed the bridge of her nose and shook her head. "Jeez. I can't believe you've been bunking out here with Tatum and Reddy and that crew for the last—"

"Far too many days," Claudia said with a wry grin. "Is there any chance I can find someplace ashore?"

"I doubt it. If the locals are leaving, they'll be closing up their businesses. If they're staying, they're probably full. Either way, you don't have much time to find out one way or the other." She fished in her pants pocket and pulled out her room key. "Here, take this. It's the Gulls Inn on the east end, room number five at the back. You can use my room."

"Oh, that's okay, I don't want to put you out."

"I won't be using it very much anyhow. You might as well have a place to keep warm and dry, but it's close to the beach, so keep an eye on the weather."

Claudia cocked a hip and smirked. "You didn't really just say that to me, did you?"

Austin grinned. "Yeah, I did. Now would you please hustle out to the bird and get out of here."

Claudia shrugged into her raincoat and picked up her briefcase and laptop case. As she passed Austin, she slowed. "Be careful, will you? Saving the company a few million dollars isn't worth getting hurt for."

"I don't think you want Eloise to hear you say that."

"Oh, Eloise…she's not that hard to handle."

Austin stared after her, trying to imagine anyone handling Eloise. Maybe Claudia Spencer was just the person.

❖

"Well," Eloise said with a resigned sigh, "we pretty much always knew this was coming."

"Did you get the permits to burn?" Austin asked, walking around the control center and shutting down equipment as she talked.

"Yes, when I advised the various agencies, I put the paperwork through just in case. Do you have any idea yet how big it's going to be?"

"So far the surface accumulations are pretty small, but they're steady. We're set to corral them with the booms and start the burn. I'll give you an update when we do."

"How long do you think you'll be able to keep it going?"

"You know the stats. Once the wind gets over twenty to twenty-five knots or the waves hit five feet, we're not going to be able to contain the oil. We'll try skimming and whatever else we can as long as we can."

"We need Tatum's crews to get that external shaft in place," Eloise said. "No leak, no spill, no burn. Make that happen."

"Hurricane, Eloise. There's a hurricane coming. I'm evacuating the rig."

"You might have discussed it with me."

"There's nothing to discuss. You know the projections as well as I do. Time's up."

"Damn it," Eloise said quietly. "All right, just keep a lid on things."

Austin thought of NBC News camped out on the shore. At least they were fifty miles away. "Right, I'm on that."

After a last look around, she picked up a two-way radio from the console on the counter, shut off the lights, and locked the door behind her. Time for the endgame. She flicked open the channel to Tatum. "Ray, it's Austin. Are your crews away?"

"The last bird just left. It's only us fucking pigeons left behind."

Austin chuckled. "Are the ships ready?"

"Under way."

"I guess it's time for us to rendezvous."

"The launch is ready to go."

"On my way." Austin clipped the two-way to her belt, zipped her jacket, and grabbed a fire emergency pack from the on-deck emergency bin. Slinging it over her shoulder, she jogged across the rig, slowing at the sound of a helicopter circling overhead. She shaded her eyes against the glare of the floodlights on the upper sections of the platform, wondering why Benny or Rio had returned. They had no reason—

"Damn it," she muttered. The colorful news logo flashed on the side of the helicopter, its spotlights scanning over the surface of the rig. Even from a distance, she could see it buffeted in the wind. The news pilot was probably experienced, but she doubted he had much practice being this far out to sea with the kind of unpredictable tailwinds they were looking at over the next few hours.

A cone of light raced across the rig and focused on her. She made a *go back* motion with her arm, but the helicopter continued to hover. Shaking her head, she joined Tatum and Reddy at the top of the lift.

"Who the hell is that?" Reddy asked.

"That would be the news," Austin said.

Tatum muttered, "Well, fuck me."

"Yeah." Austin had to agree—an audience was not what they needed right now. Eloise was so not going to be happy.

Ignoring the hovering craft, Austin climbed into the lift bucket and held on as the cage descended to the platform. The thirty-foot launch was moored to the side, and Reddy took the wheel while she and Tatum cast off.

"Hold on," he shouted, "it's gonna be a rough ride."

The launch arrowed across the chop toward one of the big containment ships, and Austin sheltered behind the cockpit as much as she could. Icy water whipped across the deck, drenching her all the same. The news copter followed them, undoubtedly filming all the way. Two ships circled slowly several hundred yards apart, the booms strung between them, enclosing the area Claudia had mapped out as the locus of the surface oil accumulation. Once they started the burn, the ships would close the loop and slowly drag the confined puddle of burning oil away from the rig. All that remained was for Austin to give the final word to start the burn.

When they reached the ship, an elevator descended along with lines to secure the launch. The captain and Phil Renuto, the burn chief, were waiting for them on deck.

Austin shook hands with the captain and Phil. "All set?"

"Ready to go. You want to take a look?"

"Yeah," Austin said.

Renuto glanced overhead. "I guess we'll have company for the whole thing."

"It looks that way."

He grunted. "I wonder if they know they'll be breathing smoke up there in a few minutes."

"Somehow, I doubt it." When she'd finished reviewing the protocol with Renuto and was satisfied with the boom placement and the direction the ships would drag the burning oil, she climbed back down to the launch. As Reddy steered them toward the spill, she gave Phil the go-ahead.

Austin braced both arms on the rail, the helicopter trailing them, as they set the sea afire.

❖

Gem poured coffee, her tenth cup of the endless evening. At just after midnight, her body felt as if she'd been shoveling for a year. Her arms ached, her back ached, even her ass ached, but she reminded herself she ought to be grateful. They still had another twelve hours to reinforce their barricades, at least if the present predictions held. She closed her eyes, leaned against the counter, and sipped, not even caring about the taste. Hot was good enough. She hadn't heard from Austin, and even though she hadn't really expected to in the midst of everything going on, the silence was unsettling. The disconnection, not knowing where she was, set her adrift and an uneasy tension simmered in her middle.

Emily and Joe came in, trailing a few FEMA guys, comparing notes as to what was done and what needed to be done, and Gem opened her eyes. Austin was a pro, she'd be fine. Too bad her stomach didn't quite believe it.

"Hey," Emily said, heading straight for the hot chocolate.

"Hi," Gem said.

Joe flicked on the news on the small television.

As he walked over to get coffee, Gem glanced at the screen. Her heart jumped. "Wait! Can you turn that up? Hurry."

Joe spun around, grabbed the remote, and jacked up the volume.

Linda Kane's image, a still photo, appeared beside video of two ships and a column of blazing orange against a midnight sky. Kane's voice-over exclaimed with a trill of excitement, "This is Linda Kane, reporting live from over the Atlantic. GOP, one of the world's largest oil companies, has just commenced an open ocean burn to contain an oil spill from Rig 86, an offshore drilling platform just miles off the coast of Maryland. As you can see, we are presently circling above the containment ships, and the oil leaking from the drill shaft continues to explode to the surface."

Gem stared at the two ships that seemed to be steaming ahead directly in the ring of fire. She knew that couldn't be the case, but her stomach tightened all the same. A group of smaller craft circled around the edges of the burn. Austin was out there.

"God, that looks insane," she murmured.

Emily rested her hand on Gem's shoulder. "They know what they're doing. They planned for this, you know."

Gem's throat was dry and she swallowed. "I know."

"It's a good thing, right? If it never gets to shore, we'll be fine."

Gem laughed shortly. "Oh, sure, assuming the hurricane doesn't flatten everything and flood the sanctuary."

"Well, yeah, assuming that."

"I don't see why she has to be out there in the middle of it."

"Probably for the same reason you're here. Because no one does it as well and you wouldn't be happy unless you were doing it yourself."

"Not the same thing. It's not like she had to light the match herself."

"Uh-huh. And you probably don't need to be shoveling sand, either."

Gem cut her a look, appreciating her friendship now more than ever. "I really don't like it when you're right all the time."

Emily grinned. "How's it going? Still being mature?"

"Not exactly." Gem hadn't been able to get the dark, desirous look in Austin's eyes out of her mind, or the feeling of being touched just from being seen. Softly, almost as if saying it would change things, she said, "She told me she was falling in love with me."

"Well, points for her for being smart enough to see what a great catch you are," Emily said with obvious approval. "I knew I liked her."

"You do?"

"Hey, she had me sold when she started filling sandbags. Those oil rigs are a fact of life, and you know what? We need them. I'm no economist, but I'm pretty sure oil independence is a real plus in today's world. So we need people like her to deal with things like this. Because sometimes, shit happens."

Gem nodded, searching the tiny images of the ships as if she could actually see Austin somewhere. Plumes of thick gray smoke rose against the midnight sky, illuminated from beneath by orange tongues of burning oil. "I just want her to get off that damn boat and get back here."

Joe walked over with a sandwich in one hand. "Hell of a fire. Better it happens out there than in the marsh."

"Yes," Gem murmured, knowing Austin was their best hope for sparing the sanctuary, at least until Norma arrived.

CHAPTER TWENTY-FIVE

The gray light of dawn was barely recognizable beyond the orange flames and black smudges of roiling clouds coating the sky above the launch. Austin flexed her fingers and toes, trying to keep the circulation flowing, and directed Reddy to circle out beyond the containment ships. They'd kept the burn going all night and she wanted to check for new accumulations of oil and to gauge the efficiency of the burn. She braced her legs and gripped the rails as the launch bumped over the waves.

Tatum edged up beside her and shouted above the wind. "It's coming in fast."

"I know. The captain just relayed a weather update from Claudia. We'll have to call it off pretty quick."

"If she comes in hard," Tatum said, "maybe she'll wear herself out fast and we can get back out to the rig and stop this fucking leak for good."

"I'm for that." Austin grinned, squinting into the icy blow. The NBC News copter had been joined by another, probably local news, and the pair trailed after them, swaying and bouncing like a pair of dragonflies. They hadn't quit following them all night except for a brief interval when the NBC bird disappeared, likely to refuel and change pilots. If Linda Kane was still up there, Austin had to give her points for toughness. With the way the birds dipped and rocked in the heavy winds, everybody aboard must have a cast-iron stomach. At least they were dry up there, so she didn't feel too sorry for them.

"We're getting oil over the booms," she said, pointing off the bow.

"Yeah," Tatum said, "waves are getting too high to keep it localized."

Austin radioed Renuto. "Let it burn out, Phil, and pull your crews back to the ships."

"You pulling the plug?" Reddy yelled.

"Yeah," Austin called. They'd have to count on the shore booms to catch the rest of it, until they could safely burn again. She signaled Reddy with a wave and pointed back to the nearest containment ship. He nodded, gunned the engine, and cut a wide arc to head back.

Austin watched the sheen of unburned oil stream out and away, hoping the heavy seas would disperse most of it before it ever reached the final barriers offshore. That was where the endgame would shift. Gem and her people would have a massive cleanup job handling the aftermath of a hurricane. She didn't want to see oil added to the calamity. Clambering forward, she called to Reddy, "As soon as we refuel, let's get to shore."

"Roger that," he called back.

She needed a status update on the shore preparations, but more than that, she wanted to see Gem. She wanted that even more than she wanted a meal and a couple hours' sleep, both of which her body screamed for. She just needed to be in the same space with her, even if they couldn't touch, couldn't share a private word. Being near her was enough to make everything else right. The rush of anticipation warmed her despite the icy water soaking her from head to toe.

"Fuck," Tatum exclaimed.

A ten-foot swell crashed over the side of the launch and Austin barely got a hand on the rail as the craft wallowed in the trench. Tatum shouted again and lost his footing. Austin grabbed a strap on his PFD, willing her frozen fingers to hold on, and the two of them bobbed on a rush of water for a couple of seconds. As the launch righted itself, she got her feet under her.

Tatum, eyes wide, shouted, "Fuck me."

"Yeah!" She laughed, nerves screaming. "Looks like Norma's knocking at the door."

"Fuck me twice," Tatum called, looking upward.

She followed his frantic gaze. One of the copters tilted, dropped twenty feet, and shot up again, rolling wildly. For a second it looked like the pilot found some steady air, and then the rotors quit and it dropped like a stone.

"Reddy," Austin shouted. "Reddy, head for them."

The copter hit the water with a loud boom and a geyser of water catapulted into the air. Sirens blared from a dozen ships. Floodlights suddenly speared through the darkness, illuminating the dark surface of the ocean. The helicopter bobbed on its side, half-submerged but intact.

Reddy pushed the launch to full speed, engines screaming in protest as the craft shot up into the air and dropped bow first into the troughs over and over. They were fifty yards away from the downed copter but making almost no progress against the stormy seas. Austin gritted her teeth, her heart pounding.

"It's gonna sink," Tatum yelled.

"Grab the life jackets." Austin tightened her grip on Tatum's vest as he released one hand from the rail and opened the locker against the sidewall.

"Get ready to toss them in," she called as the launch finally drew within twenty yards of the helicopter. The door on the upper surface pushed open, and a figure emerged. Arms windmilling, the person fell into the ocean. Austin leaned forward, eyes stinging from the salty spray, searching for some sign of him. For an instant she thought she saw a figure in the water. She pointed. "There! Throw the jacket!"

Tatum lofted the PFD and it splashed into the waves, disappearing from view. Austin held her breath. A lifetime later a head reappeared, then an arm clutching the PFD. The spotlight from the ship picked him out and stayed on him.

"Where's the rest?" Tatum said.

Austin shook her head, watching the helicopter for some further sign of life. "Reddy, can you get us closer?"

"Hold on," he shouted, and steered for the rapidly sinking helicopter.

As they approached, Austin could make out a man waving frantically from the open cabin doorway, one arm looped around another motionless form. He dragged the unconscious person free of the cockpit just as the helicopter dropped into the sea.

"Where the fuck did they go?" Tatum said.

"Give me the jacket," Austin yelled, climbing onto the rail. Sighting the last spot she'd seen the struggling figures, she grabbed the PFD and jumped.

❖

"Hey," a young blonde in a FEMA windbreaker yelled as she jogged up the shore. "Helicopter just went down out there."

Gem dropped her shovel and spun around. "What? Where?"

"Out by the oil rig," the girl said excitedly. "I just heard a maritime alert on our scanner."

"Who was it?" Gem said, her stomach dropping. "Did they say? Are they all right?"

The girl shook her head. "Don't know. Search and rescue's on the way now."

Gem stared out to sea, as if she could actually see as far as the rig. Sometime in the last hour the dark night had slipped into day, although the charcoal sky seemed only slightly lighter than the dead of night. All she saw were the familiar containment ships holding anchor offshore and, beyond them, endless miles of ocean. It couldn't be Austin. Of course it couldn't. Fate wouldn't be that cruel.

She pulled out her phone and texted Austin. Maybe it was fruitless, but she had to try. *Are you all right?*

She gripped her phone in numb fingers, her heartbeat so loud it drummed out the surf. The empty screen stared back, taunting her, reminding her with its blank face and foreboding silence how mercurial time and life could be. What had she been waiting for? Why had she been so afraid to face her own desires? Why hadn't she told Austin the truth? *I want you too.*

She'd have time to tell her that, and so much more. Of course she would. Please, just give her the time. She tried Alexis. *What's happening? Helicopter down?*

She didn't expect an answer from her sister, either, but she still hoped. Still willed the words to form. *All good.* But none came. The silence filled her head with a roar of panic. She couldn't just wait, pretending her world wasn't shattering.

Jettisoning her shovel and half-filled sandbag, she trotted over to Emily. "I have to go back to the center. Something's going on out there, there's been an accident of some kind. I need to see the news."

"Go. You've been out here all night anyhow."

"We need to pull everyone in. Soon."

"I know. I'll talk to the FEMA guys. I'll take care of it. Go."

Gem pulled her phone out and checked again for a text as she ran.

Nothing.

CHAPTER TWENTY-SIX

The frigid shock took Austin's breath away. One instant she was underwater, the next she tumbled headfirst through empty air, tossed from the crest of one angry wave into the adjacent trough before catapulting up and over another wall of water again. Clutching the extra PFD, she spat out salty water and blinked furiously each time she surfaced, searching in the endless black for the tiny figures she'd seen drop into the sea. The only sound was the crash of wind and waves. If the launch was nearby, she couldn't hear it. If anyone shouted for help, their words were lost in the roar of Norma's fury.

She kicked and flailed, beating back against the pummeling waves, her only goal to keep her head up long enough to spot the survivors and to keep from drowning in the process. Finally she caught sight of a thin beam of light lancing down from the sky. Not thinking, driven by instinct alone, she struggled toward it, tossed and turned and upended every few feet. She'd never realized the ocean packed the punch of a battering ram, and understood how the shore surrendered in the face of such an onslaught, receding inland, releasing its tenuous grip on the divide between sea and earth. She wasn't giving up. And she damn well wasn't going to let Norma win. She fought her way toward the arrow of light.

A wave carried her up like a giant's insignificant plaything and tossed her down again. When she kicked to the surface, light blinded her for an instant, and there, an arm's breadth away, two pale white ovals bobbed and sank beneath the surface.

Faces.

She kicked again, one arm through the PFD, the other reaching, and touched flesh. Cold, immobile, fragile, and fleeting.

"Help," a reedy male voice called.

Closer now, Austin saw he was dragging another form, a listless body with arms outspread.

"I'll get him," Austin yelled, doubting her words carried even the short distance between them. She kicked closer, looped an arm around the inert form, and shoved the PFD at the flailing man beside her. "Hold on to this. No matter what, don't let go!"

"I won't," he croaked.

Austin squinted up into the sky and saw nothing. Her lifeless burden dragged her down and she kicked with legs rapidly turning to stone to stay above the surface.

"Stay in the light," she yelled to the man.

The body in her arms jerked alive with a strangled scream. Arms and legs flailed. A towering wave crashed down on them, and she went under again, her grip on the survivor slipping. With numb fingers, she clutched a fistful of fabric and battled for the surface again. Her lungs ached, her limbs now too sluggish to move, her blood so cold her mind was blank.

The light dimmed and time slowed.

Gem sprinted the half mile to the center, pushed through the doors, and raced down the hall. A half dozen people ringed the small television set.

"What's happening?" She pushed forward. "Sorry, sorry. What are they saying?"

"Local news is reporting a helicopter down in the area of the burn," a voice she recognized answered.

Gem glanced to her left. Claudia Spencer, her face set with worry, nodded to her. "Do we know who?"

"That's it right now. No details."

"Have you heard from Austin?"

Claudia shook her head. "No, not for a few hours."

"Was she in the air?"

"I don't know. The captain was relaying my updates to her. Last I heard she was heading out in the launch boat."

Gem focused on the television screen, grasping at the fragments of information. The launch, not the helicopter. Not Austin. A grainy image on the TV came into sharp focus. Two ships, the flaming sea, and a ring of smaller vessels.

"The NBC News helicopter is no longer visible," a male reporter announced, a tremor of excitement in his voice, "but we were able to capture this dramatic footage just before the craft disappeared."

The image cut to another grainy clip of tiny figures, antlike, falling from the dot of the helicopter into the vast sea. At the bottom of the frame, a launch arrowed toward the rapidly disappearing helicopter.

"We don't know the occupants of the launch," the reporter continued, "that arrived on scene just before search and rescue. We believe at least one of the occupants attempted to reach the survivors. We have lost sight of all of them."

The image on the TV screen tilted and jittered.

"Conditions here have deteriorated as Norma bears down on us. GOP has apparently suspended operations to contain the oil spill at this time."

"As if that matters now," Claudia muttered.

"The launch…it's GOP's, isn't it," Gem said, a leaden sense of foreboding gripping her.

"Has to be," Claudia said. "No one else is out there."

"You don't think—"

Claudia cut her a sympathetic look. "There are hundreds of crewmembers out there, a lot of them in launches supervising the burn. There's no way to know."

For the first time, Gem registered the drumming of rain on the roof. "They have to hurry."

"In two hours," Claudia said, "this whole area will be experiencing hundred-plus mile an hour winds and storm-surge surf. Did you pull your people out?"

"Under way," Gem said, eyes riveted to the screen. The news feed switched back to the local station desk, where a cheery young man assured everyone News 6 would stay on the scene for up-to-the-minute updates. "What are you doing here?"

"The Gulls Inn wireless leaves something to be desired. I've been monitoring the storm course from here." Claudia handed her a key. "You ought to take this."

Gem glanced at her. "Sorry?"

Claudia smiled. "Austin's room key. I think she'd much rather bunk with you when she gets in."

"I…" Gem swallowed around the panic. "Yes, thanks. If you hear from her first…"

"I won't, but if anyone else has word, I'll let you know." Claudia reached into the briefcase by her side and handed Gem a sheet of paper. "This is yours too. Sorry, I picked it up by mistake."

Images of her, far more beautiful than in life, drawn in Austin's bold hand. Sketches filled with Austin's passion and desire for her, and so much more she'd been trying to pretend she didn't want, didn't need. Gem's eyes filled, and she carefully folded the paper and tucked it inside her jacket to keep it safe. "I am such a fool."

"Doesn't look that way to me," Claudia murmured.

The on-scene reporter broke in on the studio news anchor, and the camera cut away to a shaky, out-of-focus live view of the ocean. "A Coast Guard search-and-rescue helicopter has just arrived. Still no sight of survivors."

"That's my sister," Gem said, knowing it in her bones. "If there's anyone out there alive, she'll get them."

"I can believe it." Claudia gave Gem's hand a squeeze. "You should too."

CHAPTER TWENTY-SEVEN

Rain pounded the roof, the clatter on tin the only sound in the room. No one spoke. Even the reporter's tones were eerily hushed. Gaze fixed on the small screen, Gem barely breathed. They were out there, they had to be. If they weren't, she'd have heard from them by now. Besides, neither of them would *want* to be anywhere else. The big Coast Guard search-and-rescue helicopter hovered, bouncing and buffeted, above the black ocean. Tiny figures dropped on nearly invisible cables toward the roiling water and disappeared in the waves.

One of those fragile figures was her sister, exposed and vulnerable and all too human despite the superhuman actions. She wanted that to be Alex, if it was Austin in the water—no matter who was in the water. But she didn't want it to be Alex, either. She'd rather Alex spend her time onshore behind a desk, but that wasn't her sister. That wasn't Austin, either. She was an artist, but she would never be totally happy tethered to a desk. She was an adventurer at heart, and risk was part of it.

"Where are the ones in the water?" someone asked, nerves making his voice high and thin.

"They'll get them, they'll get them," Gem muttered.

"Look," Claudia said, pointing as everyone leaned forward, closing the circle around the TV, unconsciously bonding. "There's one. They have one!"

The coastguardsman's red jacket and PFD were easy to follow as he emerged from the water towing another person beside him.

They rose, swinging in the air toward the belly of the helicopter, to where a long narrow toboggan-like basket hung from one of the skids. The coastguardsman guided the victim into it. The camera panned back down to the water, and another figure emerged with a second survivor in tow.

"How many? How many are there?" Gem said.

"I think there were three in the helicopter," someone said.

Two safe then, and two more. The rescue officers dropped down again.

"They're so small," Gem said. How could they find anyone in all that vast ocean. Helplessly, heart pounding painfully, she waited for word from the two most important people in her life while Norma drove toward land.

❖

"Hold on." A dark form plummeted into the water next to Austin. A man said, "Give him to me."

Her, Austin thought blearily. She held on, afraid if she let go Linda Kane would be washed away. Linda had gone silent again, the only sign of life a weak flicker of a limb when a wave lifted them into the air before dropping them.

"I've got her, trust me," the man beside her shouted.

"Other ones," Austin gasped, her voice so weak she feared he couldn't hear over the screaming wind. "Two more."

"Already aboard." A strap slid around her chest and cinched beneath her arms. Momentarily confused, she struggled, clutching Linda tighter.

"Austin, Austin, it's okay!" Another voice. A woman.

Gem's face appeared, wavering in her unsteady vision. "Gem?"

"It's Alexis Martin. You're okay. We've got you both."

Not Gem. "Where's Gem?" A spurt of panic. "Is she here?" Austin thrashed against the strap on her chest. A hand gripped her shoulder.

"She's ashore," Alexis said. "She's okay. Relax. Let us get you up."

The man pulled Linda away, and Alexis tugged Austin closer, rapidly clipping another strap between her legs.

"You're going to be fine. Hold on to me," Alexis said, attaching a cable to Austin's harness. "We're going up. I'm right here."

Too exhausted to do anything else, Austin closed her eyes. Gem's face appeared, smiling, welcoming, warm. "Gem...call... her."

"Not long now," Alexis shouted, unable to hear Austin's faint mumbling.

Austin's feet broke free of the water and her body swung and spun in midair. The harness dug into her chest, a comforting, securing presence. Beside her, Alexis rose in tandem, one hand gripping Austin's safety harness. With every foot that grew between her and the ocean's surface, her head cleared. Still cold, she could at least feel her fingers and toes again. Her face, frozen in the icy blow, was stiff and wooden, and words came slowly.

"Alive?"

"Got them all," Alexis yelled. "All three. You saved the woman."

"Lucky."

A basket dropped from the belly of the helicopter. The roar of the rotors replaced the wind, just as loud, but providing a barrier against the freezing air currents below. Austin flexed her arms and legs, working to heat up her core. Now that she was clear of the water, her strength started to return. She could think again.

"We're going to get you strapped in here for transport," Alexis said as they pulled even with the sled.

"No. I'm okay, I'm good," Austin said. "Just cold. Let me ride inside."

"You sure?"

"Hell, yeah. Get me in there."

"Okay, hold on," Alexis said, and said something into her headset.

In another minute, they'd been winched aboard, the cabin doors slid closed, and the helicopter angled off away from the smoldering oil. Alexis knelt, opened a med kit, and pulled out a thermal blanket.

She wrapped it around Austin's shoulders, and Austin pulled it tight, shivering violently.

"You sure you don't want to lie down?" Alexis asked.

"Just need heat."

Alexis cracked a pack of instant hot against her thigh and held it out. "Drink this."

"Thanks." Austin swallowed the instant brew, the best damn coffee she'd ever tasted. She finished it off while Alexis checked her over, taking her pulse, recording her blood pressure, checking her temperature.

"Your core temp's 95. You ought to feel like crap."

"I do." Austin laughed shakily. "Reminds me a lot of Alaska. Hate the cold. Got any more coffee?"

"You must be cold if you want more of that." Alexis grinned, snapped another pack open, and held it out. "You'll live, looks like."

"Thanks—for down there."

"No problem."

"I need to reach Gem."

"Don't worry. She's great at her job."

"Not about that." She had to text her, let her know she was okay. Gem would have heard, would wonder, would worry. All hell was about to break loose, and she needed to get to Gem before the storm cut her off. She just needed her.

Alexis studied her intently and must have seen it all in her eyes. "That way, is it?"

"Very much that way."

"Stick close to me when we land."

The helicopter began its descent and Austin peered through the sheets of rain streaming across the small window behind her. A Coast Guard vessel pitched on the rough seas just below them. "I need to get to shore before Norma hits."

Alexis's grin was feral. "Norma's here, babe. This show's already started."

CHAPTER TWENTY-EIGHT

I'll wait," Alexis said, turning in to the nearly empty parking lot adjacent to the Gulls Inn.

"You don't have to," Austin said. "You've done plenty already. I appreciate you pulling strings to get me here."

Alexis drummed her fingers lightly on the wheel and grinned. "It helps, you being the big-shot oil rep and all that. The brass were happy to accommodate, especially seeing as how you've been all over the TV after that crazy-ass stunt out there when that helicopter nose-dived."

"Yeah," Austin said wearily. "I'm feeling like a pretty big deal right now."

"You're going to be the golden girl as far as network news is concerned after saving their star."

Austin snorted. "For twenty-four hours, maybe."

"Probably." Alexis laughed. "But hey, take what you can get."

"Let me see if Claudia is still here," Austin said. "She'll probably know where Gem is."

"You know they'll have evacuated the sanctuary by now."

"I know, but I'll find her." Wherever she was, she'd find her.

"Don't doubt it," Alexis said. "But I can at least drive you around until you do."

"You must have better things to do."

"I'm officially detailed to your first-response team, remember, and I'm technically off duty for the next eight hours anyhow. Plus, I want to find my shore team, get an update on the storm preparedness, and brief them on what's going on out there at 86."

"That's what we all want to know," Austin said darkly, "but there's no telling until Norma gets done with us and we can get back out there."

At one p.m. the sky was dark as midnight. Five-foot waves crashed on the shore, their foamy aftermath climbing ever closer to the underpilings of the buildings closest to the beach. Debris had begun to swirl through the empty streets, scattered and tossed by the rising winds. And still, the full force of the hurricane had yet to make landfall.

"By tomorrow morning," Alexis said, "she'll have blown over us, and we can all get down to the business of tidying things up."

"As soon as we can get back out to the rig, we'll brief on the status of the leak and the projected interval to shut it down."

"Go see about Claudia, and if you can stay awake," Alexis said, "we'll go find Gem."

Too short on energy to argue and figuring it wouldn't do her any good anyhow, Austin relented. "Okay. Give me five."

"I'll text my sister again. Maybe I'll hit a pocket of reception."

"Thanks." Austin had been texting Gem since the search-and-rescue team had rendezvoused with the Coast Guard vessel. She hadn't really expected to get through to her from out at sea, and she hadn't, nor at the airport, nor during the car ride back into town. She'd find her, though. One way or the other.

Hoping Claudia was still around so she wouldn't have to hunt down the manager for a key, she knocked on the door to her room. Fatigue sat so heavily on her shoulders, she leaned against the doorjamb just to keep upright. Not much longer. When she found Gem, she could rest.

The door swung open. Austin blinked. "Gem?"

Gem smiled softly, grabbed Austin's hand, and tugged her inside. "Stand right there for a minute."

"You're here?" Austin asked, just the slightest bit fuzzy. The door closed behind her and the sound of Norma's arrival faded.

"Shh." Gem gently ran her hands through Austin's hair, over the sides of her face, along the curve of her neck, and down her shoulders. She pressed the tips of her fingers to Austin's lips, stroked her palms down her chest, over her abdomen, and settled onto her hips. "You're all in one piece. You're safe."

"You're really here." Austin gripped Gem's shoulders and yanked her close, taking her mouth like a drowning man taking air. She groaned, warm again for the first time in forever. She cupped the back of Gem's head, held her in place, and drank her down, her exhaustion burning away on the crest of desire.

Gem threaded her arms around Austin's neck, molded herself to Austin's frame, banishing the smallest space between them. She opened for her, welcomed her in. When Austin drew way, breathing heavily, Gem murmured, "That was you, wasn't it. Out there in the water."

"Yeah," Austin whispered, cupping Gem's face, kissing her again. "God, I need you."

"Don't ever scare me like that again," Gem whispered, kissing her back just as urgently. "I don't want to lose you."

"You won't, I promise." Austin cradled Gem's hips, kept her tight against her. "I'm fine, I swear. Alexis too." Austin jerked. "Fuck. Alexis is waiting outside."

"No, she isn't. I texted her back just a few seconds ago. Told her I was here. We're alone for the next twelve hours or so, except for Norma."

"To hell with Norma," Austin said, walking Gem backward toward the bed.

"You can barely stand up. You need to get some sleep."

"You're not leaving," Austin said quickly, desperation spreading through her. "Please, I—"

"Hey, no. No! I'm not going anywhere. I'm staying right here."

Austin leaned her forehead against Gem's and closed her eyes. "All I could think about was getting back here to you."

"I've been dying, waiting for you to come back." Gem caressed her. "You need to get a shower, get warmed up, and get into bed."

"I showered on the ship." Austin tightened her grip, heat scouring through her. "And I'm already plenty warm. Come to bed with me."

Gem laughed shakily. "Oh, I intend to."

"All I want is you."

"God, yes," Gem gasped, folding down onto the bed and pulling Austin on top of her. "Are you sure? I can wait—"

"Can you?" Austin kissed her throat, opened the top buttons on her shirt, and kissed lower. "Because I can't."

Moaning as her skin electrified, Gem wrapped her legs around Austin's, pressing her center to Austin's pelvis. "No, no, I can't. I've never wanted like I want this." She arched, the tension tightening in her pelvis. "Like I want you." She framed Austin's face, searched for the safety of her dark gaze. "I love you. I don't know why I didn't tell you before."

Austin pushed up on both hands, fighting through the mist of desire to focus on Gem's eyes. They were clear, certain, strong, and sure. She came alive inside, a sensation she finally recognized as completeness. "I love you." She laughed. "I love you. It feels so good."

"It does, doesn't it. Like the sweetest, most exciting, most amazing thing ever." Gem tugged Austin's shirt free from her pants, unbuttoned the waistband, and slid down the zipper. She pushed the clothes off Austin's hips. "It feels wonderful. *You* feel wonderful. And I want to feel you all over me, right now."

Austin pushed off the bed and shed her clothes with lightning speed as Gem removed her shirt and jeans. Austin stilled, taking her in as Gem stretched naked, the faint glow of the bedside lamp sending flickering fingers of gold across her skin. "You're so damn beautiful. I could look at you forever."

"You can look at me as often as you like, but right now, I want you on top of me." Gem held out a hand. "I need you to make me yours."

"You *are* mine." Austin covered her, sliding one leg between hers, framing her shoulders with an elbow on either side, kissing her as she fit their bodies together. She might've gone on kissing her for hours, lost in the taste of her, floating on a sea of exquisite sensation, if Gem hadn't caught her hand and guided it down her body and between her legs.

"I need you," Gem whispered against her ear. "I want you inside me. Everywhere. Please."

Kissing the fragile spot on Gem's throat where her pulse beat madly, Austin cupped her, caressed her, and when she arched and cried out, slipped inside her.

Gem clutched Austin's shoulders, her head twisting to one side, her breath a ragged gasp. "Can't wait." Pushing down, tightening as Austin stroked deeper, over and over, she rode the whirlwind to the crest. "You make me want to come so much."

Austin lost herself in Gem's pleasure, swept beyond sight and sound to a place only they could go. "Anything. Always. I love you."

"I'm yours," Gem groaned. "Oh. Now. Now. You're making me come."

Austin watched the ecstasy break across Gem's face, felt time stop. Nothing would ever be the same. Outside the boarded-up windows, Norma raged. But here, here in Gem's arms was home. Unassailable, indestructible, hers.

❖

Gem drifted, listening to the keening of the storm and Austin's soft, rhythmic breathing. She stroked her hair, her back, the curve of her ass. The urge to protect her, keep her safe, filled her with tender fierceness.

Something—a branch, a broken board—bounced off the plywood covering the balcony doors with a loud crack.

Austin twitched, and her body tensed.

"You're okay," Gem murmured, kissing the side of her jaw. "You're okay."

"Damn," Austin said. "I fell asleep, didn't I."

"You did," Gem said with infinite satisfaction. "Inside me, in fact."

Austin groaned. "I'm sorry."

Gem laughed. "Oh, I'm not at all. That was maybe the sexiest thing I've ever felt."

"I'm pretty sure I can top it."

"Really?" Gem stretched, every muscle loose and warm, and a heavy ache in her depths to be filled again. "If you can, I might not survive."

Austin leaned up on an elbow and grinned. "I bet you can."

"Well, we'll see, won't we." Gem couldn't quite get used to seeing Austin this way, so completely hers. She basked in the intensity of Austin's gaze, absorbing her attention like rain on parched soil. "I love the way you look at me. Like I'm everything."

Austin kissed her. "That's because you are. I love you."

"I love you too. When I look at you, I feel as if I always have."

"You know this is the beginning, right?" Austin said. "Of us, together. When the storm is over, when the sanctuary is safe, when our work here is done, we'll go on—you and I."

"Us," Gem said, for once in her life not caring about the details. Only knowing what was true. "I want you, now and always."

"I'm yours, now and always."

"We've got a few more hours," Gem said, shifting until Austin rolled onto her back. "And I have something I want to say."

"I'm listening."

Gem smiled. "You always are." She straddled Austin's hips and cupped her breasts. Brushing her thumbs lightly over Austin's nipples, she said, "This time, though, hear me inside."

"I'm not going to last long."

"Try." Gem squeezed slowly, her eyes narrowing in satisfaction as Austin jerked. "I know you can do anything you want to do."

Groaning, Austin gripped the sheets in both hands, desire slashing through her. Gem's mouth was molten, her hands flame. By the time Gem kissed her way slowly down the center of her stomach, her breath was gone and her heart a wild thing trying to beat its way out of her chest. When Gem settled between her thighs and took her into her mouth, lightning seared her senses. When she came in Gem's mouth, she soared, an eagle on the wind.

CHAPTER TWENTY-NINE

Gem woke wrapped in the curve of Austin's body, Austin's arm around her middle and a knee tossed protectively over one of her legs. They'd lost power when Norma'd slammed ashore, and she lay on her side staring into the dark, relishing the sensation of simply being held. A kiss, warm and soft and wordlessly possessive, pressed to the back of her neck. She smiled and made a purring sound in her throat. She found Austin's hand and linked their fingers together.

"The wind has dropped," she said.

"I know," Austin said, her voice low and languorous. "About an hour ago."

"Rain sounds pretty steady."

"Mmm, Claudia predicted heavy throughout the day, but if the wind stays down…"

Gem's chest tightened and she held Austin's hand harder against her breast, as if the beat of her heart, of the love that filled it, could somehow flow into Austin and keep her safe. "You'll head back out to the rig?"

"With Tatum in the launch or the birds, if they can fly." Austin nuzzled her neck. "The sooner we do, the safer the sanctuary will be."

"I don't want you to take risks." When Gem heard herself say that, she laughed wryly. "And now *there* is an unlikely possibility."

"No, it isn't. I've never been reckless, just willing to take a calculated gamble." Austin leaned over and lit the candle Gem had left by the bedside the night before, guided Gem to her back, and kissed her. "But I won't bet on the long shots any longer. I promise."

Gem studied her face in the candlelight, bold and strong and beautiful. "I wish I could draw the way you do."

Austin smiled. "What would you draw?"

"You—when you're sleeping...the way you look at me...the way you watch me when I come."

Austin's eyes darkened, got that hungry look that said she wanted her.

Gem's blood raced, the thrill of being desired turning her liquid inside. "I have something of yours."

"You have everything of mine," Austin said.

"All I want is your heart."

"It's yours, along with all the days of my life."

"Claudia gave me some drawings of yours. Something I'd like to keep, if you don't mind."

Austin's brows drew down as if she were searching her memory. "Ah—the sketches."

"I'm not nearly as beautiful as you made me appear, but I'm glad you see me that way."

"I told you I was in love with you from the first moment. When I couldn't have you—when I was afraid you wouldn't want me—drawing you was my way of making you mine."

Gem pulled Austin on top of her, entwined their legs, and kissed her. "It's true. I'm yours."

"And you're even more beautiful than I could ever capture," Austin murmured.

"When I look at your drawings," Gem said, "you make me feel beautiful."

"Then I'll have to sketch you nude next time."

Gem laughed a little self-consciously, but the idea excited her. "As soon as we can escape together somewhere alone. If I'm getting naked with you watching me the way you do, I'm going to want you to make me come."

"That's a promise."

"I don't want to let you go," Gem whispered against Austin's throat.

"I don't want you to." Austin kissed her slowly until Gem was breathless. "I'll come home. Wherever you are, I'll always come home to you."

Thirty-six hours later

"Hey, Gem," Emily called. "Your hottie's on the tube again."

Someone in the break room chuckled.

Gem shoved the coffeepot back onto the burner and spun around, a welcome surge of energy flooding her weary body. Her head ached, her eyes were gritty, and her limbs had gone numb hours ago. Or was it days?

The sandbags had kept the worst of the storm surge out of the estuaries and the marshes, but the beaches were badly eroded, and FEMA and Gem's crew had been filling the worst of the trenches with the sand from the bags they'd spent hours filling. The rain had mostly stopped, and for brief blessed patches, the sun actually shone. GOP's vessels trolled up and down the coastline, monitoring the booms and the course of the oil. None had reached shore.

Best of all, the birds had begun to arrive.

On the screen, Linda Kane looked as elegantly coiffed and camera perfect as she always had. No one would believe she'd nearly drowned a few days before. She stood with Austin on the platform of Rig 86. A brisk wind ruffled Austin's hair but seemed to have no effect on the reporter's.

"What can you tell us about the status of the oil spill?" Linda said.

Austin faced the camera, as comfortable as if she were addressing a handful of friends.

"We're happy to report the leak has been sealed and there is no further evidence of oil reaching the surface. We expect to cease the surface burn later today."

"Are you saying that the threat to the shoreline and coastal waters is over?"

"Fortunately, there was never any significant threat. The booms we proactively placed trapped the small amount of surface oil driven shoreward during the hurricane, and we've been able to skim that off completely."

"And you're confident that the wildlife sanctuary and the beaches are secure from any potential contamination?"

"Absolutely. Due to GOP's extensive safety protocols and the early deployment of rapid response teams before any actual spill occurred, the minimal amount of oil that reached the surface was completely and safely eradicated."

Linda looked toward the camera. "I can personally verify that GOP is not only committed to harvesting our economically essential natural resources in a safe and responsible manner, but their personnel are highly skilled and selfless in their dedication to protecting our environment."

Emily turned from the screen and glanced at Gem. "Looks like Austin has a new fan."

Gem laughed. "She deserves it."

When the news feed cut away to another story, Gem texted Austin. *Nice job. Mine now?*

The response was instant.

Always. Back soon. Owe you a sketch.

Gem smiled, suddenly not the least bit tired. *I love you. I'll be waiting.*

About the Author

Radclyffe has written over forty-five romance and romantic intrigue novels, dozens of short stories, and, writing as L.L. Raand, has authored a paranormal romance series, The Midnight Hunters.

She is an eight-time Lambda Literary Award finalist in romance, mystery, and erotica—winning in both romance (*Distant Shores, Silent Thunder*) and erotica (*Erotic Interludes 2: Stolen Moments* edited with Stacia Seaman and *In Deep Waters 2: Cruising the Strip* written with Karin Kallmaker). A member of the Saints and Sinners Literary Hall of Fame, she is also an RWA/FF&P Prism Award winner for *Secrets in the Stone*, an RWA FTHRW Lories and RWA HODRW winner for *Firestorm*, an RWA Bean Pot winner for *Crossroads*, and an RWA Laurel Wreath winner for *Blood Hunt*. In 2014 she was awarded the Dr. James Duggins Outstanding Mid-Career Novelist Award by the Lambda Literary Foundation.

She is also the president of Bold Strokes Books, one of the world's largest independent LGBTQ publishing companies.

Find her at facebook.com/Radclyffe.BSB, follow her on Twitter @RadclyffeBSB, and visit her website at Radfic.com.

Books Available From Bold Strokes Books

24/7 by Yolanda Wallace. When the trip of a lifetime becomes a pitched battle between life and death, will anyone survive? (978-1-62639-619-7)

A Return to Arms by Sheree Greer. When a police shooting makes national headlines, activists Folami and Toya struggle to balance their relationship and political allegiances, a struggle intensified after a fiery young artist enters their lives. (978-1-62639-681-4)

After the Fire by Emily Smith. Paramedic Connor Haus is convinced her time for love has come and gone, but when firefighter Logan Curtis comes into town, she learns it may not be too late after all. (978-1-62639-652-4)

Fortunate Sum by M. Ullrich. Financial advisor Catherine Carter lives a calculated life, but after a collision with spunky Imogene Harris (her latest client) and unsolicited predictions, Catherine finds herself facing an unexpected variable: Love. (978-1-62639-530-5)

Dian's Ghost by Justine Saracen. The road to genocide is paved with good intentions. (978-1-62639-594-7)

Soul to Keep by Rebekah Weatherspoon. What won't a vampire do for love… (978-1-62639-616-6)

When I Knew You by KE Payne. Eight letters, three friends, two lovers, one secret. Can the past ever be forgiven? (978-1-62639-562-6)

Wild Shores by Radclyffe. Can two women on opposite sides of an oil spill find a way to save both a wildlife sanctuary and their hearts? (978-1-62639-645-6)

Love on Tap by Karis Walsh. Beer and romance are brewing for Tace Lomond when archaeologist Berit Katsaros comes into her life. (978-1-62639-564-0)

Whirlwind Romance by Kris Bryant. Will chasing the girl break Tristan's heart or give her something she's never had before? (978-1-62639-581-7)

Love on the Red Rocks by Lisa Moreau. An unexpected romance at a lesbian resort forces Malley to face her greatest fears when she must choose between playing it safe or taking a chance at true happiness. (978-1-62639-660-9)

Tracker and the Spy by D. Jackson Leigh. There are lessons for all when Captain Tanisha is assigned untried pyro Kyle and a lovesick dragon horse for a mission to track the leader of a dangerous cult. (978-1-62639-448-3)

Whiskey Sunrise by Missouri Vaun. Culture and religion collide when Lovey Porter, daughter of a local Baptist minister, falls for the handsome thrill-seeking moonshine runner, Royal Duval. (978-1-62639-519-0)

Dyre: By Moon's Light by Rachel E. Bailey. A young werewolf, Des, guards the aging leader of all the Packs: the Dyre. Stable employment—nice work, if you can get it…at least until silver bullets start to fly. (978-1-62639-662-3)

Fragile Wings by Rebecca S. Buck. In Roaring Twenties London, can Evelyn Hopkins find love with Jos Singleton or will the scars of the Great War crush her dreams? (978-1-62639-546-6)

Live and Love Again by Jan Gayle. Jessica Whitney could be Sarah Jarret's second chance at love, but their differences and Sarah's grief continue to come between their budding relationship. (978-1-62639-517-6)

Starstruck by Lesley Davis. Actress Cassidy Hayes and writer Aiden Darrow find out the hard way not all life-threatening drama is confined to the TV screen or the pages of a manuscript. (978-1-62639-523-7)

Stealing Sunshine by Tina Michele. Under the Central Florida sun, two women struggle between fear and love as a dangerous plot of deception and revenge threatens to steal priceless art and lives. (978-1-62639-445-2)

The Fifth Gospel by Michelle Grubb. Hiding a Vatican secret is dangerous—sharing the secret suicidal—can Felicity survive a perilous book tour, and will her PR specialist, Anna, be there when it's all over? (978-1-62639-447-6)